WHEN THE SIDE N*GGA CATCH FEELINGS

JESSICA N. WATKINS

Jessica Watkins Presents

Synopsis

When The Side Nigga Catch Feelings is the story of two women who are unfaithful for two totally different reasons, yet wind up with the same catastrophic outcome.

Meet Heaven: a young girl who is loving, submissive, and beyond appreciative of her husband, Ross. As a teenager, Heaven lived solely for her sister, Divine, and her daughter, Sunshine. Because her mother is mentally ill and her father ran off, Heaven had to do some unimaginable things just to feed the family. Then came Ross, and everything changed. He wasn't some filthy rich, dope boy that some young girls dream of, but Heaven felt like Ross was her blessing. Yet, Ross turned out to be a wolf wrapped decadently in sheep's clothing. Still, Heaven was willing to take the bad just to keep the good. The drama was all worth it for the luxuries of food, clothes, and shelter, not just for herself, but, more so, for Divine and Sunshine.

And then there's Treasure. How is it that a woman can have a good man and still not be satisfied? Treasure is far from as submissive as her best friend, Heaven. As a teenager, Treasure had always been the type of girl to juggle two or three boys. Once she was older and met a real man, Vegas, she tried to commit. All of that went out of the window, though, when she met the one that allowed her to be the ride or die chick that she had always fantasied about being.

Treasure isn't the only promiscuous woman in this story, however, because Heaven eventually succumbs to the wooing of a man that wants to treat her far better than her ain't-sh*t-husband. She knows that Ross deserves her infidelity. He had never been loyal or faithful to her. However, one thing he had never done was cheat on Heaven with someone in their circle.

In this tale of lust, lies, and mayhem, Heaven fights with the feelings that she has for her side dude, while Treasure basks in hers. That is, until all hell breaks loose. These two-side dude's that Heaven and Treasure have fallen for pretended as if they could play second to another man... until their feelings got in the way. Then, egos clash, bonds are broken, and, with two beasts like Vegas and Ross, a life is lost in this group's tight-knit circle... all because these ladies chose wrong.

Jessica Watkins Presents is the home of many well-known, best-selling authors in Urban Fiction and Interracial Romance. We provide editing services, promotion and marketing, one-on-one consulting with a renowned, national best-selling author, assistance in branding, and more, FREE of charge to you, the author.

We are currently accepting submissions for the following genres: Urban Fiction/Romance, Interracial Romance, and Interracial/Paranormal Romance. If you are interested in becoming a best-selling author and have a FINISHED manuscript, please send the synopsis, genre and the first three chapters in a PDF or Word file to jwp.submissions@gmail.com. Complete manuscripts must be at least 45,000 words.

PROLOGUE

TREASURE

I couldn't sit in that house. I needed Vegas, but he wasn't answering the phone. I had driven by every spot where I thought he would be, but I didn't find him. So, I gave up. I called Heaven over and over again, but she wasn't answering. I couldn't go home, so I was on my way to her house since I knew she was home the last time I had talked to her.

I gasped when I pulled onto Heaven's block and saw police cars and ambulances surrounding her house.

"Oh my God!" I pressed the gas and sped towards the house. But I could only get so close because the police had a portion of the street barricaded. I threw my car into park and bolted towards the house. The commotion had drawn neighbors out of their houses. I had to push my way through the crowd to get as close to the house as I could.

The house was illuminated with red and blue lights. I watched in fear as police officers walked back and forth. My fear was magnified to horror when I saw the yellow tape enclosing the backyard.

A scream suddenly left my throat and pierced the air. I now had everybody's attention. I ran past the blue barricade towards the driveway but was quickly stopped by a police officer.

"Let me go! Let me go! What happened?! Tell me what—"

I suddenly stopped when I saw Vegas watching me. He was talking to an officer a few feet away from me. I ran towards him. "What happened?!"

He barely looked at me.

"Vegas, please?" I begged. "What happened?"

He grimaced and told me reluctantly. "I'm trying to see myself. I came over here to holla at Ross and all this was happening."

"Fuck is you doin' here, motherfucker?!" Ross' voice suddenly shouted behind us.

I spun around, hoping that Heaven was with him, but she wasn't. Ross was being escorted out of the house alone by an officer. He charged through the lawn towards Vegas, spewing, "Get the fuck away from my house, bitch!"

"Ross, what happened? Where is Heaven?" I asked.

He didn't hear me. He just kept spazzing out. "Yo' bitch ass tried to kill me and you got the nerve to be at my house? Fuck all you snake motherfuckers!!" He was barking like a fucking maniac.

"Ross!" I tried to go to him, but the police officer near me stopped me. I looked at her, pleading, "Please? My best friend is in there. She's like my sister. Please?" I cried as I zeroed in on the yellow tape behind her. "What happened?" I asked the officer. "Did somebody get killed?"

I didn't need her answer. I knew that somebody was dead. I knew what yellow tape meant. The officer actually looked so sympathetic for my tears. Her mouth opened and closed repeatedly. My eyes begged her for an answer just as I could see paramedics coming out of the backyard. My knees buckled as I saw the black body bag. The officers caught me. I gripped her arms trying to gain my composure. I looked for Ross, hoping to get an answer from him, but both he and Vegas were frozen. Ross' anger subsided as they both stared unbelievably at the body being carried towards the morgue van.

Through my tears, I looked desperately at the officer holding me. "Please, tell me," I begged. "Who is it? Who got killed?'

❧ I ❧

HEAVEN

♫ Smoke one, one time (smoke one)
Drink one, one time (drink, drink)
Lemme fuck something one time (smash)
Turn the club up one time (turn the club up)
Smoke someone time (smoke)
Drink someone time (drank)
Lemme fuck something one time
Turn the club up one time (ugh) ♫

"This party is so lit!" my best friend, Treasure, squealed into my ear. She was leaning over into my bar stool, twerking with her hand in the air and her tongue out. She was all the way turned up.

"I know, right?" Looking around, I saw that this party was more than lit. This motherfucka was crackin'! Treasure and I had snuck our young selves into 7even, this club in downtown Chicago that cracked on Friday nights. It was especially crackin' this particular Friday night because this well-known baller from the city, Gotti, was having his birthday party there. Treasure and I had seen the flyer all over social media for the last two months. All of the senior chicks were talking about sneaking in because they wanted to meet some dudes with money. Treasure and I had managed to get in by dressing in little-bitty dresses that our overly matured bodies spilled out of. Once we got to the front of the line, those bouncers didn't even ask us for ID.

"And these dudes in here are fiiiiine," Treasure sang. She swayed back and forth, swinging her long, twenty-inch, soft swept ponytail.

"Ain't they?" I agreed as I smiled looking around.

Treasure was right. 7even was full of Chicago-bred hustlers who looked like Common and Kanye to King Louie, G Herbo, and Lil' Durk. They were draped in locs, diamond-encrusted chains, and Rollies. They smelled of good kush. At the moment, I was eyeballing a few sexy guys who were too busy looking at bad bitches to even see me.

I leaned over and spoke into Treasure's ear. "You think these dudes can tell how young I am?"

Still dancing, Treasure shook her head. "Nah."

"So, I look twenty-one?"

She frowned and laughed. "Hell no. I didn't say *that*."

I pouted but still laughed. "Fuck you, friend."

"You don't look seventeen, though. That ass and those titties look twenty-one, but that baby face gives you away. Those bouncers just wanted to hit that; that's why they let you in."

I giggled. She was probably right. While Treasure had a mature, exotic face, mine still gave off that young, innocent look, no matter how much of Treasure's makeup I'd put on.

I kept twerking on my bar stool to the Migos, enjoying being out for the first time in, I didn't know how long. I was also watching the clock because I had to be back home no later than midnight, even though it was a Friday night.

I watched with a smirk on my face as Treasure made eye contact with a few dudes as she smiled, licked her lips, and twerked. When she caught me staring, her smile got bigger. "I'm 'bout to bag one of these ballers in here, girl."

I just shook my head with a smile of admiration. Treasure had always been the one between us who got the guys. While I was struggling to keep a good dude, Treasure was taking guys down left and right. A lot of girls in school called her a hoe. But since I was her best friend, I knew that her mind just worked like one of the guys. While a lot of girls in school were thirsty for a boyfriend, Treasure was happy with juggling one dude after the next after the next, with no commitment to or from any of them. She was allergic to commitment.

"Aye, Miss Lady, can I buy you a drink?" I could feel the baritone voice tickling my neck as a guy spoke to me.

I smiled with relief as his voice eased into my ear. When I had first walked into the club, I didn't feel like any guys would holla at me. Even though Treasure had loaned me one of her dresses and some makeup, my weave was cheap, store-bought, and self-installed. All of these other chicks were rocking foreign lace fronts or royal, natural looks. Every girl in there had professionally beat brows and faces painted with MAC. I never had make-up to play in, so I had done what I could with Treasure's Walgreens brand collection. Looking at their faces, clearly, my attempt to beat my face had failed. From the neck down, I was cold. My body was voluptuous and so naturally curvy that guys got dizzy looking at it. But from the neck up, I was struggling like a motherfucka. If it wasn't for my cute, baby face and grown-woman curves, I would have been popped.

However, I put on the best sultry smile I could muster and turned around. I found the most mature, brown eyes staring back at me with a bit of twinkle in them. He was handsome, but I was kind of let down because he looked older. I mean, I was looking to meet an older guy who had more going on for himself than the boys at my school. But this dude looked *way* older than twenty-one.

"How old are you?" I asked. There was a squint in my eye that told him that I knew he was questionable.

His smile was so adorable as he pretended to clutch his chest. "Damn, is it an age requirement to buy a lady a drink in this motherfucker?"

I blushed. "No. Sorry. I just wanted to know. You look too old for me."

"Ain't it rude to ask a man his age?" he joked.

I blushed at his attempt to tease me. "I think it's actually rude to ask a *woman* her age."

He stepped closer, closing the space between us. He was so close that I could smell his earthy, fresh cologne. With a quick glance up and down my body, he licked his full lips and then asked, "Well, since you're being rude, I'll be rude too. How old are *you?*"

"You first," I teased.

"Twenty-five."

Damn, twenty-one was my limit, since I was turning eighteen soon. I cringed inwardly while our eyes locked. Despite him being obviously much older than me, it was something about him that made me look past all of that and see how sexy he was. He was just as chocolate as me. Despite being about 5'10" in the four-inch heels I was wearing, I still had to look up to him. He had a thick, athletic build. He was wrapped in a fitted tee and jeans. He looked like money. So, I let the age thing go. Besides, I never expected to see him again after that night anyway. So, I figured what would be the harm?

"Sure, you can buy me a drink."

Stroking his neatly lined beard, he shook his head. "Nah, lil' mama. Your turn. Then I'll buy you a drink."

I rolled my eyes, appearing annoyed. But he knew I was pretending by the playful smile on my face. "I'm twenty-one."

He nodded and then licked his lips very slowly this time as he looked me up and down yet again. His stare was so intense that I felt insecure under his eyesight.

"Tell the bartender what you want." He then glanced over and saw Treasure leaning against the bar while smiling at our conversation. He looked back at me and asked with a chuckle, "This your girl?"

I playfully smirked at Treasure's nosiness and nodded at him. "Yeah."

"Get her one too then."

⚝

"Shit! Divine is going to kill me! Fuck!"

Treasure sucked her teeth as she drove the old Neon, which her mother had handed her down, through the south side of Chicago. Englewood to be exact.

"Calm down," she told me. "It's only fifteen minutes after twelve."

I didn't even respond because Treasure had no idea what I had going on at home. That was my fault, though, because I hadn't told her. I was too ashamed to tell anyone.

My heart was beating a mile a minute as I tore myself out of the dress that I had borrowed from Treasure. I then threw back on the dingy jogging suit that I had originally worn to walk over to Treasure's house after my baby had gone to sleep.

"I don't understand why you have a curfew anyway. You're seventeen! It's lame as hell that you have to be in by midnight. You get good grades, and you're always in the house with your baby. I don't see what the issue is."

I was too embarrassed to respond. I just hurriedly threw all of my stuff into my book bag. Then I flipped the visor down and wiped the lipstick off of my lips.

As Treasure sped through a yellow light, I shook my head, thinking about how I had so stupidly forgotten the time. I was too busy all up in that old man's face. He had so easily made me forget the time, with his jokes and good conversation. I was constantly losing myself in the twinkle in his brown eyes. Now, I was about to probably have to pay for it.

Within minutes, I finally felt some relief because we were pulling up to my house.

Once Treasure threw the car in park, I leaned over and hugged her. "See you later, girl."

Treasure hugged me back while sucking her teeth. "Yeah, whatever. This is some bullshit. You were finally having fun."

"I'm sorry," I hurriedly said. Then I quickly opened the door and jumped out. I slammed the door in a haste and then took off for my front door.

As I rushed towards the house, I noticed that all of the lights were off inside. So, I was grateful, and my heart rate slowed down a little. Once I reached the front door, I looked back and quickly waved goodbye to Treasure. She honked the horn and pulled off. I quietly put my key in the lock and tried desperately to quietly open the old, wooden door.

I was successful. I sighed discreetly once I was able to close and lock the door just as quietly as I had opened it. With relief, I kicked my shoes off, in order not to make any noise as I tip-toed through the living room towards my bedroom.

Just as I reached the hallway, I felt a hard tug on the Dream Weaver bundles I had managed to sell just enough of my mother's Link to buy.

"Aahhh!" left my mouth in a yelp of pain, but no surprise, because I knew exactly who it was pulling my fresh sew-in from the root. "Mama, it's me! It's me!'

"Intruder! Intruder!" she chanted crazily as she tossed me around by the hair. "Somebody call 9-1-1!"

I fought desperately to keep my head from banging against something in the darkness. "Mama, stooooop!" I wailed.

I began to cry as I felt my hair ripping from my scalp while her big ass tossed me around. I wasn't crying from the pain. I was used to this, my mother spazzing and putting her hands on me. I was crying because I felt that I had let my sister, Divine, down. The demons in my mother's head always told her that anyone coming in the house after midnight was coming in to kill her. That's why I had the midnight curfew. I had let a cute, old man cause me to slip. Now, me and Divine were about to experience my mother's crazy antics yet again.

"You're coming to kill me, bitch!" she shrieked as she tossed me around in the darkness like a rag doll.

"Mamaaaa!" I clawed at her hand as it gripped my hair.

I had gotten my large assets from my mama. I was a miniature version of her. At seventeen, I was one-hundred and ninety pounds of ass and hips. At fifty, she was three hundred pounds of the same. So, it was hard to get her big, crazy ass off me.

We tussled and wrestled in the darkness of the hallway. Loud thuds could be heard as our large bodies banged against the old drywall. I prayed that my mother's hysteria wouldn't wake up my baby or Divine. But I was already sure that Divine had been so afraid that I wouldn't make curfew that she wasn't going to allow herself to fall sleep until I got home.

Finally, my mother's arm passed over my mouth. So, I opened it and bit down hard.

"Arrrrgh!" she screamed and finally let me go.

I wasn't trying to hurt her. I felt sorry for her, no matter how many times we had gone through this.

I stood in the darkness trying to find some light as I stared at her. Because of the moonlight coming through the broken blinds on the living room window, I could see her standing there gazing peculiarly at her arm and then at me.

Holding the back of my head where she had most definitely pulled some cornrolls from the root, I glared at her.

"Mama, it's me, *Heaven*." I tried to reason with her again, now that it seemed like the bite had brought her back to reality. "Go to bed."

"Heaven?" She finally looked at me and winced. "You hurt me."

"I know. I'm sorry."

"I'm going to go now," she mumbled in a confused state as she turned her back to me. "I think someone is trying to shoot me."

I didn't even bother watching to make sure she went back upstairs. I scurried a few feet down the hall into my dark bedroom. I swiftly closed the door and locked it.

I leaned against the door, taking a long, deep breath.

Don't cry, Heaven.

I didn't even bother to change my clothes. Mama had sucked all the life out of me. I just climbed into the bottom of the bunk beds Divine, Sunshine, and I shared and snuggled next to my baby.

"You okay, Heaven?" My youngest sister's sweet, sleepy voice came out of nowhere.

I cringed. "Yeah, I'm okay, Divine. I know I promised to be home by midnight. Sorry I'm late. Go to sleep."

"K." There was only a few seconds of silence before I heard her tears. "I'm sorry too."

I sighed long and hard. I stared at the bed above me as if I could see Divine's face. "You don't have anything to be sorry about."

"Yes, I do. She up woke because of me. I had to pee. She heard me flush the toilet."

My heart ached as I heard Divine's voice crack from the tears. I quickly got out of the bunk bed, climbed the ladder and fought to see her face in the darkness. I couldn't see her little chocolate face because of the blankets we had as curtains hanging from the window. I heard her tears, though. I felt around to find her cheek. When I did, I rubbed it, wiping her tears away. I bent down and quickly kissed her cheek.

"It's okay," I tried to promise her. I didn't even sound convincing to my damn self, though.

"It's my fault she hurt you."

"Stop crying. Okay? I'm okay. See?" I then smiled as if she could see me. "Go to sleep, and in the morning, I will take you to McDonald's for breakfast. I got a few dollars. We can get stuff off the dollar menu, okay?"

"Okay," she cried.

My heart broke.

I slid down the ladder, climbed back into the bed next to Sunshine, and silently cried. Divine was wrong. This was not her fault. It was mine. I usually would have never left out of the house. I just wanted to live a little for once.

This was also the fault of the son of a bitch that had murdered my only other sibling and big sister, Angel. It was his fault that we were stuck here with my mother's crazy ass.

My mother was a schizophrenic. She hated to take her medication because it made her feel "dead." Because she never took her medicine, she couldn't work. She also couldn't keep my father happy, so he'd left when I was fourteen. Angel was eighteen then and left soon after him. Divine and I wanted to go with her, but she'd said we couldn't because she didn't have a place to stay herself. She came to visit us every day, however, eating and showering because she was homeless on the street. However, she was much happier in the filth of homelessness than in the house with our mama. Every day, Angel promised that she was doing everything she could to get a place to stay so that she could come back and get us. Then the rest of us could get away from our mother too.

After six months on the streets, Angel met my bro, Caesar, just before DCFS came and took me and Divine away when my mother was hospitalized after spazzing out in a grocery store. When Angel came to get us from the state, she took us to this apartment on 79th and Hermitage. It was Caesar's place. She had just moved in a few weeks prior. Luckily, he was feeling Angel enough that he was willing to take me and Divine in as well.

That was three years ago, and it was the happiest that I had ever been in my life. Caesar was a hustler, so he had a little money, and he spoiled all three of us. We were "his girls", and he treated us like queens. So, I finally felt like a kid. I wanted for nothing and needed for nothing. I didn't have to go outside begging on the streets. I didn't have to be a mother to Divine. I didn't have to physically and verbally fight with my mama every day. Life was good. We were just living in a three-bedroom apartment on the south side of Chicago in the hood. People were getting shot right outside our front door, and cluckers littered the streets. Yet, the fact that we had clean clothes and cooked food made life feel like a fairy tale to me.

But that fairy tale only lasted up until a year and a half ago, when Angel was killed in a drive-by shooting on the Bishop Ford Expressway. She was driving Caesar's Cadillac truck, so everyone assumed the bullets had been meant for him. Yet, he'd died as well in the passenger's seat.

The day they were killed was the day that I died emotionally as well. My life was over. I was pregnant at the time, so I asked my baby's father, one of Caesar's customers, if I could stay with him. That's when his bitch-ass told me that he was actually in a relationship with kids of his own. He told me to get an abortion and never talk to him again. I took his three hundred dollars, but instead of having an abortion, I took care of me and Divine on the streets for as long as I could. The money eventually ran out, and we were forced to find my mother. She was out of the hospital and back at home. The state had reinstated her custody because she had taken her meds in order to get us back. That was something one of her many personalities was pressed to do. But once we were back, she was back to her sporadic self, not taking her meds, and Divine and I were back begging for food and clothes.

Mama's schizophrenia only seemed to get worse as time went on. At this point, she was manic. She was always paranoid. She swore somebody was trying to kill her. *Some* days, she was a normal mother to us. *Most* days, she felt like we were monsters trying to eat her. But I was too scared of getting her help because that meant Divine, my baby, and I would become wards of the state again and possibly split up. So, I took the brunt of mama's bullshit. I shielded my baby and Divine from it all. I had given birth to Sunshine, but I was Divine's mama too. Hell, we took care of each other. I looked after her, and on nights when I wanted to be a teenager, she kept an eye on Sunshine for me behind the locked door of our tiny bedroom.

🌸

TWO DAYS LATER, I WAS WALKING THROUGH THE HALLWAYS OF MY school when I spotted Treasure. She immediately rolled her eyes to the ceiling. At the same time, she looked relieved to see me. So, I knew the look on her face meant that she had some tea.

"Girl, here."

I looked strangely at Treasure as she approached me, handing me her cell phone. "Why are you handing me this?"

"That dude, Ross, has been calling you all weekend."

I smiled from ear to ear as I took the phone and started to follow Treasure to first period. Ross was the older dude at 7even Friday night who had bought us drinks. When Ross had asked me for my number, I had to give him Treasure's because I didn't have a cell phone.

"Eeew," Treasure teased me as she peeped my smile. "I knew you liked his old ass."

"He's only twenty-five."

"He looks a little older than that."

"He's sexy, though."

"Sexy as fuck," Treasure added. "Call him. I told him you had left your phone in my car that night, but I wouldn't see you until today."

I stopped outside of the classroom door where our first period was held at Simeon. We weren't supposed to have our cell phones out, but I didn't see any teachers or security guards. Plus, I was willing to risk it to call Ross back. Besides being sexy as fuck, he was cool as hell and the only man I had had any real contact with since my baby's father. All the boys who usually tried to holla at me were my age, but I had been through too much in life to be attracted to them. We didn't have anything in common. Those lil' boys were worried about if their parents were buying them the next X-box game. Meanwhile, I was worried about how I would feed Divine and Sunshine when my mama's Link ran out because I had had to sell most of it to get tissue and maxi pads, since we had used all of the tissue up, using it in place of maxi pads.

I scrolled through Treasure's call log. Once she pointed out his number, I hit the call button and waited for him to answer.

"Hello?" When his deep voice rumbled through the phone, I instantly started cheesing.

Treasure playfully rolled her eyes. I leaned against the locker next to Treasure and tried to sound the sexiest and most mature that I could. I let a soft and feminine, "Hey," swim from my overly glossed lips.

Treasure started cracking up laughing at my attempt. "Ahhhhh! Hell nah!"

I covered up the phone and narrowed my eyes at her.

"Damn. Your girl finally got you your phone back, huh?" Ross asked.

"Yeah," I lied. "Sorry about that. I was too busy all weekend to come get it from her."

"It's cool, lil' mama. It's good to hear your voice now, though. I've been thinking about you since that night. You cool as fuck with your pretty self."

I blushed again. I had been thinking about him all weekend too. We were having a nice conversation that night until I had to rush out of there. It was obvious that he was attracted to me. Once I left the club, though, I figured I wouldn't be the only girl he bought drinks for that night and he would have to fight hard to remember through the fog of his hangover the next morning.

"I been thinking about you too," I told him.

"What you doin'? Lemme take you to breakfast."

I perked up. "Breakfast?"

"Yeah. You busy?" Before I could respond, he went on, answering his own question, "You sound busy. What's all that noise?"

"I'm dropping my sister off at school," I quickly lied again.

"You busy after that?"

"No," I insisted almost too much. I damn near sounded thirsty.

"Okay. Well, you wanna meet me, or you want me to pick you up?"

"Ummm..." *Think, Heaven. Think.* "You can pick me up. I'm not driving."

Treasure's eyes bucked as she listened closely. I playfully stuck my tongue out at her.

"What school does your sister go to?" Ross asked.

"Simeon."

"Bet. I'll be there in fifteen."

"Okay. Cool." I was straight up cheesing as I gave Treasure back her phone.

"You're going to breakfast with him for real?" she asked me with a grin.

"Yeah." I figured why not. That would be the only highlight of my life for God only knew how long.

Treasure jumped a little, cheering me on, "Yaaaaaaaasss!"

"If you see Divine, tell her I will be outside at the bus stop waiting for her."

"Here. Take my phone. You don't know that dude, and you may need to call somebody."

I smiled. Treasure was my girl. We had met freshman year and had been BFF's ever since. At the time, I was living the life because Caesar was still living. But when Angel and Caesar were killed, all I had told her was that I had to move back in with my mama who was broke. I was too embarrassed to tell her the whole story. But it kept her from coming over to my house, and I was grateful for that. Treasure's parents weren't balling. She had two parents in the household working nine-to-fives, however. But like most people in the hood, they were struggling to keep ends met. However, she was fucking with enough card crackers to get whatever she needed and then some.

Treasure eyed my uniform and asked me, "You got a change of clothes?"

I realized what I was wearing and pouted. "Damn. Nope."

"Then how you gonna go meet him with your uniform on? He thinks you're twenty-one. Duh."

I was stuck. She was right.

Treasure then smirked slyly. "You lucky I'm always prepared. C'mon."

After we ran to her locker, she opened it and took a PINK jogging suit from her book bag. I then ran to the nearest bathroom and changed. By the time I was done fidgeting with myself, I ran out of the school just in time to see a Range Rover running in front of the entrance.

"Damn," I mumbled to myself as I froze.

This dude was in a Range. Suddenly, I felt out of my league. But, hell, a dude in a Buick was out of my league. I didn't have *shit*.

I forced myself to keep walking. I figured this would probably be the only date I would have in a long time, so I went for it.

⚜

BY THE TIME EVERYONE WAS GOING TO LUNCH AT SCHOOL, I WAS AT Ross' house feeling guilty as hell.

We'd eaten breakfast at White Palace. I'd had the best breakfast I'd had in a long time. He talked my ear off about himself, trying to impress me, not even realizing the omelet I was scarfing down had my panties wet all by itself. Then, I rode around with him while he ran errands, and we got to know each other some more. As the day went on, I peeped that he was a hustler. I was from the south side of Chicago, so I knew a street dude when I saw one. But whatever he was dealing was not drugs. I could tell from the code words he was using when talking business. But, still, I couldn't get a grip on what exactly he was dealing.

When Ross stopped at the liquor store, I assumed I knew where this day was going. As I drank the 1738 and his hand slipped on my thigh, I *most definitely* knew for a fact that he was about to try to get some. Because of the way my life was set up, I rarely was in the presence of a guy, especially with one touching me. So, his mere hand on my thigh felt so good. So, I decided to just roll with it.

But once we got back to his crib, I saw how he was living. This was a real man. I could tell. So, as he started to make out with me, guilt was slipping in.

"W-wait," I breathed into his mouth as I lightly pushed him away, tearing his lips away from mine.

He sat next to me on the couch looking at me like I was the young girl that I truly was.

"What? What's wrong?" he asked.

"I-I...I'm only seventeen," the liquor allowed me to blurt out.

He backed up so fast that you would have thought he was trying to get away from a monster.

"What the fuck?!" he barked.

"I'm sorryyy," I cringed. I immediately started reaching for the PINK hoodie he had taken off of me.

"You trying to get me locked up?! I'm thirty-one-"

I immediately froze, which made his rambling stop. I stared at him with bucked eyes. "Wait. What?!"

Now, he was staring at me; stuck.

My mouth dropped. "You told me you were twenty-five!" I spat.

He shrugged. "You told me you were twenty-one!"

For one second, we looked at each other with weird, questionable glances... until we broke out into uncontrollable giggles.

And, right then, at that very moment, I knew that no matter what, this man would be in my life forever.

THREE YEARS LATER...

🪙 2 🪙

HEAVEN

Me and Ross did not have sex that day, but that day is when we fell for each other. He was leery of getting sexually involved with someone my age. But destiny brought us together time after time. A connection was formed that he couldn't deny, and a few months later, we did have amazing sex that made me fall in love with him.

Now, three years later, I was his wife.

"Ross, you're trippin'! He was not flirtin' with me!"

And no one could have ever told me that day I ditched school to go to breakfast with him, would be one of the worst mistakes I had made in my life.

"That's bullshit!" Ross roared from the driver's seat of his Lexus truck. "Don't fucking play with me, Heaven! That nigga was all in your face!"

"He's your friend, Ross," Treasure cut in from the back seat. "Of course, he was in her face. He was in all of our faces. He was just talking to us."

I sucked my teeth and said, "Thank you, Treasure." Then I laughed and shook my head at how silly this argument was.

Why did I feel froggish enough to do that, though?

Bow! That was the sound his hand made as he backhanded me.

"Unt uh! Stop, Ross!" Treasure immediately spat.

"Fuck, here he go," his partner, Vegas, mumbled from the back seat next to Treasure.

Ross had hit me so fast and hard that my head smacked into the passenger's side window before I even saw that shit coming. Instantly, I tasted the saltiness of blood leaking from inside my lip.

My head was ringing over Ross' barking, "You laughin'?! You think this shit funny?! You think I'm a motherfucking joke?!"

I just sat there holding my face, feeling my head pounding violently. My face was on fire. Tears were stinging my eyes as I stared out of the window.

I had gone through this so many times before that I was numb to it. The first time he'd hit me three years ago, I was astonished. My heart was broken as I stared at my black eye in the mirror in his bedroom the next morning. But I was seventeen and in love with a guy who was rescuing me from my fucked up life. I didn't even think about leaving him then. And that was the first of many times that he had put his hands on me.

It didn't even make me mad anymore. This was Ross. This was how he showed his frustration and jealousy. This was how he expressed his anger and his insecurity of being married to a young, beautiful girl while being surrounded by friends and employees that he felt could take me away from him if they tried. No matter how much I tried to show and tell him I loved him, his insecurities were stronger than what I said and did. So, he tried to kick, punch, slap, and beat me into never looking at another man.

I didn't blame him. This was how he had been taught. He had told me so many stories of how his father used to beat his mother. It was like he was training a puppy to act right and be obedient. But the difference between his mother and me was that she was a hoe that stayed cheating on his father... God rest her soul.

I sat in that seat, Ross' barking being overshadowed by my thoughts. I hated that he put his hands on me sometimes, but to me, it was a small price to pay for what he had done for me and mine. Four months after the day he took me to breakfast, I turned eighteen and he moved me, Sunshine, and Divine into his home. I felt like fucking Cinderella, especially when he started to control me. But I rode with because, besides that, my life was lit. I had managed to bag "Caesar reincarnated," and he was in love with me. I was in love with him too. It wasn't just about the money. In the past three years, Ross and I had developed a connection that no one could deny. We finished each other's sentences. I knew what he was thinking before he said it. He was my king. I loved him so much, and he showed me that he loved me. Yet, he didn't love himself enough to realize that I wasn't going anywhere. He never realized that, no matter the next younger dude that came along with money, I wasn't fazed because I loved him. The moment he realized that, was the moment he'd stopped putting his hands on me. I knew it. Until then, I forced myself to look past the random moments when he acted out like this in order to keep this life for not only me, but Sunshine and Divine as well. I had dealt with the same from my mama for the same reasons. Now, it was like second nature.

I felt a soft pat on my shoulder and heard Treasure say, "C'mon, girl. Get out."

I finally focused on my surroundings and saw that Ross had pulled into our driveway. I waited for him and Vegas to get out before I grabbed my purse. Before I could open the door, Treasure had hopped out, opened it, and reached to help me out like I was helpless. I fought not to look into her eyes, but I couldn't help it. She was my best friend. I knew what she was thinking and saw it when I looked into her disappointing, exotic eyes.

"I'm okay," I told her as she looped her arm through mine.

"That eye isn't, though. C'mon. Let's get some ice on it."

As we walked towards the house, I noticed that Ross had already gone inside, not even waiting for me. I just shook my head. He was definitely in one of his moods tonight. Vegas was standing in the doorway waiting for us, however.

"Bae, why don't you talk to your motherfuckin' friend?" Treasure spat in a whisper. "I'm sick of him."

"Aye, man," Vegas whispered back and shrugged. He left it at that because we could all hear Ross nearby in the den at his bar. He was banging bottles and glasses around, still acting a fool.

Treasure eyed Vegas evilly. He just shook his head and went into the den after Ross.

Treasure blew her breath. Her nostrils flared with irritation. "Let me go check on Sunshine and Divine for you. Go put some ice on that eye. I'll be back."

I just nodded as I headed towards the kitchen and Treasure approached the staircase that led to the second floor.

Once inside of the kitchen, I cringed when my eyes met the nanny's. "Esperanza, what are you doing up?" I asked, trying to appear cool.

She obviously saw what Treasure had seen on my face, and her pale skin turned beet red. Her thin lips pressed together as she threw the kitchen towel down on the counter and folded her arms tightly across her large chest.

Esperanza was like a mother to me and Divine and a grandmother to Sunshine. Don't get it twisted. Ross wasn't so filthy rich that he could afford some highly paid nanny. Esperanza was the mother of a hype, Julio. He was the dude Ross used to have do odd jobs around the house when he needed the money to get high. That's how Ross had met Esperanza. She used to come around looking for her son. One day, she asked Ross for work, and he offered her a decent pay to watch after Sunshine when we needed her, which wasn't often since Ross didn't want me working. But she always made herself useful by cooking, cleaning, and doing any other chores to keep the money coming from Ross. Shit, she was a nanny to all of us in a sense, which had earned her the right to take over one of the two guest bedrooms in our five-bedroom, brick house on the south side of the city on 73rd and Vernon.

I ignored Esperanza's chastising glare and opened the freezer. Just as I grabbed a pack of frozen vegetables, Vegas came into the kitchen with worry and sympathy flooding his baby blue, heavily and girlishly lashed eyes.

Reaching out to me, he said, "That motherfucka drunk. He trippin'. You okay, baby girl?"

I fell into his embrace, and he hugged me tightly.

"Yeah," I said weakly. I wasn't in physical pain. I was emotionally hurt. I just couldn't understand why Ross didn't trust me after all this time.

As Vegas gently rocked me from side to side, his Versace tee smothered me and his masculine, yet sweet, scent swam into my nostrils and soothed me. For a white dude, Vegas had so much swag. He stayed looking good, fresh as fuck, and smelling good. I swear.

His deep whispers roared into my ear, "You too pretty and good to him to let him hit on you like that."

"Yeah?" I asked sarcastically. "Did you tell him that?"

Vegas scoffed as he replied, "Hell yeah."

The click-clack of heels could be heard nearing the kitchen. Vegas let me go and prepared for the tongue lashing from Treasure. She quickly appeared in the doorway with the same attitude that she'd had on her face when she went upstairs.

She fixed her face, though, when her eyes fell on Esperanza.

"Oh, hey, Esperanza," she said. "I didn't know you were here. Had I known, I wouldn't have gone to check on Sunshine."

"I'm always around somewhere, dear," she replied, her words laced with her Spanish accent. She then eyed me with the same chastising glare that she had when she first saw my face.

"Good night, Heaven. We'll talk in the morning."

I cringed with fear like she was my mother. "Good night, Esperanza."

"Good night," Treasure and Vegas said in unison.

As she disappeared from the kitchen, I kicked off my heels and padded towards the nearest stool at the island. I then plopped down on it and put the bag of vegetables on my face.

I could feel Treasure's attitude steering my way.

"Treasure, please..." I tried to stop her rant, but, as always, she gave zero fucks.

"Fuuuuuuck all 'lat!" she immediately started to fuss. I groaned, but she kept going in on my ass. "He always puttin' his fucking hands on you-"

"It's not always-"

"I don't give a fuck if it's once a year! It ain't right!"

I looked at Vegas for some sort of help to shut her up, but he just shook his head and walked out. He knew better than to fuck up his ride home and any potential pussy he would be getting that night by saying a word. My night had already gone to shit, however, so I just sat on that stool and let Treasure tell me for the umpteenth time that I was better than Ross putting his hands on me, all while a medley of broccoli, carrots, and cauliflower melted on my face.

ROSS

I sighed when I saw the defeated look on Vegas' face as he came back into the den.

"She mad?" I asked.

Vegas blew his breath hard and the wrinkles in his forehead came out as he ran his hand over his disheveled ponytail that held up that stupid-ass man bun. "Fuck, I don't know. Treasure mad enough for her. She really won't let Heaven get a word in."

I groaned and clutched the glass of cognac in my hand tighter.

Vegas approached the bar as I leaned against it from the opposite side. He sat on the stool and grabbed the glass of cognac that he had abandoned when I sent him back into the kitchen to evaluate just how mad Heaven was at me.

Vegas shook his head slowly as he brought the glass to his lips. He stopped short to say, "You gotta stop that shit, man." He took a sip after he gave me his advice.

"I know," I immediately agreed with him.

"She didn't do shit."

"I know."

"Dub didn't really do shit either. He was just talking to all of us. It's been three years. When are you going to get used to your people being around your woman?"

Just the thought of these niggas eyeing my woman made my mouth tighten. "Never."

Vegas chuckled and shook his head. "You sound crazy as fuck. Yeah, you got a beautiful, young, woman on your arm-"

My eyebrow raised, and I cocked my head. "You sound like you wanna fuck her-"

Vegas' face balled up as he barked, "Don't fucking insult me."

But no matter how hard he tried to look with that beard and hella tattoos, that fucking man bun didn't put no fear in my heart at all.

But I quickly told him, "I was fucking with you." I was, for real. The only motherfucker I trusted my woman with was Vegas. He had been at my right hand for years and he had never crossed me.

"Yeah, but you gotta stop fucking with her. That girl loves you. She don't see no other man but you. It's been that way since the day y'all met. You know that. So, stop acting like an insecure bitch."

A smile slowly spread across my face. "I'mma let you get away with calling me that because I'm drunk and tired."

Vegas waved his hand, the diamonds accenting his white gold Gucci watch sparkling as he swatted my threat away. "Yeah, whatever. You gon' let me get away with that because you know I will drag your ass if you tried to backhand me."

I waved his threat off. "Whatever."

Vegas threw back the shot of cognac left in his glass and stood up. "I'm out, motherfucka."

He reached his hand out to shake up with me, and mine met his. "Cool. Let yourself out. Tell Treasure don't be talking no shit on the way out either."

On his way out, Vegas chuckled and shot over his shoulder, "Doubt I'll be telling her that."

I laughed. I didn't give a fuck how big and tough his white ass was or how lethal his body count was, when it came to Treasure, that motherfucker was a punk.

HEAVEN

"Treasure, let's roll."

I got so sad as soon as I heard Vegas' voice in the foyer. Treasure was my voice when I was too busy appreciating this rent-free house and the father figure for Divine and Sunshine to tell Ross that he was acting like a stupid, insecure bitch.

Treasure saw my sadness and asked me, "Want me to spend the night with you?"

I sucked my teeth and looked at her like she was stupid. "Hell no."

"I will if you want me to," she swore.

"I know. But, no, I don't want my bullshit to fuck up y'all night no more than it already has. I think he's calmed down now anyway."

"You sure? I will stay. Fuck Vegas. That motherfucka can jack his dick," she insisted.

I laughed, and she finally cracked a smile for the first time since Ross had smacked the shit outta me with his big-ass hand.

"Yes, Treasure," I said with a giggle. "Go home and give your man some pussy."

She smiled at the sound of that. Then she gave me a quick hug before leaving out of the kitchen and meeting Vegas in the foyer. I watched as they walked through the foyer and toward the door. Treasure was fussing at him in whispers that I couldn't hear. But, since we had been friends for so long, I knew she was fussing at him about Ross. I shook my head, embarrassed that my man's insecurities were even fucking with my best friend's relationship.

I stayed seated on the stool at the island with the veggies melting on my face. I wondered if I even wanted to bother going into the den to talk to Ross about what had just happened. I wanted to fix it, but I for damn sure wasn't trying to get in another fight.

Earlier that night, we had been at a club partying for one of his homeboy's birthday. Everything was all good at first. The club was crackin'. Even though Treasure and I were only twenty, Ross and Vegas had gotten us fake ID's years ago. That night, we had been at V75. All of the dope boys, card crackers, and hustlers were in the building. A good time was being had by all until Dub's drunk ass held a conversation with me a minute too long for Ross' taste. Ross was all the way across the bar, but as Dub talked to me, I could feel his eyes on me. The moment I looked up and across the bar, my eyes met the fire in his. I knew it was gonna be one of those nights.

Just thinking back on the bullshit had me irritated. I was ready to go into the den and snap on his ass. However, my face was hurt enough. I wasn't about to make my head hurt as well by having the same conversation with Ross. Besides, those conversations always only led to him still forgetting how loyal I was to him as soon as the next man looked at me or spoke to me too long. So, I opted to just leave him in the den and tiptoe upstairs to snuggle up with Sunshine.

With a long, deep, sigh, I looked around the kitchen before I stood up. It was beautiful. In fact, this whole house was perfect. That day, three years ago, when Ross picked me up from school and I saw this house, I thought it was a mansion. And it was compared to the tiny box I had been living in. That day, Ross told me he had bought this house for forty-five thousand dollars cash and renovated it with his own money. It had an open floor plan, high-end wood trim, and rich, dark hardwood floors throughout the first and second levels. Custom white cabinetry was in the modern kitchen with chrome light fixtures, quartz countertops, stainless steel appliances, and a sunroom off of the kitchen, leading to a private fenced-in backyard and garage. The finished basement was tiled with beautiful wood grain like tile. Soft grey colors painted the walls throughout the entire house. Each bathroom had marble tile with custom white cabinets. No detail had been overlooked in the five bedrooms and three bathrooms of the tons of living space on all three levels of the home. Now, his forty-five-thousand-dollar investment was worth well over two hundred thousand dollars.

I loved Ross and could never see a reason to leave him. But this house was another reason why I stayed with him. It was another reason why I looked past his temper tantrums. This house that I paid no bills in and the 2016 Acura truck that I didn't have to pay a note for were reasons why I was so submissive and loyal, despite the bullshit. Ross' hustle hadn't earned him millionaire status, but he definitely had enough money to take care of me, Sunshine, and Divine without either of us lifting a finger except to get it manicured. That was something I was not willing to take for granted. So, I was willing to go to bed without arguing with Ross about it, without telling him how I felt, or how his insecurities hurt me.

However, just as I stood from the stool and grabbed my Louboutins from the floor, I felt his tall, dark shadow over me. I slowly stood up, looking him in the eyes and setting the bag of vegetables on the counter.

"I'm sorry, baby," he whispered in a tone laced with a small crack as he handed me a glass. And no matter how much of a devil he looked like in that car, I had never heard those words spoken so genuinely.

The last thing I wanted was another drink that night, but for the sake of keeping the peace, I took it. I always did what I had to do to keep the peace.

When I looked at him, that crazy, insecure little boy was gone, and my loving man had reappeared. So, when he moved towards me, I didn't flinch. He wrapped his arms around me and kissed the top of my head in the loving way he always did.

"I love you." And I had never heard those words spoken so genuinely either.

Still holding him around his waist, I looked up into his light brown, slanted girlish eyes with the same genuine love for him in my eyes. "I know, but you don't know that I love you."

I could see his soul cringe as he took my hand and walked me back toward the island. "That's not true. I do know how much you love me. You show me every day, every hour, and every second. I'm just a stupid old man-"

My giggles interrupted him as he helped me back up on the stool. "You're not stupid," I joked.

"Oh, but I'm old?" I just laughed, so he kept pressing with wide eyes, "I'm old, babe?"

I smiled, relaxing in this atmosphere. This was us. All that physical abuse and arguing was not us. It wasn't what made me fall in love with him. It wasn't what I had to deal with the majority of the time.

"No, baby, you're not old."

That was not a lie. I was not just saying that to gas him up.

The moment Ross and I connected, we became exactly the same age; the years between us disappeared. I never saw age when I looked at Ross. I saw a man who loved me. I saw a man who saw enough in me to not only take in me, but to take in my baby and my sister and love on them as if they were his own.

Looking up at him with a faint smile on my face, I also never saw the horrible choice I'd made when I married Ross. But the day would come when I would see it. The day would come where it would be clear the terrible mistake I'd made when I said, "I do," to Ross.

❀ 3 ❀

TREASURE

"**M**ove, Vegas." I frowned and swatted his hand off of my thigh. I was staring out of the passenger's side window of his Porsche truck. All kinds of attitude was all over my face. I could feel Vegas' baby blue eyes digging a hole in the side of my blonde, curly, pixie cut.

He quickly glanced at me and then looked back at the road. This sexy-ass smirk was on his face as he squeezed my thigh. "Stop it. You ain't mad at me. Gimme a kiss."

The only good thing about Ross was that he had introduced me to bae's ass. Never would I have thought that after being raised in Englewood that I would fall for a white boy. But since he was raised in Terror Town, he was tougher and had more swag than any of the guys that I had fucked with in the past. The only thing white about him was his skin. But that could hardly be seen because his skin was covered in colorful drawings that symbolized the GD's he ran with as a teenager, his Italian heritage, and his dead homeboys. But besides his lightly-tanned skin, everything about him said "Chitown" and "hood nigga".

He and Ross had worked side by side for eight years, since Vegas was seventeen. Vegas wasn't nearly as old as Ross' ancient ass, though. Vegas was now only twenty-five. He had started working with Ross when he bought a car from Ross' chop shop. Back then, Ross was only flipping cars. Vegas was selling drugs, so he was one of Ross' repeat customers. Then Ross expressed interest in expanding his business. That's when Vegas introduced Ross to his uncle, Vinny, who was the connect. He wasn't the drug connect, however. He was a *gun* connect. Ross and Vegas distributed weapons, not drugs. They went in half on that first shipment of firearms, and it was a wrap from there.

I met Vegas soon after Ross and Heaven started fucking around. It turned me on how his white ass was the coolest motherfucka that I had ever met. I had never had a problem getting guys because I was a Leo. We are known as hoes, but in all actuality, we are just free spirits when it comes to sex. We like a variety. And Vegas was definitely a taste that I had never acquired before. But he didn't like my mouthy ass. For once, a dude didn't want me, so I chased him for a year. The moment he finally succumbed to this pussy, he owned it. We had been together ever since. That was two years ago. He had actually made me put down my player ways...for the most part. I had gone from juggling two or three dudes to being committed to just him. And it was well worth it. Vegas was the first man who had shown me what unconditional love was. When most street dudes were trying to have me in the streets right next to them, Vegas had me on this pedestal that made me feel like a prized possession.

I ain't gonna lie. That promiscuous girl from the streets was still in me. I knew Vegas loved me, but there had been a few moments when I had to do me.

Vegas squeezed my thigh again. "I said gimme a kiss."

I pushed his hand away and smacked my lips. "I ain't."

He faked looking legit hurt. "What you mad at me for?"

Snarling, I told him, "Because you're actually best friends and working with that motherfucker."

"I might not be for long."

My head whipped towards Vegas. He had the nerve to keep his eyes on the road and away from me. He knew I was looking at him like he had lost his fucking mind.

I had to hear him wrong...

"What did you say?" I asked.

"I might not be working with him for long."

"W-why not?" I had just seen a grown-ass man backhand the shit out of my best friend, but *this* was the first time that night that I had been blown away. That was because seeing Ross act out like a bitch was the usual, but hearing Vegas talk like this made me feel like I was in the twilight zone. This just didn't sound real.

"What you mean you might not be working with him for long?" I asked.

For the first time in a long time, I saw Vegas look hurt and worried. "I think he's stealing from me."

My face balled up in confusion. "Why you think that?"

Vegas shrugged like this was everyday shit. "I heard he out here spending mad cash, and money ain't adding up."

I shook my head, still in complete disbelief, even though I had heard him loud and clear.

"Y'all been partners for years. He's like a big brother to you. I don't think Ross would steal from you."

"That ain't what other motherfuckers sayin'."

My eyes narrowed at him. "Other motherfuckers like who? Princess?"

He sucked his teeth. "C'mon, bae, don't start. What she got to do with this?"

"I saw that bitch in your face!" I spat.

He had the nerve to chuckle and stroke his beard. "Now, you sound like Ross."

I hit his shoulder, and he leaned over towards his window to dodge me.

I closed my mouth and then spat, "Fuck you! Ross a fucking psycho, but I *know* what I saw. That bitch is always on you."

Princess was a THOT bitch in our circle that always found a reason to be around my dick, giggling and shit. I had no worries that Vegas had fucked around on me with her. He had not given me a reason to think that. But Princess had been throwing that pussy at him like a baseball for the last year, after she broke up with her man for having a baby on her.

"Because I work closely with her brother and his friends," Vegas explained.

I rolled my eyes towards the roof of the car. "Whatever—"

"Any fucking way, nah, Princess didn't tell me no shit like that. Don't you think it would have been a reliable source that I heard it from if I actually believe it?"

Fine. If bae's ass wanted to change the subject, I would for now because this was way more important than Princess' THOT ass.

"But Ross is your family, babe."

Again, he shrugged nonchalantly, keeping his eyes on the road. "Family shit on each other all the time."

I sat up a bit like that would make him believe me. "Vegas, you're wrong. Who got you talking like this?"

"Just trust me, babe."

I groaned inwardly. That was always his answer. He never really told me the ins and outs of his and Ross' business. I knew what they did, but when it came to details, he treated me like a little kid that he was protecting. Vegas didn't want a ride-or-die bitch out there committing crimes with him and taking cases for him. He wanted his beautiful woman at home, safe and out of the way of all the bullshit that he and Ross got into.

"Mmm humph," was my reply.

"Don't worry," he said, putting a hand on my thigh again. "I got an accountant looking into it to make sure before I make any moves. So, we'll see."

"And if he is?"

His blue eyes darkened with uncertainty. "Then I guess we'll have to see about that too."

HEAVEN

The next morning, the feel of Ross' beard tickling my ass pulled me out of my sleep.

"Mmmmm," I moaned as I began to stir in my sleep and feel his tongue licking my sweet crevice.

As I began to move, I felt his grip on my thighs getting tight. He locked me in place and started to suck on my clit, jolting me completely out of my sleep.

"Mmmm! Shit..."

He began to moan into my pussy as he sucked my clit into an orgasm. I had an amused smile on my face as I stared at the ceiling, biting my lip. Ross thought he was slick. He had tried to eat his way out of the dog house last night, but I was too drunk and tired to let him get some. Now, I guess he was just going to take it.

My back arched and my nude, matte, coffin-shaped nails gripped the sheet as I felt the intense pressure of an orgasm barreling through my body.

"Fuuuuuuck!"

"Mmmm humph," Ross moaned into my pussy as he sucked and licked my clit simultaneously. I could feel his intense suction as his tongue played with the hood of it at the same time. I closed my eyes tightly, trying not to cum so fast.

I enjoyed head from Ross the most. His dick was good, but that mouth of his is what got me to fall for him initially. At eighteen years old, I hadn't had many men eat my pussy, or eat it well at that. Dudes my age still thought eating pussy was nasty. But the first time Ross and I had sex, he showed me that a grown-ass man wanted to taste the cat as much as he wanted to be inside of it. His soft big lips felt like a massage. He sucked my soul right out of me. And when he put his fingers in my pussy and ass at the same time, I swear, it was better than sex. That's why I married him a year later. Luckily, I didn't have many family members to argue with me about marrying a man that was over ten years older than me. Of course, Treasure thought the idea was genius because not only did Ross love me, my sister, and my daughter, but he was also filthy fucking rich, to us. She thought I would be stupid if I didn't jump at the chance of securing my future, securing the fact that I would never have to return to selling food stamps just to be able to have clothes on my back.

Our wedding day was the best day of my life. He had taken me, Divine, and Sunshine, along with his family and friends, to the most beautiful resort in Cancun, Mexico. Not only was I marrying the man of my dreams, but for the first time in my life, I had flown on a plane and saw white beaches and blue water. Nothing was more beautiful that day than when the sun went down and Ross and I made love on the white sand.

"Baby! I'm cummiiiing!" I was actually disappointed. Like I said, I loved Ross' head. So, the last thing I wanted to do was end it. Sometimes, he would eat me into another paralyzing orgasm. As I came, I hoped this would be one of those times, but unfortunately, he sat up on the edge of the bed, giggling and wiping my juices from his beard as I shook uncontrollably

"Shit, "I sighed. That's when I rolled over onto my side and felt the pain on the side of my face as I lay on the pillow. That's when I remembered what had happened between Ross and me the night before.

I guess that is when Ross remembered too, because he stood up and walked towards the dresser. I saw him pick up his wallet and dig inside. He pulled out a large knot of money and laid it on the nightstand beside me.

"Why don't you go shopping today?"

That's how he always fixed it whenever he flipped out and hit me. He made up with me by using sex and money. He still had so much to learn about love because he didn't even understand that I didn't need either of those two things to forgive him or to continue to love him. I had forgiven him last night. Ross hitting me was like a kid throwing a tantrum. Was it right? No. Absolutely not. But just like a kid throwing a tantrum didn't mean he didn't love his parents, Ross hitting me didn't mean that he didn't love me. I knew that.

"You're about to leave?"

When I should have felt anger when he put his hands on me, I was now pissed the fuck off because as usual, Ross was getting ready to leave for the day. He would be gone for most of the day, and I just knew he would be with another woman.

"Yeah, I'm about to ride. I have some business to take care of."

That was what he always said; that he had business to take care of. But that was some bullshit, and I knew it. Yeah, he probably had a few things to do concerning his money during the day, but Ross had escalated to a level in his business that he barely had to do any real work. At this point, Ross had created a hustle where he had employees doing most of his work. Now, I had never gone to college, and because of how my life was set up, I didn't pay attention much when I was in high school. But I was no dummy. I knew that Ross was not *so* busy every day all day. That was what hurt. The emotional pain of knowing he was cheating on me was way worse than the physical pain. I had whooped a few bitches in my day and gotten clocked in the process. Therefore, I could take a hit. But the emotional pain of Ross being with another woman hurt like a motherfucker. This thing between us was more than love. He knew how much our marriage meant to me because he knew where he had rescued me from. So, the fact that he would lie to me hurt like a motherfucker. I didn't have evidence that he was cheating. But I didn't need to walk in on him with his dick in another bitch for me to know what was going on. That was what hurt; that he was the one cheating on me, but he would put his hands on me at the mere thought of another man looking at me.

As he started to get his toiletries together for his shower, I didn't say anything, though. After all the bullshit last night, the last thing I wanted to do was start this day with another fucking argument and fight.

"Oh, and Mello is coming home in a few days," he added.

I rolled my eyes behind his back and bit my tongue. He was just bringing up Mello to avoid the conversation about where he was really about to go. He knew that shit was on the tip of my tongue.

"I know," I forced myself to say instead. "He told me."

"I want to throw him a welcome home party. Can you make that happen?" He picked up his wallet again, grabbed some more money, and placed it next to the knot he had already given me. "Make it real nice. I know you can do that. I trust your judgment."

"Okay."

Ross always said that he had three kids: Mello, Sunshine, and Divine. But Mello was Ross' only biological child. Embarrassingly, his son and I were the same age. Ross and his baby's mama had conceived a child at the very young age of fourteen. Twenty years ago, it wasn't as common for kids so young to have babies, so when they found out she was pregnant, Mello's mother's very Baptist parents moved down to Florida to get her away from Ross. Being a kid himself, Ross was not able to fly down to Florida to be a part of Mello's life. Ross' parents were too poor to travel anyway. By the time Mello's mother's parents divorced thirteen years later and the mother moved back to Chicago with Mello and his mother, the damage had already been done to Ross and Mello's relationship. Mello felt like once Ross was old enough that Ross should have tried harder to be in his life. Ross was too busy making a name in the streets to do that, though. He had become accustomed to giving his all to the streets. That's who got his unconditional love. He knew nothing about the fatherly bond he should have had with Mello. Over the years, Mello tried to establish that bond, but it was always a fail. Ross was just never the emotional person Mello needed as a father figure. For years, Ross only made sure to show up on the holidays, birthdays, and graduations. Then, at sixteen, Mello started getting into some trouble. The one thing Ross did attempt to teach him was the streets, which started to lead Mello down the wrong path. Luckily, Mello was smart enough to get the fuck out of Chicago. I had never even gotten the chance to meet him because he had gone back to Florida to college soon after Ross and I got serious. But he and I had had many conversations and video chats over the phone and on Facebook. Ross always felt like money fixed everything, including love, so he would throw Mello some cash before he would give him the conversation he wanted whenever he called home. But I was the one who kept him abreast of everything going on in his father's life over conversations that went on for hours sometimes. Eventually, he stopped calling for Ross and just asked for me.

I never called Mello my stepson because that was just weird. But he was definitely a friend and he was family, so, I was happy to throw this party for him and welcome him home.

◌╳◌

A few hours later, I was headed to Sadie's Soul Food Palace to place the catering order for Mello's party. Holding Sunshine's hand, I headed towards the garage with Esperanza and Divine following behind me.

Esperanza had been quiet all morning while she cooked breakfast. I could see in her face that she was still upset about what had happened the night before. She had spoken only a few words to me and even fewer words to Ross. I appreciated her being quiet about it and sparing me the embarrassment. But as soon as I got in the car, she started in on my ass.

"So, he did it again?"

I sighed deeply and readied myself for her reprimand and inter-rogation.

"Who did what?" Divine asked, and I cringed. "Did Ross hit you again?"

I probably shouldn't have, but I never kept anything from Divine. She was my younger sister, but we were equals in what we had gone through as kids. She was just as much as my best friend as Treasure was. So, I never kept anything from her. Therefore, when she would ask me why I had a scratch or bruise, I was honest about it. But having gone through hell with me, Divine understood exactly why I stayed.

"Yes, he did," Esperanza answered for me just as I got a text message. I checked my phone and smiled when I saw that it was Mello replying to the text that I had sent him before leaving out of the house.

Mello: *He what?*

I laughed as I typed back: *He's throwing you a welcome home party.*

"Leave that bastard—"

"No, Esperanza, don't call him that." I cut Esperanza off.

"Ross is a great man. Don't get me wrong, but he should *not* be putting his hands on you!" she urged as she turned red. "You are a great woman to him...a *great* woman. It's unacceptable what he does."

"I know, Esperanza. He just—"

Her sneering interrupted me. "Don't take up for him."

I quieted obediently after saying, "Okay," just as I got a reply from Mello.

Mello: *He don't even fuck with me, but he wanna throw me a party? Stuntin' ass nigga.*

I laughed to myself. I honestly didn't blame Mello. Ross was my husband, and I did love him, but he honestly did not know how to show love. If he didn't know how to love me right, I understood how his son could feel the same way.

As I approached a red light, I quickly sent a text back: *Be nice.*

Esperanza's eyes rolled up to the sky as her arms folded across her large chest. "God, at least fight him back."

"Exactly," Divine cut in. "You fought Mama all the time. All of a sudden, you can't fight back?"

Just as the light turned green, I saw Mello reply back: *I will. But only for you.*

"I didn't have anything to lose when I was fighting Mama," I told Divine. "Now, I got everything to lose. I don't take the hits for just me. I take it for all of us; you, me, and Sunshine. You two are like fucking princesses. You are a long way from having to babysit our crazy-ass mama and eating fried baloney sandwiches. Even you, Esperanza; I take the fights and the bitches for you too, because if we weren't with Ross, you wouldn't have a job."

Her lips were pressed tightly into a thin line. She wanted to argue with me, but she knew I was right. I knew that when Ross hired her, she was looking for a job in order to obtain her citizenship and take care of her children and grandchildren. The money that Ross gave her was a blessing.

Shaking her head slowly, Esperanza groaned, "Roosevelt doesn't know what he has in you."

I didn't agree. I didn't see myself as some angel. I had lived my life sacrificing for myself in order to ensure the safety of *my* others. But I did laugh at the sound of Ross' government name. I hadn't heard it more than a handful of times, and it only came out of Esperanza's lips.

Luckily, Esperanza didn't have anything else to say.

A few minutes later, we arrived at the restaurant. Treasure was standing in front of the door waiting in a beautiful maxi dress. I recognized it from when we had gone shopping two days before in Akira.

Damn, I knew I should have copped that.

The sun was shining so bright that it looked like it was baking her light skin. It was a very hot, June day, so Treasure looked miserable as she stood there fanning herself as we parked.

"Took you long enough, bitch," she cursed as I climbed out of the car.

After Esperanza got out, she stayed back to take Sunshine out of her car seat, as Divine and I sashayed toward Treasure.

"Good to see you too, best friend," I said.

I could tell that she was about to say something, but something behind me had caught her eye.

"What are you doing here?" she asked. That made me and Divine turn around to see Damo headed our way with a smile on his face. Damo was one of Ross and Vegas' customers who had become one of their homeboys over the years.

"What up, Damo?" Divine greeted him with a hug.

He kissed her on the cheek and told the rest of us, "What up, y'all? Good afternoon, Esperanza."

We all spoke as he bent down and playfully pinched Sunshine's cheek as she held Esperanza's hand. She giggled and told him, "Stooop," while Treasure continued to give him this odd look.

"I just came to get me something to eat," Damo answered her inquisitive expression as he playfully pushed her. "Dang, I can't eat?"

"You can eat," she sassed. "Just making sure you ain't following nobody. I just saw you at the crib and told you that I didn't know where Vegas was."

"I know. I'm following you for Vegas, making sure your ass ain't out here on no hoe shit."

Treasure sucked her teeth and smacked his arm. "Yeah right. Stop playing."

As me and Divine laughed, Divine asked him, "You buying us something to eat too?"

"Hell nah. You with the money right here," he said, looking at me and opening the door for us. "She got it. She got us all."

ROSS

"Everything go all good with those African motherfuckers?"

"Yeah, boss," one of my workers told me through the phone. "Money came in real smooth. Twenty-thousand a piece for the Benzes."

I nodded as if he could see me. "Bet."

"You comin' into the office today?"

"Not today. I got some shit to take care of. I'll holla." As I hung up, I saw the smile on April's face as she rode on the passenger's side of my truck. I knew what I had just said would make her happy. She had been bitching about getting some time all week, so I was giving it to her today to keep her from acting a fool.

I knew I wasn't shit for beating on Heaven for even the possibility of her doing the exact same thing that I was doing, but a woman's place was at home being committed and obedient to her man. I had been juggling women since I broke my virginity at the age of twelve. Having money and women was what defined a man out here in these streets. I had the hoes, the badass wife, and the criminal organization that had a name that was ringing bells. Vegas and I were on our way to being the new Black Mafia Family. We dealt a little with drugs, but mostly with the importing of guns and the resale of stolen foreign cars out of the chop shop that he had eventually gained a partnership in. We sold hot commodity foreign cars to customers all over the United States. My chop shop broke down stolen cars and welded them together to make a brand-new untraceable foreign luxury vehicle. Basically, I had little niggas out there hitting up rich dudes all over the U.S. for their half-a-million-dollar cars, just to disassemble them and sell them to some cheap dudes for half the price. I started as a teenager after the drug game became too intense for me. I don't know about these other motherfuckers, but I made this money to enjoy living a long life. These niggas out here were selling drugs and risking their lives to end up in the grave or in prison just for their wives and baby mamas to live comfortably with the money that they worked their lives and lost them over. Not me. I took my drug money and started a chop shop before I was twenty. At first, we were stealing Chevys, Cavaliers, and other low-end vehicles. Now, I was selling foreign cars and shipping them all over the United States. We used high-tech hacking equipment to steal modern cars, so my employees didn't even need a key to steal them. Then I had tech geeks on lock to make the new keys.

Gun trafficking was just as lucrative as the chop shop. Through the connections I had obtained through Vegas' uncle, I got the hookup on gun shipments. When guns came into the U.S., I had somebody on lock waiting to steal them at the ports. Then I resold them to anybody from gun dealers to personal buyers. It was quite a lucrative business, earning me as much as ten grand for three automatic rifles.

It was a lucrative business that had awarded me and Vegas a comfortable life by now. I was able to take care of my family with ease. Heaven's only job was to be my wife and not be a hoe. Therefore, no matter what *I* was doing, she needed to know she never had that option.

❧ 4 ❧

HEAVEN

♫ *My bitch too foreign, need a visa (ooh,) I don't need her (huh?)*
Pull up drop top with a eater (skrrt,) two seater (skrrt)
New bitch wanna fuck to my AP (AP, ice,) new freezer (ice)
I woke up thinkin' 'bout bands (bands)
Hop off a jet to a check when I land (yuh)
My bitch too foreign, need a visa (bitch,) I don't need her (huh?)
Pull up drop top with a eater (yeah,) two seater (skrrt, skrrt)
New bitch wanna fuck to my AP (bitch,) new freezer (new freezer)
I woke up thinkin' 'bout bands (new freezer)
Hop off a jet to a check when I land (dat way) ♫

A WEEK LATER, THE BACKYARD WAS FILLED WITH OUR PEOPLE
dancing to "Freezer" by Rich the Kid, eating soul food, swimming, and
playing basketball. With the help of Treasure, the backyard had been
transformed into a man cave. During our many conversations, Mello
had told me that what he missed most about Chicago was the women.
He said the women at school were lame and boujee. So, I had made

sure to invite a bunch of girls. Big booty bitches were twerking on the dance floor that I had created by hiring someone to pour cement in the middle of the large yard last summer. Then there were more big booty bitches in swimsuits and bikinis in the pool and lounging on the deck in the beach chairs that surrounded it. Beautiful canopies covered the outside sofa seating arrangements that I had rented. Underneath another canopy, along the privacy fence, was a whiskey bar because that was Mello's favorite. Then there was another fully stocked bar with free liquor for everyone in attendance. I had hired one of Chicago's hottest deejays, DJ Hi-Speed, to spin for the day party that looked like it was definitely going to go way into the evening and early morning. Mostly all of Ross' family, friends, and business associates were filling up the yard. Most of Mello's homeboys were in the alley playing basketball with their shirts off and sweating in this hot-ass June sun.

"Damn, Mello know he fine as fuck," Treasure said, swooning as she fanned herself with a paper plate. We were sitting on one of the sofas under a canopy. So, I wasn't sure if she was fanning herself because the weather was making her hot or watching Mello was. So, I just laughed. It was already bad enough that Dub was at the party. The last thing I needed was for Ross to now be mad because I was looking at his son too hard.

Shifting her weight to lean into me, Treasure peered over her sunglasses. She discreetly watched Mello dribble the basketball. "I ain't laughing. I am *so* for real. He is fine as hell with his lil' chocolate ass."

"*Little?* He's our age," I corrected her.

"Oh, I said that just to be funny. Ain't nothing *little* about him. Look at his body. He's wide, tall, and built up just like Cam Newton. And do you see that print in them basketball shorts?"

"No," I quickly denied.

I was lying, though, because I saw it clear as day. Anybody could see that bulge. Hell, Stevie Wonder could see that motherfucker. Teyanna, Mello's girlfriend, was one lucky bitch.

"Well, *I* do," Treasure insisted. I looked over and caught her licking her lips and shaking her head as she pushed her sunglasses back up.

"You better stop looking because his crazy-ass girlfriend is here," I warned her.

"Fuck that bitch! I can look. I don't want her man. I got my own."

"And you don't want nobody looking at his ass either." I laughed.

She instantly snarled. "A bitch better not."

"You better tell Princess that then," I said as I stared over at the bar.

"What?!"

My head tilted towards the bar. "She's over there giving Vegas the eye while she makes his drink."

Treasure groaned, balling up her fists. "Oooh, I hate that bitch. Who asked her to fucking bartend anyway?"

"Ross. He said she would look good behind the bar. You know the bitch don't ever wear no clothes after she bought that body over in the Dominican."

She sneered as she stared at Princess show all thirty-two teeth to Vegas. "Stankin' bitch. I know she wants my man."

"Shit, I know she wants him too. Everybody knows that."

"I'll be back."

I laughed, but before I could say anything, she was outta there, rushing towards the bar through the grass, trying not to bust her ass because her four-inch heels were sinking into the dirt.

"She so crazy," I mumbled to myself as I shook my head and watched. I was ensuring that she didn't go over there and fuck up the party by punching Vegas or Princess in the face. But she had taken the other route by putting her arms around him from behind, standing on her tiptoes and kissing him passionately once he turned to see who it was.

"Pettyyyy..." I laughed to myself at Treasure just as a shadow came over me. I looked up, assuming it was Ross. I hoped that it was, because for that last thirty minutes, he had been having a conversation with April, Mello's mother. I knew that the conversation was innocent, but I wanted my husband to be next to me.

It wasn't him, though, and I was even more disappointed because it was Dub.

"What up, Heaven?"

Shit, I thought to myself as he sat beside me.

"Hey, Dub," I spoke without even looking his way. I was scanning the crowd, looking for Ross. When I found him, I saw that he was still holding that convo with April. Even though I knew he and April had been over for over twenty years, it irked the fuck outta me how they had been in one another's face all day. If it had been me in the face of a member of the opposite sex, he would be pissed the fuck off.

I was sick of Ross' one-sided rules and regulations. The day he woke me up eating my pussy, he left and didn't come back home until three in the morning. There ain't no business to be taken care of for that fucking long. Then he laid in the bed and didn't touch me. His dick didn't even get hard when he pulled the covers back and saw that I was completely naked. That was because he had been fucking all day. I knew it. So, when Dub sat down, I didn't even budge.

If Ross was gonna wanna fight again, I didn't care. I had spent my life fighting, so, it didn't scare me like it should have.

"Fuck, it's hot out here," Dub complained.

"I know, right? It's gotta be like ninety degrees out here."

In response, Dub continued to fuss. "And it's only the beginning of the summer. *Shit.*"

"Exactly. That pool looks like it feels so good. I wanna get in so bad."

"But you know Ross is gonna flip the fuck out if you let all these dudes see you in a bikini. He like Top Flight Security over yo' ass, old Barney Fife-lookin' ass."

We both laughed. In fact, I laughed so hard that I leaned over a little and slapped Dub's thigh. I thought it was fucking hilarious that everyone else could see how crazy Ross could be at times, except Ross, himself.

"Heaven, come here," Treasure called me.

I looked towards the bar and saw her calling me over with her hand. She was still standing next to Vegas with her other hand literally in his back pocket. She was so fucking petty, and I loved it.

"I'll be back," I told Dub as I stood up.

In my high-waist jeggings, cropped tank, and flip flops, I walked through the crowd of people towards the bar. The heat was beating down on my brown skin as I danced through the crowd to my jam, "Love" by Kendrick Lamar, that the deejay was now playing.

♫ *Just love me*
I wanna be with you, ayy, I wanna be with
I wanna be with you, ayy, I wanna be with
I wanna be with you
If I didn't ride blade on curb, would you still (love me)
If I made up my mind at work would you still (love me)
Keep it a hundred, I'd rather you trust me than to (love me)
Keep it a whole one hund', don't got you I got nothing ♫

Suddenly, I could hear the lyrics being sung behind me as a hand grabbed my elbow. "*Ay, I got something (I got something). Hol' up, we gon' function, no assumptions.*"

I turned around with a smile on my face because I recognized the voice. It was Mello, swaying from side to side, stepping and snapping his fingers with his other hand as the one holding my arm brought me closer to him. I started to step with him, but when his sweaty arm brushed against mine, I freaked.

"Eeeeeewe!"

"My bad, my bad," he chanted as he wiped the salty moisture from my arm.

I frowned as I stared at the pool of sweat rolling from his head, down his face, and onto his chest. "You need a shower."

"I know, right? I'm sweaty and thirsty as hell."

"C'mon. I was on my way to the bar anyway." I continued toward the bar with him beside me. I asked him, "You havin' fun?"

"Hell yeah. This party is dope as fuck. Thank you."

I smirked and shook my head. "Don't thank me. Your father paid for it."

"You always do that. Always talking yourself down. I already know you did all the work to make this happen."

I giggled. "Yeah, I did."

"Then, like I said, *thank you*. And thank you for being there for me while I was gone. Good looking out."

"That was your father's money."

"But *you* made sure to send it to me and you talked to me for hours at a time. I needed all that shit. I felt lonely as fuck down there with those nerdy motherfuckers."

I side eyed him and asked, "Nerdy motherfuckers? I think *you're* the nerd with that 4.0 GPA."

He mannishly blushed and licked his lips. "Yeaaaah, I'm kind of a genius."

That was an understatement. Mello was so smart. The streets of Chicago had raised him. He had hella swag. But he was so smart that he had finished undergrad early. He had majored in Computer Systems Analyst. He was a genius when it came to computers. He could hack anything.

"Are you going back to school to like to get your master's?" I asked him as we finally made it to the line at the bar.

He frowned and shrugged. "Man, I don't know. I doubt it. I'm sick of school."

"That's cool, but don't stay here."

"Why not?" he asked me as Treasure walked up to us with Vegas behind her.

"I don't want you getting in trouble in Chicago or worse, *killed*. It's always the innocent ones who get caught up in the bullshit."

Mello smirked. "I'm far from innocent. Don't let the collegiate shit fool you."

"I know." I really did know. He had told me so much about his past during our many conversations. "I'm just saying."

He just shrugged, leaving it at that. Then we finally gave Treasure and Vegas our attention.

"Why the fuck you standing in line?" Vegas asked me. "You bought this shit. You ain't gotta wait," he fussed.

I shrugged, saying, "I'm not trying to be rude."

"Fuck, I will," he cursed. "What you want?"

Mello and I told Vegas what we wanted, and then he marched towards the bar.

I laughed as Treasure was sure to keep her eyes on Princess.

"Stop it," I told her as I kept laughing.

"Fuck that. I don't trust that bitch." Still, I was giggling. So, she said, "You ain't gon' be laughing when Ross gets a hold to your ass."

I rolled my eyes slightly to the sky. "What I do now?"

"He was glaring at you while Dub was sitting next to you."

Fuck. Here we go again.

5

MELLO

She was so beautiful, even when she was afraid.

I playfully pinched her arm, any excuse to touch her. "What are you scared of?" I asked her. "That old man ain't gonna do nothing to you."

When she and Treasure exchanged this weird look, I asked them, "What?"

Heaven immediately shook her head and answered, "Nothing."

"*Anyway*," Treasure said. "I told you that bitch, Princess, be all on my man..."

Their conversation faded out as I stared at Heaven. While I had been away from Chicago, I thought that my attraction to her was just physical. Being raised in Chicago on the South Side, I was attracted to a particular type of female. So, those chicks down at school didn't hold a candle to the ratcha-sophisticated women that I liked. Those chicks in Florida were too boujee, too skinny, and far from hood enough. It was some ghetto shit about a Chicago chick that I liked. I loved the fact that they could pick some greens and fry chicken, then go cook some dope, and at the same time drop the dope off for you, and then come back home and suck your dick until you cum. So, when Heaven was the only Chicago-bred female I had contact with over the years who wasn't on my nerves, I thought that the connection I felt with her was because she was the only chick around who was familiar. Yeah, I talked to my baby mama, and my girlfriend stayed flying to Florida coming to see me. But their company and conversation was always a headache because those bitches stayed into it with each other, even though I wasn't even in Chicago. But every time I saw Heaven's face on Facetime or heard her voice, she was telling me something encouraging and telling me how proud she was of me. She was always encouraging me to stay in school. She was the only chick around that felt like home. Not to mention, on top of that, she was beautiful. Her baby face hadn't aged over the years. But her curves had matured into some mountains that I wanted to climb. Her smooth chocolate skin looked like brown butter. Then she was wearing her hair in those long curls down her back that looked like that expensive hair that all the hood bitches wanted and sold their Link to get. Ever since my mother showed me her Facebook page, talking shit about my father settling down with some young chick, my young ass had been having fantasies about her. But the more we connected while I was away at school, my attraction intensified.

Now, I was a grown-ass man and I could appreciate and envy the submission and loyalty she had for a dude that didn't even deserve it. Heaven had never told me a single bad thing about my father, but the fact that I could talk to her until three in the morning and he was never around, I knew he was on some other shit. Heaven didn't deserve that. Heaven was a down-ass chick. She was loving and appreciative. She was everything that no woman in my life had ever been. Not even my mother, who was too busy still chasing after my father, who didn't give a shit about her or me when we were younger and still didn't. Heaven was a fucking breath of fresh air. She was a cool breeze on this scorching summer day. But she was my father's wife. Even though I didn't fuck with him like that, Heaven was still married to him, which made her off-limits. And looking at my woman stare at me from across the yard, I knew I had my own shit going on. For those two reasons, I knew I would just always have to admire Heaven from afar.

A light push on my shoulder got my attention. "Move your tall ass out the way. I'm trying to get a drink."

I turned around to see Divine smiling up at me.

"You too young to drink, ain't you?" I asked her.

"Yeah, she is. Stop playing, Divine," Heaven cut in. "Where you been anyway?"

"I was done swimming, so I went to shower and change my clothes."

"Where is Sunshine?"

"With Esperanza playing in the water."

Divine was seventeen and looked a lot like her sister. I would have had better chances crushing on her. I would have at least been able to act on it, but the heart wanted what the fuck it wanted, especially when it couldn't have it.

"Oh God." Heaven's groaning got my attention. Looking at her, I noticed she and Treasure were staring across the yard. Then deep voices could be heard getting loud, which triggered everybody to start running in that direction. Then the music suddenly stopped.

"Ooooohhh shiiiiiit!" I heard some dude chant as I ran towards the mayhem that was unfolding.

"Move! Get out the way!" Treasure fussed as she, Divine, Heaven, and I tried to make it through the crowd.

The closer we got, I heard my mother screaming, "Stop, Ross! *Stoooop*! What the fuck is wrong with you?!"

Hearing my mother's voice, I started knocking niggas over to get to the middle of the scene. I was relieved when I was finally able to lay my eyes on my mother. She was fine. She was just standing there with wide eyes and her hands over her mouth as she looked down at my father beating the shit out of the dude that I saw sitting next to Heaven a few minutes ago.

I was 'bout the only dude in the backyard bold and big enough to stop my father, so I bent down, grabbed his ass around the waist, tossed him to the side, and stood over him. He was reaching for his gun in his waistband until he realized it was me. I bent down, reaching for his hand and helped him stand. He was glaring at the dude he had just whooped as Vegas helped him to his feet too.

"Yo', Pops, be easy," I said with my palm on his chest, lightly pushing him back.

"Punk-ass bitch! I'll kill you!" he barked, still glaring at ol' boy.

"Man, Ross, you trippin'," the dude said in return. He was only able to glare back at Ross through his good eyes while holding the other that was leaking blood.

My father tried to get through me to get back at the dude, but I didn't let him.

"Get him the fuck up outta here!" my father shouted at anyone who would do it.

Treasure walked up on him with the same glare in her eyes that Ross had for ol' boy.

"Really, Ross?" she snapped. "What he do? Why you fightin' him and shit?"

My father didn't even look at her as he told her, "Mind your business, Treasure. This is about business. It ain't got nothing to do with you."

Treasure sucked her teeth and spat, "Yeah right."

I think the only other motherfucker in that backyard that didn't fear my father, besides me, was Treasure.

She stomped off in Heaven's direction before Ross could say anything else. Luckily, Vegas was walking the dude my father had beaten up out of the backyard.

"Deejay, turn the music back up!" my father yelled. "It's still a fucking party."

He started saying something to me, but honestly, every word was going over my head. His back was to Heaven, so I was able to stare in her direction without him seeing me watch her go back and forth with Treasure. She looked irritated and hot as she shook her head, running her fingers through her hair. She still looked good, though...real fucking good.

HEAVEN

Twenty minutes later, I was upstairs in the master bathroom soaking in the Jacuzzi. Treasure had left the party because Ross had blown her mood. I didn't blame her and I totally agreed with her. Ross had tried to make it seem as if he had hit Dub over some business, yet she and I knew that it was because he felt like Dub had overstepped his boundaries with me again. It was ridiculous, and since Ross was in one of those moods, I had made my exit along with Treasure.

As I sat in the tub soaking off the sweat and smell of outdoors, I smiled, thinking about the words Mello had said to me. He was so sweet. When he finally arrived at the party, even though I was meeting him for the first time physically, it was like I had known him all my life. He wasn't just Ross' son. To me, he was now a close friend. We may have never met physically before today, but we had spent so much time getting to know each other over the phone. He possibly knew more about me than my own husband, because he spent way more intimate moments with me late night on the phone. The only secret between us was his father's abuse and my sister's death. I was too embarrassed to tell anyone outside of my home and Treasure that Ross was beating me. And I never talked to anyone about Angel. Just the thought of her made me sick to my stomach. I missed her so much. It destroyed me every time I thought about her in that grave. She didn't belong there. And a lot of the things that Divine and I suffered when we were kids was because of the motherfucker that had killed her. The rage and sadness were just so unbearable that I never spoke to anyone about her, not even Treasure or Ross.

Just as I was adding shower gel to my loofah, the bathroom door swung open so violently that it hit the wall behind it with a hard bang. Ross came through it, making long strides towards me. I sucked my teeth, rolled my eyes, and instantly started to defend myself. "Ross, don't start. Dub was only—Aaaah!" I was only able to let out that scream before he came lunging down towards me with the most malicious look in his eyes. My eyes bulged as he grabbed the back of my head and forced my face into the hot bath water.

I hadn't had the chance to hold my breath very well before the water seeped into my mouth and nose. I fought to loosen his grip as I choked on the water seeping into my lungs. I fought desperately against his tight grip, but it felt like all two hundred and eighty pounds of him were on top of my head. I kicked and swung as much as I could for what felt like minutes.

I just knew that I was dying.

But within seconds, he was pulling me back up, barking at me as I coughed violently and gasped for air. "Stop fucking playing me! I bet' not 'eva see you with your hands on another man!"

I was too busy hacking, heaving, and clearing the water from my eyes to see what he was planning to do next. But luckily, through my coughing, I heard the bathroom door slam shut.

Still coughing and gasping, I felt my heart continuously beating frantically.

Ross was losing his mind. Things had gone from bad every now and then, to worse every day. At first, he had only put his hands on me two or three times in the course of a year. But it seemed as if the longer we were together, the more insecure he was becoming. I was starting to think that my loyalty was going to get me killed. I was sure that he wasn't just trying to kill me with a backyard full of witnesses. He was trying to scare me straight. But what if he *had* killed me? What if one day, he was so mad that he took my life? I missed Angel, but I didn't want to see her again...not yet.

MELLO

By now, the party had started back up again. Heaven had disappeared, and I was disappointed that I didn't have her beautiful self to look at. I was dipped off on a couch smoking a blunt with Vegas, avoiding the shit outta my woman, Teyanna. She had been trying to be all in my ass since she got to the party. She was trying to make sure I didn't pay too much attention to all the ass running around this motherfucker.

But what she didn't know was that I wasn't paying all this ass no mind. My eyes had been stuck on Heaven. She was the best-looking ass in this bitch.

"So, what you gon' do for the summer?" Vegas asked me.

I shrugged, blowing a light cloud of loud through my nostrils. "I don't know. I guess get a job."

"You gon' be here all summer?"

"Maybe longer than that. I might stay here for good. I hate being away from my son. So, I might go to grad school here. I don't know. I need a job first, though."

Vegas looked surprised, and I didn't blame him. For the years that I had been in school, I had never come back to Chicago, opting to take classes during the summer as well. Teyanna would fly down to see me and Paris would do the same with my son, TJ. I just did not want to come back to "Summertime Chi." So much shit went down in Chicago in the summer, and at the time, I didn't have any willpower to keep myself outta the streets, so I stayed in Florida. That's why I had been able to get my degree in three years instead of four.

My father frowned like I had said some disrespectful shit. He had just joined us, after returning from checking on Heaven, and I was annoyed as fuck by his presence. "A job? You're too smart for a job."

I shook my head as I passed the blunt to him. I knew what he was getting at.

"Me and Vegas could use your intelligence and expertise in our organization. Get you some real money." He stared at me, waiting for an answer as he hit the blunt.

Still shaking my head, I chuckled. "Naaaah, Pops. I'm straight."

His face was still balled up as he asked, "Straight? On this? This life? Look around you. Don't you want this for you and your girl?"

"I can get this legally." I could. Unlike my father, I was street *and* book smart. I was a genius at this computer shit. These young motherfuckers thought they were doing something with this card-cracking shit. I would have been able to do some things on a whole new level. The only thing keeping me from doing that was my son and the desire to be out of jail being a better father to him than mine was.

"How?" my father tested me. "How much money can you make with a bachelor's degree? I make all this without a piece of paper."

"That's cool for you, but I'm good."

I didn't have anything against hustling. I just preferred to make smarter choices for my son. What I *did* have was something against was my father. I tolerated him whenever he chose to act like a father, but I didn't fuck with him. He never fucked with me like he should have. As a shorty, I wondered why my pops wasn't there for me like he was for the streets. Then after having my son, I wondered *how* he couldn't be there for me. I couldn't imagine never being around for my seed. The only time Ross fucked with me was when he was either shoving some money in my face or getting me into some bullshit. The last time I ever even kicked it with him, he had me in the middle of a shootout. So, nah, the last thing I wanted to do was give him any of my time and intelligence to help him get more money.

Fuck outta here.

❧ 6 ❧

MELLO

After the party, I headed to my crib, took a much-needed shower, and met Teyanna back at her spot.

"Oh my God, Mello," she breathed. "This dick is so goooood!"

I was drilling shorty from the back. She was face down, ass up in her bed. That big ass was spread open wide for me too.

"I want to take aaaaall this dick. Give it all to me. Yessss."

She was taking it good too. Had my dick rocked up.

"Shit! It's so fucking deep, baby." Teyanna then went from resting on her elbows to up on her hands and started to throw that ass back on me.

"Yeah, that's it," I encouraged her. Then I reached up, held her shoulders with both of my hands and started to fuck her back just as hard as she was throwing that ass on me.

"Oooooh my Goooood!"

"Yeah, that's it. Give me that pussy."

"Shiiiiiit!"

"You 'bet not fucking stop. Gimme that shit. I'm cumming."

Holding on to her shoulders tighter, I pounded into that pussy, listening to the sound of me digging in her juicy pussy, similar to the sound of stirring macaroni and cheese.

"Aaaaaaaaaaaargh!" I pumped out the nut and then grabbed the base of my dick as I pulled out, making sure the rubber didn't come off.

Teyanna collapsed on the bed. Her light booty jiggled as she lay on her stomach. I forced myself to look away from her because had I kept looking at her, my dick would get hard again. I couldn't afford that since I had somebody waiting for me.

Teyanna rolled over onto her side and had a real-ass mean mug on her face as she noticed I was getting dressed. "You not spending the night?"

"Nah. Not tonight. I promised TJ I would pick him up after the party so we can play video games at my crib."

Teyana sucked her teeth. "Why can't y'all do that over here?"

I stopped while pulling up my pants and stared at her. "C'mon now. You know why."

"I really don't," she sassed.

I just looked at her as I kept getting dressed. She was playing fucking stupid. Then she had the nerve to buck her eyes at me as if she really wanted an answer.

"Because you and Paris don't get along. C'mon now. You know that shit."

Paris and Teyanna had been getting into it since I got with Teyanna. It was like no matter how much I showed Teyanna that I wasn't on shit with Paris, she still insisted that Paris wanted me or that we were still fucking around. She was jealous of Paris, straight up, when she didn't need to be. Paris was a beautiful girl, don't get me wrong. But she had fucked up with me the moment I found out that TJ existed. Me and Paris were fucking around when I was sixteen for a few months when she just disappeared. Two years later, she popped up in my Facebook Messenger showing me a picture of TJ, talking about her boyfriend had made her get a DNA test because TJ didn't look shit like him. The test had come back negative, and I was the only other possible father. I didn't even know she had a boyfriend when we were fucking around, and I wasn't ready for no shorty. Even though Paris was sure I was the only other option, I got the DNA test anyway. Come to find out, TJ *was* mine. Paris' boyfriend ended up leaving her, but there was never anything to us after that. At the time, I had just got serious with Teyanna. Teyanna swore me and Paris had to be fucking because Paris and I had a close parenting relationship. My dumb ass still kept fucking with the girl, not realizing how obsessed she was with Paris, until it was too late, and I was two years in with her crazy ass. The fights between the two of them had gotten so bad that Paris didn't even trust Teyanna around our son. I couldn't say that I blamed her.

"She being petty as fuck," Teyanna kept fussing. "She is just trying to keep you away from me. Because you always with TJ, so when you supposed to spend some time with me?"

"We been together all day," I reminded her.

She hissed, "Fuck you, Mello."

Finally, I was done getting dressed. I leaned against the wall behind me and asked, "Damn, for real? All because I wanna go spend time with my shorty?"

She had the nerve to pout. "You always with him! What about *me?*"

I shook my head slowly. "You sound stupid and spoiled."

"So!" she spat, sitting up, titties bouncing. Titties had never been more unattractive to me than at that moment. "You didn't come home to be with me. You came home to be with *him!*"

I shook my head and swatted my hand at her pettiness. "Whatever. I'm going to the crib."

She sucked her teeth and waved me off. "Yeah, the crib your mama had to get you with your broke ass! Grown-ass man gotta get his mama to pay his rent. Fuck outta here."

That was a low blow. I hated being broke. I remembered being in the streets getting money. But I also remembered the bullshit. If I wanted to focus on school and keep those grades, I couldn't work and stack no paper. Teyanna knew that my mama had only gotten that crib for me because she wanted me to come back to Chicago and I couldn't afford it. My mama and Teyanna knew that once I got back on my grind that nobody was going to be taking care of me but me.

Shaking my head, I told Teyanna, "Take one broke motherfucker to notice the other."

Then I walked out on her ass. She was too cocky to chase after me. I could hear her in the bed calling me all kinds of "broke niggas". I left out of her crib, wondering how someone so beautiful could have such an ugly attitude.

Teyanna was the type of girl you would refer to as a baddie. I had met her two years ago downtown on some shopping shit with one of my guys. She was walking down Michigan Avenue in jeggings and a cropped top. Her body and face made that simple attire look more expensive than Vera Wang. Her eyes were grey, and her hair was the right color of blonde that went with her light complexion. She was 5'7", which made her look like a model when she had on heels, but with her curves, stylists would never let her walk in any shows in Fashion Week. I chased her damn near two blocks before she finally gave me her number. I was on my way to school in Florida as we started talking. To my surprise, she was cool with being my girl long distance while I was getting an education. But what she wasn't cool with was Paris coming to Florida to bring TJ to see me. While I was at school, she and Paris were back in the Chi getting into it over me all on social media and shit, posting subliminal messages. I guess I was able to deal with it back then because I was all the way in Florida. Now, I had only been home two days and I was already ready to strangle her ass.

HEAVEN

A few days later, on a Tuesday morning, Treasure and I were at break-fast at Chicago's Chicken and Waffles. Esperanza would have cooked for us, but I was looking for any reason to get out of the house. Ross had hit me before, but when he had the audacity to push me under that water, it left me feeling uneasy around him. I was starting to wonder how far he would go next time. I was more hurt than usual. At this point, I felt like he was punishing me for *his* wrongdoing. I was loyal and submissive. I had done everything right. Yet, he still took every opportunity to put me in my place with his hands like I was some fucking puppy that he was training when *he* was the one who needed his ass whooped.

"You okay?" Treasure asked. She peered at me over the glass of orange juice she was now gulping down.

I sighed as I stirred my shrimp and grits. I was really just playing in the food. I didn't even have an appetite. "Nah, not really."

"What's wrong?"

"Ross is getting on my nerves." I would have never told her hot-headed ass about Ross trying to drown me. I would have never heard the end of it. "He's going too far now."

Smacking on her bacon, Treasure nodded and said, "Yeah, that shit he did to Dub was bogus."

"It's like he's losing his mind." I then sighed and forced myself to eat a spoonful of the grits.

"Right."

"I'm so happy he's going out of town. I need a break."

I could feel the relief already, and he wasn't even gone yet. I loved Ross to death, but after that stunt he'd pulled in the bathroom, I realized I couldn't let him love me *to death*. I couldn't put Divine in the position that Angel's murder had left me in. I didn't want her to have to take care of herself and Sunshine because I was gone. The pressure of all that was making me so unhappy when Ross was home. I was tired of wondering what imaginary things he would make up that I he thought I was doing next. I was living in fear. I felt like I was back in the hood living with my crazy, irrational mama.

"Where is he going?" Treasure asked.

"To New York to handle some business for like two weeks. I'm so happy."

Treasure tilted her head and frowned. "Two weeks? Damn. That's a long-ass time to handle some business."

I shrugged and forced myself to eat another bite. "It is, but I didn't even ask for details. I am just happy to get a fucking break from his ass."

Treasure's perfectly arched eyebrow raised. "You think he's going to go see a chick?"

I frowned. "I don't know, and I don't care, to be honest."

She sighed and took a moment to sip from her orange juice. Then she asked me, "You think the only cheating he does is on you?"

Now, I was tilting my head and watching Treasure curiously. "What you mean?"

She leaned in and asked, "Like, if he would cheat on you, you think he would cheat in business too?"

"No. He ain't shit when it comes to his dick, but he don't play when it comes to money."

"I agree," she said with a nod.

"Why would you ask me that?" I pressed, pushing the grits away. I couldn't force myself to eat anymore.

Treasure shrugged as she answered, "I was just wondering how deep his disloyalty goes when it comes to the people he's supposed to love."

I sighed as a thought came to mind. "To be honest, I think the only person he is disloyal to is *me*."

Treasure shook her head. "And that's fucked up."

I nodded. "It is."

"So, why are you with him, Heaven?"

I didn't even need a moment to think about it. "Because he's my family, Treasure. Besides, Sunshine and Divine, he's all I got."

"But I think you have been so used to suffering in order to take care of Sunshine and Divine that you think what he does is normal. You lived your childhood fighting your mama, and now you gotta live the rest of your life fighting your husband? That ain't cool."

Sometimes I hated that I had finally been honest with Treasure a few years ago about my living situation. I had to finally tell her, though, when she wondered why me *and* Divine were moving in with Ross back then. I felt like it would make her understand better, and it did, but it also just made her assume that I *let* Ross hit me because I was used to getting my ass whooped all my life.

It might have been true, but whatever.

"He rescued me, Treasure. I fucking went from nothing to everything. I feel like fucking Cinderella. My sister needs for nothing. She has her own car at seventeen. When I was seventeen, I couldn't even afford a bus card." Just the memories made tears well in my eyes. I swallowed them back as I kept trying to make Treasure understand why I could ignore my pain for my family's happiness. "My child has a nanny. I have a roof over my head and nice clothes that I didn't have to borrow or beg for."

Treasure looked as if she felt sympathy for me. But she still asked, "And that's worth the abuse and the cheating?"

I shrugged. "Some people would say yes, especially those who don't have shit like me."

Treasure looked so sad for me as she shook her head and just shrugged. She didn't have anything else to say. I sighed hard into the glass of apple juice that I was about to drink from. What Treasure didn't know was that though I felt like the cheating and fights were worth it to me, Ross possibly killing me wasn't. These were the times that I missed Angel the most. Having this talk with Treasure was cool, but she was hot-headed. I needed some motherly advice. I had never been able to get anything sound or rational from my crazy-ass mother, but Angel had always been such a nurturing mother figure to me. If she were still alive, she would be able to tell me what to do, if what I was feeling was right.

TREASURE

After breakfast, I hopped into my Lexus and hurriedly made my way to my next destination. As I drove, I still had that funny feeling in my stomach that I got when Vegas told me that Ross was supposedly stealing from him. Ross was a son of a bitch, but Heaven was right. No matter how he treated her, he was loyal as fuck to his crew. Heaven was my best friend, and I told her everything. So, it was fucking with me that I couldn't tell her how Vegas was feeling or what he had been told. But even though I wasn't one-hundred-percent loyal to my man, that was one out of two secrets I had to keep from Heaven, since he'd asked me to. She was so loyal and submissive to Ross that he didn't trust that she wouldn't repeat it. And until Vegas found out if Ross was really stealing, she couldn't know what was going on.

I didn't like this beef that was brewing between them at all. It was a recipe for disaster. Vegas and Ross were both beasts. So, a beef between them would be catastrophic, at the least.

I shook off the unsure feeling that it all gave me, turned the radio up, and tried to keep my mind off of that and concentrate on the bullshit that I was on my way to handle.

♪Done with these niggas
I don't love these niggas
I dust off these niggas
Do it for fun

Don't take it personal
Personally, I'm surprised you
Called me after the things I said
Skrrt, skrrt on niggas
Skirt up on niggas
Skirt down, you acting like me
Acting like we
Wasn't more than a summer fling ♫

As I sat there at that table back at the restaurant talking shit about Ross, I felt like the pot calling the kettle black. Ross wasn't shit for cheating or putting his hands on Heaven. But, hell, I wasn't shit either.

Once I got to my destination, I took a deep breath, turned off the car, swallowed my guilt, and hopped out. As I walked towards the house, as always, memories of my past experiences in that house came to mind and ran chills down my spine. The guilt started to fade, and the excitement started to enter. This is how it always was for a chick like me. I enjoyed the rush, the sneaking, and the excitement.

I hated that I was so bold and unforgiving with my unfaithfulness when I had as good a man as Vegas. But I couldn't help it. It wasn't about Vegas. He hadn't done anything wrong. I was just the type of woman who enjoyed seeing multiple men. Some may call it being a hoe, but men did it all the time. I just thought like a man. I loved Vegas, but I liked something on the side too. It was just something about seeing a man that gave me chills, planning my attack, going for him, and actually getting him. Once I spotted a man I wanted, there was usually nothing anybody could do to keep me from getting him. It was the thrill of the chase that turned me on and kept me going. It was the thrill of conquering some dude who thought *I* would be the one chasing him, but he ended up being the one chasing me. Committing myself to Vegas had taken that thrill from me. I liked adventure in the bedroom, but having sex with the same dick for two years had turned that adventure into a boring routine that I was too young to fall into.

I knew I wasn't shit for thinking like that. But I also wasn't some old lady ready to settle down, stay in the house, cook, and clean, only to leave when I was having brunch with my girl. I was only twenty and I for damn sure wasn't anybody's cook, maid, or wife.

I sighed long and hard and shook off the small amount of guilt as I rang the doorbell. As I waited for him to answer, I fanned myself as if that would help against this damn heat. Chicago was one extreme to the next; cold as a polar bear's ass or hot as fuck. That's it. We had two seasons; north pole and hell. No in-between.

"So, you finally decided to show up?" That's how this motherfucker answered the door, leaning against the doorway like he wasn't trying to let me in, looking good as fuck.

I ignored the way my pussy throbbed looking up at his fine ass. I ignored the way that his Dolce and Gabbana cologne was swimming through the air. Instead of throwing the pussy at him like I wanted to, I narrowed my eyes at Damo. He just stared at me while leaning against his door frame.

I threw my Gucci tote over my shoulder and folded my arms across my chest. Cocking my head to the side, I asked him, "You gon' let me in?"

He sucked his teeth. "Tuh! Fuck no."

Fuck it. "Stop playiiiiin'," I whined.

I couldn't stay mad at his fine ass. Forget his looks. Beyond how gorgeous he was, it was something about Damo's swag and ignorant attitude that turned me the fuck on. It was the reason why he was able to get the pussy in the first place eight months ago.

Vegas was perfection. He loved me to death. But that was the problem. He loved me so much that he gave me everything I wanted with no question or fight. Damo was that gangsta dude that I liked that told me what to do and to shut the fuck up at the same time. He didn't coddle me. He snatched my ass up and told me where to be. I was his Bonnie too, not his precious pet. And he was my secret, my biggest secret. I had stepped out on Vegas here and there with guys that I had only hit once, maybe twice, but Damo had survived eight long months. No one knew that I had been fucking him; not even Heaven. She knew about some of my other hoes, but not this one because I was ashamed that I had overstepped the disrespectful boundary of fucking one of my man's friends and business associates.

No matter my boredom with Vegas, I would never leave him. I wasn't that stupid. I wasn't about to hand my good thing over to the next thirsty bitch. He was mine, and Damo was just fun.

I tried to step towards the door, and he didn't move, refusing to let me in. When I pouted, all he asked me was, "Why haven't you been answering my calls?"

"Because you followed me to the fucking restaurant the other day!"

I couldn't believe he had walked up on us the other day outside of Sadie's Soul Food Palace. Luckily, I had played it off well and nobody peeped what was really going on.

"I was making sure you weren't goin' to see another dude," his cocky ass said boldly.

My eyes bucked. "I told you I was goin' to meet *Heaven!*"

He shrugged like what he had done was sane or normal. These dudes always acted like they were cool with being the side nigga, until their feelings got in the way.

"I thought you was lyin'," he replied.

"So, you followed me? You tryin' to get me caught up or something?"

He gave me a slick grin. "I don't give a fuck about Vegas catching yo' ass up and you know that." Then he literally pushed up my mini skirt and grabbed the seat of my panties, pulling me towards him. My nipples got so hard as he grabbed the back of my neck and brought my mouth to his. This was that raunchy shit that had me risking my very good man over a plaything. I didn't have feelings for Damo. He was just excitement, what my relationship was lacking. He was the small, minuscule, and nearly invisible to the naked eye part of Vegas that was missing. It wasn't worth it. When I was with Vegas, when I felt his unconditional love, I knew Damo wasn't worth it.

But as he commanded my mouth with his and his overwhelming masculinity suffocated me, I easily forgot. And as his hand softly wrapped around my neck while he boldly started to suck my tongue and brought me into the house, I didn't care.

HEAVEN

"You leavin' back out?"

Hearing his voice suddenly, I jumped a bit. Then I tried to play if off as if he didn't scare me and kept slipping my foot into my stiletto sandal.

I barely said, "Yeah," I started to move faster. I was really ready to get the hell out of the house now.

I shouldn't have even come back home. I mentally fussed as I could feel his shadow came over me.

I kept putting my shoes on as I heard him ask, "Where is Sunshine?"

"With Divine over her friend's house."

"Where are you goin'?"

"Out with Mello."

"Oh okay."

I laughed inwardly and finally look up at him. "Oh, so it's okay if I go out with Mello, but I can't hold a conversation with the next man?"

He shrugged. He didn't see the bullshit in his ways at all. "Mello ain't no threat. He may look like me, but the broke version."

Ross laughed at his own joke, but I didn't find anything funny. I sighed hard and, finally getting my shoes on, stood to leave. I tried to walk around him, but he grabbed my arm.

"Hold up?"

I sighed again, fighting the urge to snatch my arm from him. I wasn't feeling fighting him off tonight. I had beat my face and curled these inches; Ross wasn't about to mess all of that up because he wanted to fight tonight. So, I forced myself to just stand there and say whatever he felt like he needed to say.

"You still mad over that shit from the weekend?"

"No," I lied.

"I just don't think it's respectful for you and Dub to be all up in each other's face."

But you can be all in your baby mama's face...

"That shit is disrespectful as hell."

Aaaand yet you can disrespect me whenever the fuck you feel...

"Stop showing out and I won't have to."

I bit my lip until I tasted blood.

"Have a good time." This motherfucker was actually giving me permission to leave.

Whatever he needed to feel to allow me out of the house in one piece, I was going to let him feel it. I continued to talk shit in my head as I walked out of the living room and towards the front door. On my way out of the house, I cursed myself out for not having anything of my own so that I could show my dumb ass husband up at least once. I loved being submissive to Ross, but now I was starting to feel like his dumb ass little servant that only made a move when he said so.

On my way to my car, my Facetime started to ring. I cringed, hoping that it wasn't Ross trying to watch me all the way to my destination.

I relaxed when I saw that it was Mello.

I hit the answer button as I jumped in my car. When I looked into his eyes, I relaxed. It was something about his stare that made me feel safe. Every time Ross or any other man looked at me, I was in fear. I feared what Ross was thinking and I feared Ross would see the men looking. But with Mello, I just felt like I had nothing fear.

But when Mello saw my face, he started cracking up.

"Yo', what's your problem?"

"Nothing."

"Stop lying."

"I'm good," I told him forcing myself to smile.

"You lie so much, yo'. I don't even know why I fuck with you."

A sweet smile spread across his face. That's when I finally slowly smiled genuinely. "You fuck with me because I'm the only female friend you got. Who else is gonna keep you from getting your ass whooped by Teyanna?"

He was cracking up. "You funny as hell. Teyanna ain't neva putting her hands on me."

"Mmm humph," I teased

"You on your way or what?"

"Yep. Just got in the car."

"Ah ight. I'm on my way in. Meet me at the bar."

"All right. See you in a few minutes."

I hung up and backed out of the driveway. It was rare when I ever went out without Ross, so I was looking forward to kicking it tonight without Barney Fife.

Once I made it to Lamelle's, I had calmed down. I jumped out of my car and switched towards the club. It felt so good to finally be out without Ross watching my every move… even though I didn't put it past him to be in the corners somewhere lurking if he found out where I was.

Lamelle's was crackin', so I had to fight my way through the crowd. On my way towards the bar, a few guys grabbed my hand, trying to get my attention. I had only thrown on a spaghetti strapped, bodycon tan dress, but the brown stilettos, Louis Vuitton, and long hair had dressed it up.

These guys weren't looking at me, though. They were looking at my body, this ass, so I didn't pay them any mind. But then I felt yet another grab of my hand. This time it was more aggressive, so I spun around ready to snap but fell all the way back when I saw that it was Mello. He immediately pulled me into him and embraced me. His wide, large body engulfed mine. The smell of his cologne molested me as he slightly rocked us from side to side. Just like when I would look into his eyes, his embrace made me feel just as safe. I had been so happy that now that we were physically around each other, he was just as cool as he had been over the phone.

"Here, I got your drink already. You looked like you needed it."

I smiled so hard up at him. You would have thought that he had given me a bouquet of roses. But it was the simple things like this that he did to make me smile that Ross never did and never allowed any other man to get close enough to me to do. I serviced Ross, he didn't service me, unless it was in the bedroom. But not Mello. He never missed a moment to be thoughtful or sweet. If he treated me this way as a friend, I envied Teyanna.

I took the drink from him and started sipping on it, without even asking what it was. I needed a drink too bad to even care what it was, but I immediately realized that it was a long island.

♪ *Booty me down*
Take it to the ground
Bring it back up
Gimme gimme now
She a bad bitch
Make it bounce bitch
I make it rain trick
This some stripping shit ♪

As soon as K Stylis' *Booty Me Down* started banging through the speakers, the club went up. Damn near every chick in the club started twerking, including me. Sipping from my drink, I put my free hand on my knee and started bouncing my ass. Mello hopped right behind me and started dancing with me. I had always loved Mello's energy, but now that we were hanging out, I was really digging it. He had already shown me over the years that he was a real man and a real friend to me. I knew that he truly cared about me, but now that we were in each other's presence, I could feel that he was really my friend. He had always been attentive, there for me and caring, but having him do all of that in the flesh was making me look at him with even more appreciative eyes.

Being in that club with him, dancing and smiling, having a good time, made me realize how I was supposed to be treated. This was supposed to be me and Ross this happy and this cool with each other.

7

MELLO

When my phone started to ring, I hit the answer button my Bluetooth headset. "What up?"

"Carmello."

I cringed, recognizing the voice of my academic advisor from school. I had been dodging his calls since the summer started. He had finally caught me slipping.

"Harold, what's up?" I asked as I started back lining up my client.

"I hear you're in Chicago," Harold answered, sounding all stern and shit.

I put my hand on my client's head so that I could get his lining just right. "Yeah, I am."

"Why aren't you here in Florida doing that internship?"

Man, Ross might not have been a good father, but Harold had definitely made up for the lack of a father-figure while I was in college. Without me asking or needing him to, Harold had taken me under his wing. It's like he wanted to make sure that the one hood nigga in that school turned out to be something.

"Internships don't pay, Harold," I reminded him.

"No shit, asshole," he fussed. "Please tell me that you're not staying there."

"I'm thinking about it."

"Argh," he groaned. "C'mon, Mello, don't waste these opportunities that you have. You were offered a free ride to go to grad school."

"If I took the internship, but I didn't."

"If I arrange the internship for next semester, will you consider coming back?"

I chuckled. "Probably not. I need to be in Chicago with my son. And I need to take care of him. I don't have more years to give to that school. I need to be making some bread."

"Would you please just think about it?"

"Proooobably not."

"Think about it," he pressed. "I'll give you a call in a few weeks to see where your head is at."

I laughed. This motherfucker was persistent as hell. "Ah ight."

As I hung up, I went right back to daydreaming about Heaven. We had hung out a few times since I came back to Chicago. Every time I hung out with her, my feelings for her grew more and more. Last week, when we were at Lamelle's, I had her all to myself and it only further let me know that my attraction to her wasn't just physical. That girl had it right, when every other bitch had it wrong. I couldn't see what she saw in my old ass pops and wished to God that I had been the one to meet her first.

"Heads up, Mello."

I took my eyes off of the head I was cutting to look up at Mo, one of the other barbers in the shop. He was staring out the big picture window that faced the front.

"Fuck," I groaned as I turned the clippers off.

Mo laughed when he saw me cringing at the sight of Teyanna sashaying towards the front door of the shop *unannounced* like a motherfucker. I knew she was on bullshit. What woman showed up at her man's job with a face full of makeup, hair styled perfectly, and wearing an outfit like she was going to the club at twelve noon on a Tuesday? She had been blowing my phone up since I walked out on her ass a few days ago. I wasn't fucking with her, though. She needed to learn how to watch her mouth. But I guessed I should have answered one of those calls because now she was showing up at the worst time.

I tried to be cool. I cut the clippers back on and kept lining up my customer.

Vegas had just let me get a booth at his shop the day before. I used to cut hair at his shop, Kutz Barber Studio, before I left for college. I was nasty with the clippers. That talent had helped keep some money in my pockets while at school. Now that I was back in Chicago, I was back in the shop, until I figured out what I wanted to do with this degree I had earned.

But first, I had to figure out how to defuse the situation that was about to unfold.

I heard the bell on the door jingle as Teyanna entered. The shop was still going on in conversation like it wasn't about to go down. The only person who knew about the bullshit was Mo. That's why he was looking just as stressed. He tried to hide it while he buried his face in the beard that he was lining up, but I could still peep his vibe.

The closer Teyanna got to me, the more stressed out I got. I was about to fuck dude's lining all the way up, for real.

"Hey, baby." As Teyana spoke to me, I could smell the cucumber-melon fragrance on her. Yeah, she was *that* damn close.

But before I could say anything, a shrieking, "Daddy!" pierced the air. It was only piercing because it was like the ringing of the first-round bell in a heavyweight boxing match. I caught the sneer in Teyanna's eyes as she glared towards the back of the shop where TJ's voice was rising as he approached me. When her eyes grew, I knew that Paris must have been behind my son.

Teyanna was seething like a pit bull in a dogfight. "What the fuck is *she* doing here?!"

I sat the clippers down and went towards her, ready to extinguish this fire. "Chill. She just came to bring TJ to see me."

Paris was now standing beside me, not really making things any better. She had come to the shop in these little-ass shorts and a tube top. Teyanna and Paris were like night and day. They were salt and pepper. Whereas Teyanna was a light-skin baddie, Paris was a chocolate beauty who resembled an African princess. Her dark skin had been toasted in the summer sun. She wore a big braid out that made her natural beauty look even more regal. She was only about 5'3", but that short frame was holding some natural curves that every bitch in that shop was jealous of. At twenty-one, Paris had the shape of somebody's grown-ass auntie. She looked like she had been fed collard greens and cornbread, yams, and smothered pork chops all her life. But since she was so young, she still had that naturally small waist and tight stomach. She was really obsessed with keeping her figure tight, so she worked out a lot when most of these young chicks just got their work out in by running after the next dude.

"You don't have to explain shit to her!" Paris popped off before I could say anything. "How many times I gotta tell you I don't want Mello, bitch—"

That's all Teyanna needed. "Bitch?! I got your bitch!"

In a split second, everything just started happening so fast. Teyanna lunged for Paris. I was too busy trying to protect my son to keep these two chicken heads from fighting each other. I couldn't fucking believe this shit. Nobody in the shop really even gave a fuck either. Nobody tried to break them up. Motherfuckers started taking out their phones to videotape these two bitches fighting, while I ran to scoop up my son so he wouldn't be caught up in the mix.

"I'll kill you, hoe!" Teyanna promised as she tried to pull my baby mama's scalp clean off her skull.

"Fuck you! Let my hair go!"

"I'mma beat cho ass!"

They went back and forth, cursing each other out as they tried to rip each other's hair out. It really wasn't a fight. Teyanna was on top of Paris, straddling her. She had Paris' hair wrapped around her fist while *trying* to land punches on her face. And Paris had a handful of Teyanna's weave, while she was *trying* to do the same. These bitches were wrestling, not fighting.

I sat TJ down in an empty barber chair and then hustled towards these two goofballs. I was easily able to scoop Teyanna up and force her towards the front door, kicking and screaming.

And her ass was still popping off. "I'mma kill you, bitch! Swear to gawd!"

"The fuck is wrong with you?!" I spat through gritted teeth while I damn near pushed her through the glass door. Swear to God, I wanted to push her ass through that motherfucker, but lucky for her, it opened, and she tumbled out, looking at me with bucked eyes.

She charged me and pushed me, cursing, "Fuck is wrong with *you*? You got that bitch up here!"

I grabbed her little hands and tried not to crush them in mine. "She brought my son up here to see me! And you gon' fight his mama in front of him?! That ain't helping shit!"

Snatching her hands away, she spat, "Fuck you, Mello!"

She tried to walk away, but I was on her heels.

"Nah, fuck *you*! You so fucking insecure that you gon' fight my baby mama in front of my son? You ain't got no fucking respect, bitch!"

She spun around. "Bitch?!"

I laughed at her ass. "That's all you heard?" That shit only pissed her off more.

"I hate you, Mello!"

"The feeling is fucking mutual right now. Get the fuck away from here!"

Fuck this. Why did I even come back to Chicago?

Just then, I caught a glimpse of TJ through the window. *That's why I came back.*

"I ain't goin' nowhere until you make that bitch leave."

I literally picked her ass up and started walking towards her car. She started beating on my back as I walked up the block. I had all kinds of people in the hood looking at me like I was crazy. I was trying to hurry up and get this bitch away from here before the police came. I wasn't in the streets no more, so I wasn't scared of the police, but the last thing I wanted to do was bring attention to Vegas' spot.

I was a big dude, so I was able to open her car door with one hand and sit her down in the car. She didn't go willingly, though. She was still kicking and screaming, but I didn't give a fuck.

"Get the fuck up outta here, man."

She was fuming, smacking the steering wheel, and throwing a fucking tantrum. "I hate you, Mellooo!" she cried.

"For what? I'm not even fucking that girl."

"But she always around!" She stared at me with tears in her eyes. It was crazy how her anger looked so genuine. This wasn't an act. She legit was mad at me about this petty shit.

"Because I'm a good father. Don't you want me to be the same way with the kids we'll have one day?"

Her eyes narrowed into little slits. Pure anger was pouring out of those pretty gray eyes. She snapped through tightly gritted teeth. "I wouldn't know that because you made me kill *my* baby, remember?"

How could I forget? When she told me she was pregnant, I was sick to my stomach. The last thing I wanted was a girlfriend, but there I was in a relationship with Teyanna. It was cool, though, because it was long distance, though. But when she told me I had knocked her up during one of her visits to Florida, I was reminded why I initially didn't want a woman. Prior to Teyanna, I had had women, but nothing too serious on my end, even if they claimed me as their man. I was young and I wasn't stressing about commitment. A baby was a commitment like a motherfucker, though, so I insisted that Teyanna get an abortion. She didn't want to, though. She wanted that baby, but me and everybody else felt like she just wanted the baby to make sure she had me on lock. Once I started to fade to black, she got the abortion. We started to get back right, and then a month later, I found out about TJ.

Talk about bad timing.

"I was on my way to school!" I tried to explain.

But she wasn't hearing that shit. "You made me kill my baby. You acted like you didn't want any kids, but now, you put Paris and TJ on a fucking pedestal! You fuckin' Daddy of the Year now!"

"You act like I knew she was pregnant with him!"

"So!"

I took a deep breath, trying to keep calm. At this point, we had the attention of everybody on the busy main street of 69th and Western.

She had a legit reason to be hurt. I couldn't front. So, I told her, "Go to the crib. Let me finish up my client, and then I'll meet you there so we can talk."

She wiped her eyes clear of tears. It looked like she was calming down. That's all she needed to hear, that I was coming to her. All she ever wanted was me to be under her, like she couldn't rest unless I was in her eyesight.

Shit was fucking insane.

"You promise?" she asked as she put the key in the ignition.

"Yeah."

✦✦✦

By the time that I got back in the shop, TJ and Paris were gone. I finished up my customer's cut and got the fuck up outta there. Teyanna was blowing my phone up, though, making sure that I was coming and wondering what was taking me so long, even though it had only been an hour. So, I knew going back to my crib or hers wasn't an option if I wanted some peace. So, I popped up at my pops' crib.

"What are you doing here?" Heaven asked as she stood on the other side of the open front door. A dude like me rarely used the word gorgeous, but Heaven was the pure definition of that word as she stood in the sunlight, wrapped in leggings that hugged her thick thighs and a simple wife beater. Her flip-flops showed off fresh, French tip, pretty toes. Her weave was up in a high ponytail, keeping it off her neck that was sweating despite the cool breeze from the central air conditioner I felt blowing out of the house.

I shrugged, trying to act like the sight of her wasn't making my dick hard in my Nike shorts. "Just came to say what's up."

She leaned against the doorframe and crossed her arms over perky, chocolatey milky titties that the wife beater was doing a bad-ass job covering. "Mmm humph."

I chuckled. "Nah, for real. I can't go home. Teyanna showed up at the shop spazzing. I know she's lurking at my crib."

She giggled. "So, you came over here to hide from her?"

And to steal a look at you... "Something like that."

"Well, me and Sunshine are about to leave." Before I could respond, she turned and went into the house, leaving me in the doorway, staring at the way her big-ass booty was eating up those leggings.

Pops can't possibly know what he's doin' with all that.

I stepped in the house and hurried to adjust my hard-on before closing and locking the door. "Where y'all goin'?"

Heaven shrugged as she walked into the kitchen. Sunshine was at the table eating chicken nuggets.

"For a walk."

I frowned. "A walk? Ain't no fun in that. Let's take her to the zoo."

She looked up at me as she sat down in the chair in front of Sunshine. "*Let's?* As in you and me? You want to spend your summer day with a toddler?"

"Yeah." I shrugged. "I ain't doin' shit. And it's nice as hell out today."

"Cool." Man, when she looked at me and smiled, she probably thought it was the most innocent gesture, but that smile was killing me softly.

⚘

AN HOUR LATER, HEAVEN WAS STILL TORMENTING ME WITHOUT even knowing. I was starting to think it would've been a better idea to have dealt with the torment back at Teyanna's place rather than deal with all this temptation. However, I preferred the sight of watching Heaven lick on an ice cream cone instead of watching Teyanna's head spin like the exorcist.

"Look, Mommy, that's a big kitty! Can we have one?"

Heaven laughed as she looked down at Sunshine, who was standing next to her, holding her hand and pointing at the lions.

"That's a lion, baby. We can't have those as pets."

"Oooh," she sang as she stared in amazement at the lions. They were staring out of the window at us just as amazed as Sunshine was staring up at them.

I watched as Heaven took in a long, deep breath as she looked around.

I leaned over and nudged her with my shoulder. "What's wrong?"

Still looking around, she said, "This is nice. Thanks for suggesting this. I am really enjoying myself."

I was still staring at her, watching the ice cream melt on that juicy bottom lip of hers. "For real?"

"Yeah."

"I would think this was nothing compared to the things you and my pops do."

I couldn't understand why it was so much sadness in her eyes when I said that.

She shook her head and said, "Nah. The most me and Ross do is go to clubs, and that's always with our friends. We've never done anything like this."

I was shocked. I looked at her, but she was staring at the lions in just as much amazement as Sunshine was. It was like she had never seen them before either.

"Never?" I asked.

"Nope," she answered as she shook her head and started back on the ice cream.

Fuck, I wish she would just finish that motherfucker.

I forced my eyes away from the ice cream melting on her warm tongue. "Y'all don't go downtown?"

"Nah."

"He never took you to the beach?"

She shook her head. "Nope."

Then what the fuck did he do to get you? "His old ass probably outgrew all that shit."

Heaven laughed. "Yeah, probably."

"I figured Pops would've taken you all over the world, showing you off."

That's when she looked up at me. Our eyes met. We held eye contact longer than we ever had. I wanted to look away. I mean, it would have been inappropriate as fuck for me to be walking around that zoo with my hard dick sticking out of my basketball shorts. But, fuck, it was so hard to look away from those eyes.

She did, though. She smiled and then looked away, lightly tugging on Sunshine's hand. "C'mon on, baby. Mommy wants to see the gorillas."

8

HEAVEN

"It's so nice out today." I leaned against Mello's Jeep Wrangler, inhaling the summer air. I don't think it was the weather that had me feeling like this, though. It was the freedom. It was the relief of not feeling suffocated because Ross was somewhere lurking. "It's not too hot. It's perfect."

Mello leaned against his truck next to me. "Yeah. I'm not ready to go in."

I cringed, feeling myself in the midst of the weird tension that had developed between us all of a sudden. It was funny how there had never been this tension between us before. When we would Facetime, or have those countless hours of conversation when he was away at school, it felt like I was talking to a friend. I felt like he looked at me as a friend. Even as we had hung out here and there now that he was back in Chicago, it always felt so innocent. He treated me like I wished Ross would. I admit that he treated me so good that I was falling in love with our friendship even more. But it always, *always* felt like friendship.

But the way that he looked at me at the zoo earlier made me feel like he saw me differently. It was messed up how I was a married woman but had never had a man look at me like that before. I was married and had a baby but still had never been looked at as if I was so adored and treasured. It was such a different feeling.

"Me either," I said honestly.

I really wasn't. I wasn't ready to go back into that house where I spent so much time stressing and wondering why I was still with the man who had had the nerve to try to drown me when he probably was out of town with the next bitch. No, not probably; he *most likely* was out of town with the next bitch, because he had been gone for four days, and I had barely heard from Ross. He was just texting me like we were still in high school and he didn't know how to court a woman. He had disappeared; some shit that he would never let me get away with if he was at home. Let me disappear inside of the four walls that we lived in for more than thirty minutes; he would swear to God that I was somewhere on my phone talking to the next piece of dick.

"Yeah?" Mello asked. "Wanna hang out?"

"Ummmm..." I acted like my mind had drifted off as I watched Sunshine ride her scooter in the yard. But I was actually wondering if I should hang out with Mello or not. When he first showed up at the house earlier, I thought it was cool. I figured, you know, this was Mello. I thought it was okay to hang out with him like we had been doing. But as the day went on, I didn't like the way he looked at me. I didn't like the way I *liked* how he looked at me. There was no way that anything would ever happen between us, of course. But my dumb ass was still so afraid of, and at the same time still loyal to, Ross that I felt like I shouldn't be in the presence of any man who was looking at me the way that Mello was.

But this was Mello, Ross' son. He would never try me. We were friends. We cared about each other on another level. I knew I was just thinking too much into things. Or maybe I was the one so thirsty for affection that I was seeing something that wasn't there.

So, I said, "Yeah. Let me tell Esperanza we're leaving."

He nodded, and I went into the yard, picked Sunshine up, and made my way into the house. Esperanza was in the foyer mopping when I got inside.

I placed Sunshine's feet on the floor. "Go watch TV, Mama."

Without a word, she ran into the living room where the TV was still on the Cartoon Channel from earlier today.

"Hey, Esperanza. I am going to leave Sunshine here with you while I take a ride with Mello."

Her eyebrow rose as she continued mopping. "And if Ross calls?"

My face scrunched up. "If Ross calls? He hasn't called me since he's been gone."

Her eyebrow was still awkwardly arched high as she told me, "He's been calling me."

"For what?"

She stopped mopping and put her hand on her hip. "What do you think? Checking up on you. Wanting to know where you are. He called earlier, but I didn't tell him that you were at the zoo with Mello. I told him you were alone."

"What was wrong with you telling him I was with Mello? He wouldn't trip over me being with his son. Mello and I hang out all the time."

"I don't trust that. And I wasn't willing to take that risk. Are you?"

She was right. After that stunt he'd pulled in the bathroom, I really wasn't sure of how far Ross would go. Clearly, he wasn't thinking straight. And I was honestly enjoying him being away from the house. I didn't need him to feel like there was any reason for him to cut his trip short. So, I told her, "No. I'm not. Tell him that I'm sleep if he calls."

"That won't work. He'd want me to show him."

My mouth dropped. "Like on Facetime? Are you serious?!"

"Yeah."

"Then...um...then tell him I went for a drive. I'll deal with the bullshit if it comes. Maybe that'll make his ass actually pick up the phone and call me."

Esperanza laughed. "Okay, sweetie."

"Be back soon."

VEGAS

"What you got for me? What's the verdict?"

I was holding my breath. This was it. This young, genius mother-fucker was about to decide Ross' fate. Either Ross was being loyal to me and he would live, or he was cheating me out of bread... and he was going to die.

I had thought long and hard about it. Yeah, me and Ross had been bros for some years. He had been like a big brother to me for so long that I had forgotten that I actually had blood brothers. We had gotten this money together, slowly making a name for ourselves in the streets of Chicago. We weren't kingpins or no shit like that, but we were living freely and comfortably. Not only were we business partners, we were like family. I kept all of his dirty-ass secrets from everyone, including my own girl.... And that was why I was going to kill that motherfucka if he was stealing from me. I was the one who had put him on when he was trying to get into the business. He wouldn't have shit if it weren't for me.

Steve sighed long and hard before sealing Ross' fate. "You were right."

I sat back in the booth that I was sitting across from him in at White Palace. "You serious?"

Steve nodded as he took out his phone. "Yeeeep," he said slowly. "Unfortunately, Ross *has* been stealing from you."

Then, as he tapped on his phone, I asked, "How much?"

When he said, "At least a hundred thousand," it was the most painful betrayal I had ever felt. I had always thought that a woman would be the one to make me feel like this, not my bro and right hand.

"What the fuck?" I rasped in a whisper.

Steve's lips were pressed in a thin line of regret. "Here. Let me show you."

I leaned over as he tilted his phone so that I could see it. That's when he showed me statements and figures while using big words to explain the situation that only his genius ass could understand. Although some of the words were going over my head, one thing was crystal fucking clear: after a thorough investigation, Steve had learned that Ross had been stealing from me for years, using withdrawals to a phony automotive parts company as the front that was in Heaven's name.

HEAVEN

♫ Who can I run to,
To share this empty space?
Who can I run to,
When I need love?
Who can I run to,
To fill this empty space with laughter?
Who can I run to,
When I need love? ♫

I was wrong. I was really, really, *really* wrong. There was no way that I should have been hanging out with Mello. It wasn't his fault that I was feeling this way. He wasn't doing anything out of the ordinary. It was me. It was totally me. I just felt like I was in the presence of a man that looked at me in a way that I wanted Ross to look at me. Being with Mello made me realize how much shit I was taking from Ross for no reason at all. He made me see that I was taking the cheating and his abuse just to get shitty treatment in return constantly. Ross never looked at me the way that Mello was. He never took me and Sunshine to intimate alone moments like the zoo. And he had never taken me downtown on a warm summer night to simply walk the streets alone, just me and him, playing R&B from his phone.

♪And my mind is so confusing,
Who would be that special one?
Every day I'm trying to find you,
All along, I've got to know,
Is there a place for me?♪

As I listened to the words of the song, I looked up at Mello with a teasing smile. "What do you know about Xscape?"

He looked down on me and beamed as well. "My mama listens to this old shit all the time."

I blushed at the way he smiled at the mention of her. It was clear that he put his mama up on a pedestal that he had never put Ross on. Then I quieted and kept enjoying the mood.

"You okay?" Mello asked over my thoughts.

I looked up at him and saw a younger version of Ross that I wished I'd had. Mello had been so thoughtful and caring all day, seemingly without even trying. Why couldn't Ross be that way?

"I'm good," I lied.

"Why you so quiet?"

You.

But I couldn't say that. Instead, I told him, "Nothing. Just enjoying myself."

"I still can't believe you've never been down here."

"I have."

"To shop, yeah. But I mean on some shit like this. Downtown is the nicest but cheapest date that a dude could take his woman on. Got that romantic feel y'all like and shit. You can bring your own liquor." He laughed at his own joke as he waved the Mr. Pure Cranberry Juice bottle in the air that he was drinking his whiskey from.

I giggled, but I was still all in my feelings. Mello was right. This was the type of simple night I had never experienced but should have. Ross felt like because he took care of me that I had to deal with his shit while he dated other bitches. I wondered had he ever done this with the hoes he cheated on me with.

Mello was also right about this night being so romantic without either of us even trying. At ten o'clock at night, after the stores had closed and the sun went down, and after all the shoppers had disappeared, Michigan Avenue was beautiful. It was beautifully lit by the lights in the windows of the stores. The air smelled so much cleaner than in the inner city. I closed my eyes and heard nothing; no sirens, no ambulances, and no gunshots. And there was something about it that was very dreamy. The hotels, the restaurants, the skyline—it all gave you peace and tranquility that was romantic. And although we were just hanging out, it made me see Mello in a different light. I no longer saw him as the guy I talked to for hours who was off at college. He was Mello; tall, chocolate, handsome, wide stance, full of swag and charisma, thoughtful, caring, slanted light brown bedroom eyes, heavy, curly lashes, smelling good, and ... sexy. So fucking sexy.

"Heaven..."

I jumped out of my skin when he grabbed my hand. I stood there, frozen in the middle of the block on the corner of Chestnut and Michigan.

He watched my fear curiously. "You okay?"

"Yeah...I-I...I'm sorry. You just scared me. I was in my head for a minute."

"Sorry. I was just trying to get your attention."

Still, I was shaky and nervous. "I know." I nervously played with my hair and smiled. "Sorry."

He reached and grabbed my shoulders gently. "What's wrong?"

"Nothing."

"Stop lying," he replied as he stepped closer. He was too close. His smell. Fuck, that smell. Ginger, lavender, African Mandinka fruit and leather stimulate... Shit, it was suffocating me.

I stepped back.

But he stepped closer, narrowing the gap between us even more. He stared at me with the kind of intensity that scared the shit out of me.

What the hell is he doing?

MELLO

What the fuck am I doing?

I knew it was wrong. She was my father's wife, but I didn't see him as my father. That motherfucker had not been a father to me—*ever*. So, to me, he was not my father. He was Ross. He was a man, a man who wasn't treating his woman right. And I didn't see her as my father's wife, not when it mattered and definitely not right now. She was Heaven, the chick I had had a crush on for a long time. And now that I had matured, I was a grown-ass man ready to take advantage of any moment she gave me to treat her like I always wanted to. That's why I was creating this fake-ass date mood with liquor and Xscape singing in the background. She had never complained to me about Ross. But when a man is really into a woman, he can see the pain behind her smile. And every time she had smiled that day, I saw the pain. And I knew he couldn't have been treating her right, if he hadn't even given her simple time like this. She deserved days like this. She deserved to be with someone who was utterly obsessed with her.

But still, I knew what I was about to do would blow her mind and possibly mess up the bond we had built over the years. But I had been fighting the urge all day; ever since I saw that ice cream melting on her lip at the zoo, I wanted to lick it off. I wanted to kiss her. And for some reason, I felt like she hadn't been kissed right in a long time, especially if she hadn't had simple days like this.

She looked scared, like she didn't want me to...but wanted me to. It seemed as if she was scared of wanting me also. I wasn't scared, though. For some reason, I didn't give a fuck. This was my father's wife, but for so long I had felt like I could do a better job taking care of her needs than he was.

So, I went in. I was about to break the rules, but I was willing to break the rules for her.

I bent down towards her short frame as she looked up at me with eyes big with fear and anticipation like Bambi. And my mouth started to water from the chance to taste her mouth.

"W-what...what are you doing, Mello?" she stuttered. Her voice was sexy as fuck; real breathy like my dick was already in her, giving her pussy panic attacks. She looked afraid and panicked about what it looked like I was about to do, but I peeped that she hadn't moved. Not even a little bit.

"I'm 'bout to kiss you," I told her boldly.

Fuck it. I was willing to shoot the dice, feeling like I wasn't going to crap out.

She gasped, and when I thought her eyes couldn't get any bigger, they did. But still, she didn't move. She stood there. So, I closed the space between us even more. I closed the air between us until we were breathing each other's...

"*Mello!*"

Heaven and I jumped back when we heard her voice. I looked up the block and saw Teyanna jumping out of the driver's side of her car that was pulled over with the hazards on. I bit my lip, grimaced, and looked up at the sky.

I'mma kill this bitch.

9

ROSS

"Mmmmm, yes, Roooooooss! Yesssss! Please don't stop. I'm cummiiiing."

Tisha was panting and moaning while I was rodding her with this dick, on top of her, with her ankles on my shoulders. I turned my head to kiss her feet as I plunged in and out of her.

"Fuck!" she squealed as she reached down and rubbed her clit while cumming all over my dick.

I let her cum, digging in that pussy over and over again, until I felt her squirting all over my dick.

"Aahhhhhhhhhhhhhhhhhh!!! Shiiiiiiit!" She rubbed that clit in a circle, hard and fast, even after I had pulled out, still squirting. I dodged her juices as she rolled over so that they could spill on the sheet.

"Shit!" She sighed once she was finally done.

I chuckled as she lay there paralyzed. I reached for her, wrapped my arm around her waist, and pulled her under me. As I held her, I could feel the bulge in her stomach. As it had been since I got to Alabama, every time I saw it, every time I touched it, I got sick to my stomach.

"How far along are you now?" I asked her.

Even though it was dark in the room, I could see her perfect white teeth when she smiled. "Five months."

"Did you think about what I said?"

And like every time when I brought this up, I saw her smile fade.

"No," she spat through gritted teeth.

"Why not?"

Tisha's eyes narrowed at me as if she couldn't believe what I was saying. But I had been saying the same thing since she had found out she was pregnant. "Because I'm not killing my baby!"

I rolled my eyes. "Stop calling it your baby like it's not mine too."

"Clearly, you don't give a fuck about it being your baby since you want me to kill it!"

"Tish—"

"No!" She swung at me, but I blocked the slap she was trying to land on my face. "Don't! I told you I'm not having a fucking abortion! I'm five months! It has fingers, toes, and a heartbeat."

"And I told you to get an abortion before it got to this point!"

I stared at her, and she shrugged. She was acting so nonchalant as if this decision that she had made wasn't about to ruin everything for me.

Tisha said, "Well, we're at *this* point now," as if it were so damn simple.

"And I still want you to get a fucking abortion!" I urged, feeling my blood boiling.

This bitch acted like I hadn't been pressing her to get an abortion since the moment she told me she was pregnant. She had the nerve to call me and tell me she was pregnant with happiness in her voice like *she* was my wife. I may have been a cheater, but I would never hurt Heaven by bringing a baby into this world outside of my marriage. Heaven had stayed with me through a lot of shit, but one thing I knew was that she wouldn't stay with me through no shit like this. So, this baby could not be born. But Tisha wasn't hearing me. Just like a side bitch, she felt like this baby was going to keep me. But I didn't understand how she felt like that when nothing had been able to keep me with her for the last year I had been fucking with her.

I had met Tisha in Alabama when I was organizing a shipment of guns from there to Chicago. She was a woman closer to my age, nearly in her thirties, who didn't understand why she was losing to a woman ten years younger than her. Tisha felt like she could whip the pussy on me, and I would want her because she was established and had a career. She tried everything in her powers when I would see her for one or two days every other month, to get me to stay with her or to move her to Chicago, but that shit wasn't happening.

Then my dumb ass got her pregnant, and she saw the goal line.

Suddenly, Tisha started to laugh hysterically as she jumped out of bed. "I knew it!"

"You knew *what?*"

"When you told me you were coming here for two weeks to spend time with me, I knew that it was strange."

"I always come see you."

"When you come here on business, for a day or two, that's it. But you have never spent *this* much time with me. You've been so focused on me, like you really fuck with me. But you just came here to talk me into getting an abortion, so your lil' wife won't find out about us."

"*Us?*" I chuckled and shook my head. Now, I was the one being nonchalant. "There is no us."

She was so mad that she stomped her foot like a little girl. "Bullshit! There has been an us for over a year!"

"And you just said that I only see you one or two days at a time when I come here. So, if you think it's an *us*, you're as stupid as I thought you were."

She glared at the way I lay there looking at her with near disgust in my eyes.

"Fuck you, Ross!" she shouted. "You ain't shit! I don't give a fuck if there is an us or not! I am *not* killing my baby. I don't give a fuck if your wife finds out! Matter fact, just to make you stop pressuring me to kill my baby, I will tell her my—"

I jumped out of the bed so fast that she didn't even see me coming. Before she knew it, I charged at her. She tried to run, but could only back up against the wall. I was on her ass every inch of the way with eyes so fiery, she instantly became afraid.

"You ain't gon' say shit. I would never let that happen." With my voice at a low, menacing rumble as it slid through my gritted teeth, she got the threat loud and clear.

The offense that she felt was all over her face. Her heart sank, and she started to swing on me.

"*I hate you!*" she screamed as she swung. "*Fuck you!*" As I tried to grab her hands, she shouted, "I don't give a fuck! I'm having my baby and I'm telling that bitch everything!" She was trying her best to claw at my face as we tussled back and forth. I finally grabbed her wrists so tight that she couldn't get out of my grasp. So, she spit in my face, and I slapped the shit outta of her.

"Arrrgh!" she screamed as she fell back on the bed. I came towards her, and she started kicking frantically. I had hit her before, so she knew what was coming and started trying to defend herself against it. But I was a big motherfucka who easily overpowered her. I straddled her and put my hands around her neck. At first, I started choking her just to show her I wasn't to be fucked with. This bitch thought she was going to have this baby and tell my wife against my wishes? Fuck that.

But as she started to gasp for air and claw at my hands, I realized the relief I would feel if this bitch was just gone. She thought she had a place in my life and I gave a fuck about her? If I didn't want this baby, what the hell made her think I wanted her? So, I started squeezing her neck until I felt her esophagus in the palms of my hands. And the more I closed it and felt it bending in my grasp, the more she cringed from the pain and lack of oxygen. Instantly, I felt the relief of this stress in my life going away just that easy.

HEAVEN

"What the fuck are you doing here, Teyanna?"

Looking into Mello's eyes, I couldn't tell whether he was pissed that she had popped up on him or pissed that she had stopped what was about to happen between him and me.

Standing there, I watched him turn from the swagnificient dude who was about to persuade me to make the biggest mistake of my life, to a beast that was about to kill this poor girl. I wondered if *I* was happy that she had stopped what was about to happen between us or if I was disappointed.

Honestly, I was disappointed. I couldn't even lie. Even though I felt the guilt, I knew I was still disa-fucking-pointed.

"What the fuck are *you* doing here?" She glared at Mello. It was like she didn't even see me. "You were supposed to meet me back at my place!"

Luckily, it looked like she hadn't seen us about to kiss, so I discreetly sighed with relief and just stood back watching.

"So, you been following me?" He looked around like cameras were following us. "How long you been following me?"

Teyanna's hands flew on her hips. "Since you left your dad's house."

Mello chuckled. "You say that like it's cool."

She frowned as if he were being so silly. "Fuck you mean? You're *my man*, so I can do what the fuck I wanna do!"

His eyes bucked and he looked like he wanted to laugh. But her audacity had him so pissed that his glare overshadowed his humor. "No, the fuck you can't!" he spat.

They started going back and forth in each other's faces, screaming "fuck you's" and "how could you's" on Michigan Avenue at ten o'clock at night. They were ruining this beautiful summer night that was showing me the way that a man was really supposed to treat me.

"That's why I can't fuck you with, man!" Mello groaned at her. "You crazy as fuck! Following me and shit like you my mama or something!"

Teyanna was right in his face, glaring with spit flying from her mouth. "Well, you should be answering your phone!"

Mello's voice echoed into the night as he bellowed, "I ain't gotta do shit! You don't fucking run me! You need to stay in your fucking—"

"Excuse me," the sound of a deep voice came out of nowhere. I turned around and saw two officers approaching us.

Shit.

Mello had been drinking—*a lot*. I had been drinking a little, but I'd stopped because I didn't want any of my feelings or actions to be blamed on the alcohol. I had felt like the liquor was what had caused me to look at Mello differently. I thought I had to be drunk if I was feeling like he was looking at me in a romantic way. But I was now sober, and Teyanna had popped up. The atmosphere had changed... yet every time Mello glanced at me, he still looked at me the same... and I still felt the same.

"Leave now or I am going to arrest you all for disturbing the peace," one of the officers ordered.

I wasn't even thinking when I gently grabbed Mello's elbow and told him, "C'mon, Mello. Let's go."

Teyanna's eyes bucked. Then she grabbed his other elbow way less gentle than I had. "No! Fuck no! You comin' with me!"

The police officers were getting agitated, so I gave up. I needed to anyway. This shit was stupid and crazy. This night needed to end.

"Mello, just give me your keys," I told him. "I can drive myself home."

Teyanna raised her eyebrow and she smirked at Mello as if she were happy with my suggestion. She folded her arms and waited for him to come with her. The police officers were waiting too—*impatiently*.

Mello was emotionless when he said, "Teyanna, go get in the car. I'll come holla at you after I drop—"

She gasped and started to yell, "No! What—"

The police officers stepped towards her, one with his hand out. "Ma'am, you need to leave."

Mello didn't even flinch as he turned away from her and gently guided me by the small of my back up the street towards where his truck was parked.

"Mello!!!" we could hear her start to scream. "MELLO!"

"Ma'am!" we could then hear one of the officers snap. "*Leave*. NOW!"

I tried to turn around to look to see what was going on, but Mello gently nudged me back around.

I had to walk three times as fast as him to keep up with his long-legged strides.

"You can go with her," I told him.

"Fuck her," he growled, obviously pissed.

"She's gonna fuck around and get arrested."

He shrugged. "Better her ass get locked up than me getting arrested for beating her ass."

We turned down the more isolated street that he had parked on a few hours ago. He kept taking gulps of his whiskey and cranberry juice. Luckily, he didn't look as pissed off as he had just a few seconds ago. He was staring off into space as he walked like he was focused and thinking about something.

All of what had just happened should have made reality set in. It should have made me realize the mistake that I was about to make and made me grateful that fate had stepped in and stopped me from fucking things up. But, unfortunately, it didn't.

Finally, we made it to Mello's ride. He followed me to the passenger's side and when he reached from behind me to open the door, he stopped. I turned around to see what was wrong, leaning against the car and found myself right back in that space with him that I shouldn't have been.

"You okay?" he asked.

Mello was making my heart melt...melt into putty that was senseless, stupid, and irrational.

I swallowed all of the fucked up emotions that he was making me feel and forced out, "Yeah."

I was ready to go. This was bad...all bad. Anything that could feel this good without touching or kissing, with just words and eye contact, was all bad. It had to be.

"You sure?"

"Yeah." I was trying to look like all of this was normal. But I was failing like a motherfucker. I was fidgeting and shit. "Sorry."

"Why you sorry?"

"You were supposed to be with your girl, but you been with me all day and—"

He inched closer to me, which stopped the words in my throat. This was about to happen. It was definitely about to happen, and I should have stopped it. As he bent down towards my mouth, I just kept telling myself that I should stop this. I just felt like this was about to be the moment that was going to change the rest of my life. And it would not only change my life, but Sunshine and Divine's lives as well. This was not just going to end with this kiss. I knew it. It would only be the beginning of an extremely dangerous roller coaster ride.

Something was also telling me that this good feeling he was about to give me was not going to be worth it. But did I listen? No. I let him kiss me and I should have stopped him right then. I should have stopped him when his soft, silky lips landed on top of mine, but I didn't. I kissed him back. I opened my mouth and allowed his tongue to penetrate my mouth, and the kiss intensified. I started to breathe his air. His hands went under my top, and he started to caress my breasts.

Before I knew it, he was opening up the passenger's side door. He then lifted me up by grabbing my ass cheeks and put me in the back seat. I lay on my back looking up at the ceiling wondering what the fuck was happening and trying to make myself stop this. But I couldn't. I wanted to feel him just as much as I knew it was so wrong to do so.

He stood outside of the car, pulling down my leggings. All I could think about was all the hurt and stress Ross had caused me despite how loyal I had been to him. Then I wondered about the woman he was spending time with right now who had his mind so consumed that he had no idea where I was at that moment. He had spent so much time tracking me, following my every move, and making sure that no man was next to me, but whoever she was had his mind so wrapped up that right now a man was doing something to me that he wouldn't even believe.

And at no point did I feel like this was Ross' son. He was a man who had catered to me all day, making me feel adored and beautiful. As he put my legs down and took my shoes off, he watched my body as if it was something he had been waiting to see all his life. He removed my panties slowly as if he wanted to keep a mental picture of the moment. And before I knew it, he pinned my thick thighs down by each side of me to the point that my knees were in my armpits. He bent down so slowly that the anticipation was agonizing. He kissed my pussy just as slow and intently as he had kissed the lips on my face. He didn't hungrily eat at it. He ate it slow and with passion. He licked my clit deliberately and unhurriedly, after slowly opening my lips. He ate it slowly as if it were something he had been waiting to taste for a lifetime, hoping to savor every bite.

"Oh God," I cried out in a hoarse tone. My eyes were literally watering. It felt so good and so wrong at the same time. I could still feel the dull pain on the side of my face where Ross had last hit me. I also felt the terror from him pushing my face under the water. And yet, I still felt guilty. I was no longer the innocent one. He now had a reason for his actions. And even though that gave me guilt, it also gave me comfort.

We were now on the same playing field.

"Ah!" I gasped and my eyes sprung open as I felt a sudden hard and filling thrust in my pussy. My head slightly lifted, and I looked down to see the most amazing sight. Mello was standing outside of the car pulling me down onto his dick as he stood there with his shirt lifted and tucked under his neck. He was so focused as he thrust in and out of this pussy that was leaking so much that it was embarrassing.

"Shit!" I breathed and cried, "Oh my gaaaawd." Tears streamed slowly out of my eyes and down my face as I watched his beautiful manhood swim in and out of me. "Ooooh..." My moans suddenly stopped, relieved when he suddenly took it out. I could think straight. I could breathe. And then... "Shit!" He bent down and started to eat my pussy again. "Fuuuuuck!" He was sucking my clit, licking at the hood of it, and drinking my cum. "*Oh! Gawd!*" I tried to reach for something to hold onto, anything, something, but there was nothing to brace my body on as he stopped mid-orgasm, stood upright and shoved that dick back in me. "Ahhhhhh!"

❧ 10 ❧

ROSS

I had driven all the way to Neely Henry Lake with Tisha's lifeless body in the trunk of her Kia.

Once there, I left the car running. I then stepped out and used a rag to wipe everything on the driver's side free of my fingerprints. Then I went to the trunk and popped it open. Tisha's eyes were staring right up at me. That shocked and terrified expression was still etched all over her face. There was absolutely no life in her hazel eyes, though. Her yellow skin had started to look pasty and ghostly. Looking at me, she looked like a zombie that would haunt me for the rest of my life. She still had the strained look on her face as she struggled for that very last breath I had refused to allow to enter her lungs by squeezing her throat shut. Her expression still had so much life, but she was dead. I had made sure of that back at her crib. I waited an hour after choking the life out of her before deciding to get rid of her body.

I was able to easily lift her body out of the trunk. Even as dead weight, she weighed all of one hundred and seventy pounds. I smelled her urine and feces that had left her body as she lay in the trunk during the hour-long drive. My nose burned from the smell of death as I put her in the driver's seat. Then I reached over her and put the car in drive. As it started to roll slowly toward the lake, I used the same wipes to clean off the door handles, close the truck, and wipe that off as well. Then, stuffing my hands in my pockets, I watched as the car rolled into the lake and started to disappear under the water.

I felt no guilt. I never did when I had to get rid of someone who was getting in my way. And Tisha was definitely trying to get in my way. Now, she and that baby were non-existent. I had taken care of this problem. Now, it was time to get to the crib in order to cover my tracks.

MELLO

"You okay?"

I knew I sounded like a broken record. I had been asking Heaven that all night. Earlier, I could see on her face that she was uncomfortable with what was happening. But she was still there. She never left. She continued to drink and take that walk with me. And even after Teyanna showed up, Heaven was willing to let me take her home. I figured she wanted this. That was why I had gone ahead and taken the chance.

As a boy, I'd waited on this moment for years. And even when she was finally in my eyesight, I knew she was a territory I should not invade. But it was obvious that her husband wasn't on shit. So, I took her mouth and then I took that pussy. And it was so worth it. I took my time with that pussy. For an hour, in the back seat of my jeep, I got every stroke in that I had always imagined. And when she never stopped me, I knew there was something more between us than the friendship. I knew what I felt for her was genuine, and that if Heaven was only not afraid to allow herself to feel for me, she would feel the same. But until she felt that, she was going to feel this dick. And I made sure that she felt every inch of it, the entire circumference. She had gotten it all.

And now we were dressed and sitting in the front seat of the Jeep that still had not moved. It was almost eleven now. She was sitting in the passenger's seat catching her breath and staring out of the window off into space. Her eyes were saying so much, even though her mouth was saying nothing.

"Yeah," she finally whispered.

I wanted to ask her was it as good to her as it was to me. But that just seemed so immature. Honestly, I didn't need to ask that because I knew. The evidence of it was all over my dick. The evidence of it could be heard through my car and even on the outside as she yelled my praises. I knew that shit felt good to her too.

I was smart enough to know what she was thinking. What we had done was very scandalous, ratchet shit. But I didn't regret it even if she probably did.

"I don't want you to think I was taking advantage of you or no shit like that."

She finally looked at me, and when her mouth held a little humorous smile, I felt relief. "Take advantage of me? How? I gave it to you. I just... I just..."

"You feel bad?"

"No."

I was shocked. "You don't?"

"I mean, I do a little, but not for Ross, for me. I'm not this type of person, but Ross doesn't deserve my loyalty. He's done some really fucked up shit to me."

"Like what?" Instantly, I went into superhero mode. I was ready to wreak havoc on Ross for causing the pain I saw in her eyes. I was like a love-sick puppy, sitting there with my chest heaving. My homies would be cracking so many jokes right now if they could see me.

"He...he just..." She sighed deeply, tore her eyes away from mine, and looked out of the passenger's side window again at nothing in particular. "He isn't always a good person."

"He's cheating?"

She nodded slowly. "Yeah."

"You know this for sure?"

"Have I ever caught him with a bitch? No. But I ain't stupid." She had this fire in her eyes as if she was reliving every moment he had done her dirty.

"So, why are you still with him?" I asked her.

"Because he...he's a bad person at times, but he has been so good to me and my sister and Sunshine. You know my story."

"But he's cheating on you."

"Every man cheats. Ain't that what you just did?"

"You got a point." I swallowed everything else I wanted to say. Even though she had fucked me, I was still scared of finally being honest with her just for her to go back to that ain't-shit-husband.

Heaven yawned. Then she said, "I'm starving."

"Yeah, it's been a minute since I ate too. You wanna go eat?"

"I wanna go eat, but I wanna go lay down."

Bet.

"Wanna eat and lay down? We can Grubhub it."

She looked at me long and hard. Then, she finally asked, "At your house?"

"Yeah, I mean if you want to...if you feel comfortable." I was trying to be cool, but I really wanted her to. Today was like a young nigga's dream come true. It was like my wet dream as a little boy coming to fruition. And I did not want this to end. I did not want her to go just yet, because I wasn't sure if I would ever experience her again. I just wasn't ready to let go. She was looking at me as if I had asked her for a lot, but at the same time, she looked willing. She didn't want our good time to end either.

"Yeeeah," she finally answered slowly. "I...I wanna go with you."

"You sure?" I bit my lip, trying to maintain my excitement. But I wasn't able to keep myself from slipping my hand on the inside of her thick-ass thigh. It was so warm and juicy in there. "You comin' with me?"

She looked like she was damn near breathless as she stared into my eyes. "Yeah."

I wanted to kiss her again, fuck her again, feed her, lay with her, and spoon with her. All that cornball shit that dudes swear they would never do with a chick, I wanted to do with Heaven.

I watched as a sudden sadness came over her. She broke our eye contact with all this disappointment in her eyes.

"What's on your mind?"

She relaxed her head back on the headrest, closed her eyes, and then opened them again before she looked out of her window. "You're a good dude." It fucked me up when she sounded so sad and disappointed when she said that.

"Uh... Thanks." I nervously chuckled.

She chuckled as well over her sadness. "Sorry. You know I don't mean it like that. It just doesn't seem fair. I wish I would have met your first. But instead... You're...you're his *son*." Tears fell from her eyes.

"First of all, I don't see him as my father. If I did, I wouldn't have done it."

She sucked her teeth and wiped her eyes, trying to stop the tears. "But still—"

"And I don't see you as his wife. I see you as a woman I've been feeling for a long-ass time."

She looked at me again, only this time with disbelief. I threw my ego out of the window. She needed to know that I wasn't being the typical dude.

"Look, I know I may look like I ain't shit to you because of who you are and because I got a girl, but I'm not feeling Teyanna like that, so that's why I'm here with you when I should have been with her. I'm feeling you." She finally gave me her eyes again. She looked like she was searching mine for sincerity. I knew this was news to her. Before this day, I had never shown her that I was crushing on her, that I cared about her as more than a friend. "Seriously. I always have. I always had a crush on you, but I knew I could never overstep those boundaries. But today, I just couldn't help but risk that shit. You seemed like you needed it, so I took a chance."

Her phone started buzzing. She looked relieved to have something else to focus her attention on. She bent down to get her purse off the floor and rummaged through it, looking for her phone. Once she found it, she unlocked it and swiped through some apps. I could see her going to her text message inbox. She opened the first unread message. As she started to read it, her eyes grew bigger and bigger.

Then she spazzed. "Fuck!"

"What's wrong?"

She started to hyperventilate. Literally, she was taking these heavy breaths over and over again real fast. "Shit!"

"What?" I instantly started the car. Even though she hadn't said anything yet, I knew a move needed to be made fast, so I made it. "What's wrong, Heaven?"

"I gotta go! *Now*."

HEAVEN

Suddenly, my bubble of a perfect day was threatening to burst violently. My fantasy of a perfect day with the perfect guy was ending with a nightmare. Mello was no longer this bomb-ass dude who had taken me on the perfect date and ended it with the perfect night of great head and dick that I would gladly pay for with anybody's money. Suddenly, Mello was *now* Ross' son again. I was seeing the light. I was seeing my wrongs too. It was very clear what all I had risked for an hour's worth of good dick.

Mello had thrown the car into drive and sped out of the parking space. "What's wrong? What happened?"

As I tried to catch my breath, I answered, "Ross is back in town."

"What? I thought he wasn't supposed to come back for another week."

"Me too," I said in a panic.

"Did he call you?"

"No, but he's been blowing Esperanza's phone up. He texted her and told her he was catching the last flight out and would be home in a few hours. That was two hours ago. I gotta go!"

I felt so bad. I felt like shit for doing this to Mello. I honestly wanted to stay with him. I did not want to let go of the feeling he was giving me.

I was so confused. He had just told me how he felt about me, and I had never heard words spoken to me so genuinely. I didn't want to just leave him like this. I didn't have the same feelings for him, but he deserved a better response than this. But I had to get the hell out of there. Mello couldn't take care of me, Divine, and Sunshine. And who was to say I wanted him to? This night had happened, and no, I did not regret one moment of it. But though I was now seeing Mello in another light, and he had confessed his feelings for me, he nor I had said a word about taking this any further past tonight.

All night, Mello had looked at me like he wanted to be everything to and for me, but how could that happen? Ross was my husband and my provider. Mello, though adorable, full of swag, and so fucking caring, had been nothing but dick. I wasn't willing to risk my family's comfort for a piece of dick.

"I'm sorry, Mello," I finally apologized with a frustrating sigh.

"What you apologizing for?" He tried to sound sincere, but he couldn't even look at me. He just kept his eyes on the road.

"I feel bad."

"Don't." His shortness was cutting deep.

"You...you aren't going to tell anybody about this, are you?" I needed to know.

"No. Your secret is safe with me." He looked so hurt when he said it.

I felt like shit. I had just had sex with my husband's son. That reality was starting to sink in deeper and deeper as we drove south on Lake Shore Drive. The deeper it got, the sicker I felt.

What had I just done?

TREASURE

"Arrrgh, fuck!" Vegas came inside of me with a hard thrust, pulled out of me, and rolled over on his back. I giggled as he heaved hard and fast, trying to catch his breath. He reached and smacked my ass, asking, "What you laughin' at?"

The feeling of him gripping my ass made me giggle even more. "You're dying over there."

"So. I ain't shame. That's that good pussy, girl."

I laughed, "I love you, baby."

"I love you too."

I know I seemed fraud as fuck, but I did love my man. He had been the best man to me. I had never been treated better.

I just wasn't shit.

As I spooned with Vegas, he said, "I got something to tell you."

I hated the way he suddenly got serious and how hard I could hear his heart beating as I lay on his solid, big chest. "What?"

"I met with Steve, the accountant, yesterday."

"What he say?" I asked. But I could tell from the anger in his voice that whatever Steve had told him wasn't good... Not at all.

"I was right. Ross is stealing from me."

I immediately sat up, reached over on the nightstand, and turned the lamp on. Vegas' blue eyes squinted and fought to adjust to the sudden flash of light. We had been fucking in the darkness for the past two hours. Beads of sweat covered the colorful tattoos on his chest. I stared into those piercing, blue eyes, past those long sandy brown lashes that damn near looked like curtains. I was trying to find some notion of him joking, but there wasn't one.

"You serious?" I asked anyway.

It looked like it pained him to answer, "Yeah."

I then reluctantly asked, "How much?"

"A hundred thousand."

My mouth dropped. No words came out, though. I stared off into space. This hurt. Ross and his family were noticeably living a better life than me and Vegas. He and I were comfortable, but he got a smaller percentage of the business because he had only invested so much when he was younger. He had Kutz Barber Studio, which brought in cash as well. We were far from poor. We lived in a nice condo on 59th and Calumet. Yeah, we all had foreign cars, but that's because Ross owned the chop shop, so we had access to them for the low. We were far from rich too, though. Far from the one hundred thousand dollars Ross owed Vegas.

"Are you sure?" I really, really wanted him to be wrong.

"Steve showed me the transactions of Ross paying a bogus parts company over the years."

"Bogus company?"

"Yeah. It's a front company."

"How do you know?"

"Steve did some digging and found out that the company is in Heaven's name."

I cringed.

"You think she knows?" he asked.

"Hell no. Heaven doesn't know shit about what you all do."

Vegas seemed relieved.

"What are you going to do?" I asked him.

"I'm killing that son of a bitch."

I winced. Ross deserved it. And I knew Vegas wasn't bullshitting.

He had enough bodies on his hands for me to know he was very serious.

"No, Vegas," I whined.

"Fuck him."

"I know, but he's my best friend's husband. I do not want to see her hurt. If he's dead, he won't feel the pain. Heaven will."

I stared at him and I could feel him weighing his ego over his love for me. He finally shed his monster, and his loving man appeared again. He reached and pulled me down on his chest. He kissed the top of my head.

"Then what you think I should do, babe?" he asked. "He gotta feel this shit. He *got* to."

"I got a plan."

11

ROSS

"Here's your coffee, Ross."

I stared at Esperanza as she handed me the same coffee mug that she'd been handing me every morning since she started working for me. I knew she could see me staring at her. But I think the only other person in the house ornerier than me was her.

"You didn't see me calling you the other night?" I asked her.

"What night, Ross?" she asked, trying to sound dumb.

"Tuesday."

"Oh," she said in this high-pitched condescending tone. "I was sleeping."

I grabbed my fork and started cutting my French toast with a smirk. "You always answer my calls, even when you're sleeping."

"Well, I was really tired that day. Could you not get through to Heaven?" Before I could answer, she looked across the table at Heaven. "Heaven, why didn't you answer your husband's calls?"

Heaven shrugged. "Because my husband didn't call me."

I looked between them with a raised eyebrow. They were trying to play me, and I didn't like this shit at all.

"Not one call, Heaven?" Esperanza pressed.

"Noooope," Heaven sang sarcastically. "As a matter of fact, he didn't call me at all that day."

Esperanza smirked. "Humph!"

Staring at Heaven but speaking to Esperanza, I kept pressing. "So, ain't shit happen that I should know about?"

"No, sir," Esperanza swore as she walked away from the table.

Still staring at Heaven, I asked, "So, Heaven was sleep like she said she was?"

"Yep. We all had a very busy day in the hot sun, so we all went to bed quite early."

"Umph." I watched as Heaven totally disregarded me, even though I was looking right at her.

Something was up with these two that I couldn't put my finger on. It was my fault that I couldn't put my finger on it, though. When I was in Alabama, I was so busy trying to get rid of that problem that I wasn't focused on what was going on back home in my house.

Esperanza always answered my calls—*always*. But that Tuesday night before I got back into town, she wasn't answering my calls. If it wasn't for the money that I gave Esperanza, her family would be out here bogus. She sent the money I paid her back to Mexico to take care of some of her children who were still there. She also used some of it to take care of her crack-head son who came and went. Given all of that, she wouldn't fuck this money up for shit.

She rarely missed a call. I didn't give a fuck if she was comatose; she came out of that coma to answer that call. But for the first time ever, that night, I couldn't get through to her. I knew it was some bullshit behind it. And that bullshit had a lot to do with Heaven. I knew it. She had been acting up since I got back in town. She had not said much to me since I got home. She was in her own world, and she wasn't acting like I was the main priority in it. I knew that she was pissed that I hadn't called or answered her calls. but Tisha had been so far up in my ass that I hadn't had a chance to do either.

Even in death, Tisha was causing me grief in my household, but I was gonna get down to the bottom of this shit.

HEAVEN

A few days later, I jumped every time my phone rang.

Tuesday night, Mello had gotten me home just in the nick of time. I had him pull to the end of the block. Then I literally ran up the block, to the front door, and keyed into the house. As soon as I smelled the familiar fragrance of my house, if I wasn't feeling horribly guilty already, I was being drowned in guilt by being in the house. My footsteps were so heavy. I felt too guilty to go into Esperanza's room. I knew she had a lot of questions because I had been so wrapped up in Mello that I hadn't even checked on my daughter all day. But I couldn't face her.

I tiptoed into my room and closed the door, trying to lock out all of the bullshit that I had created on the other side. I stripped and showered Mello's scent off of me and jumped into bed just in time for Ross to come through the bedroom door. My heart was beating so fast that I was scared he wouldn't believe I was as asleep as I was pretending to be. I had washed my body three times in the shower, but I still felt like he could smell his son on me. I don't know if I was happy or sad that once he got into that bad, he didn't even touch me. He turned his back to me and fell asleep soundly. Nothing was on his mind, seemingly. It was as if he didn't give a fuck about me or about not speaking to me for the last couple of days that he had been out of town. He slept so soundly while I lay next to him with so many things running through my mind. But the most important thing that ran through my mind was *Mello*. All I could think about was how he would have appreciated and held me had I been in that bed with him that night. I wondered how he would have looked at me once he came in from out of town and hadn't seen me in days, because the way he looked at me once he saw me for the first time was incredible.

Mello stayed on my mind every day and every night. He was on my mind while I showered and while I fed my daughter. He was on my mind while Ross and I tiptoed around each other for three days. Mello was on my mind when I dodged every phone call and every Facetime attempt from him. And every thought of him ran thunderous chills down my spine.

I couldn't talk to him. I didn't know what to say. I didn't know if I could withstand looking at his face and not being able to be in his presence. I didn't know if what I was feeling was right or wrong, so I dodged him.

"Who is that that keeps blowing up your phone?"

I looked over at Treasure as she sat on a stool at the bar in the den. She had been drinking like a motherfucker for the last three days. Something was wrong with her, but I had been too much in my own head to even try to figure out what was wrong with her.

"Huh?" I asked.

"Your phone. Somebody keeps trying to call you."

I hit the ignore button and turned my phone over, even though she was too far away from me to see it.

I tried to think fast. "That's just some school that keeps calling me."

"School?"

"Yeah. I thought I was interested in going to college, but I don't feel like arguing with Ross about it. So, I changed my mind. But the recruiter keeps calling me."

"Fuck, Ross," she slurred. "You can go to school if you want..."

Treasure's voice faded out and was replaced by the same thoughts of Mello. I couldn't understand how to deal with these feelings that had been growing for him over the last couple of days. I had never had these thoughts about Mello before. I never thought twice about his beautiful face, his juicy lips, or how thoughtful he was. Now, all of that was constantly on my mind; that and the way he totally invaded my body and took that motherfucker over. I didn't know if these sudden feelings were just sexual, or if I just missed him because I was no longer talking to him every other day, or if I really liked him. And then I got frustrated because even once I figured all of that out, it didn't matter. That dope-ass hour of sex had ruined everything. Now, it felt like our friendship was over, but there were no possibilities of anything else.

ROSS

"Yo', Ross. What up?"

"What up, boss?"

A few of the young guys were speaking and dapping me up as I walked into Kutz. I spoke to them and shook up with a few of them as I made my way back to Vegas' office. It was some straight bullshit that I had to bring my ass up to this shop just to find out what the fuck what going on with my right hand. I had been hitting him up since I got back in town, but I couldn't get through to him.

"What's up, son?"

Shit, Vegas wasn't the only one being shady. When I spoke to my own son, he barely stopped lining up his client. He looked up and gave me a dry-ass, "What up?" Then he kept perfecting the lining.

I had more pressing matters to deal with than Mello's young ass, so I kept it moving. It was no telling what his issue was anyway. It was probably his baby mama, his bitch, or *both*. I kept it moving towards the back. Once at Vegas' office, I knocked, but I opened the door and let myself in without waiting for him to respond.

He was sitting at his desk going through the same phone that I was just calling without getting an answer from his ass.

"Damn, motherfucka, what's been up with you?" I sat in the chair facing his desk, reaching back and closing the door.

Barely looking up from the phone, Vegas answered, "Shit."

I sat back and toyed with my beard, trying to figure out what this motherfucka was on. I didn't like his disposition at all. "We got a problem?"

He finally looked at me but only for a second before looking back down at the phone. "Fuck no. Why you say that?"

"I been blowing your shit up. You ignorin' my calls like I'm one of your bitches or something."

He chuckled and finally put his phone down. He looked at me, interlocking his hands and resting on the desk with his elbows. "I just been busy. Me and Treasure been on some booed-up shit. My bad."

"Yo' bad?" Yeah, something was definitely up.

"Yeah. Thought you were still in Alabama anyway. You said you was gon' be gone for two weeks. What happened?"

"Tisha was blowing me."

"You talk her into getting the abortion?"

"Yeah." He smiled sarcastically. "You slick motherfucka. Lucky you."

"Yeah... Lucky me."

MELLO

♫ Ain't no complaints (nah)
Racks in the bank (racks)
Fuck what you think (huh?)
We got some rank (rank)
Leave your ass stank (bow)
Robbin' the bank (bank)
Pull out the banger (rah)
You was a stranger (stranger)
We don't relate (no) racks in the (rack)
Racks in the safe (safe)
Steak on my plate (steak)
My sons are dons (dons)
My bitch Amazon (bad)
My plug is hund (Offset, plug)
She fuckin' for some (smash) ♫

I was flying to my crib bobbing my head to "No Complaints" by Metro
Boomin, trying to act like everything was cool, but it wasn't. Things

were far from cool. I was starting to think that I should have stayed my black ass in Florida. I had only been back in Chicago for a few weeks, but everything was fucked up already. I was still cutting hair in the shop, not working some cushy-ass job with a fat-ass salary like I was expecting once I graduated early from college. Me and my girl were at each other's throats, which wasn't technically out of the norm, but it was worse now more than ever. Ever since I walked away from her downtown, every attempt to communicate with her ended with "fuck you's" and "I hate you's." I hadn't even seen her since. And that was by choice. I still didn't like how she had put her hands on my baby mama in front of my son. It had me ready to put my hands on her. So, I didn't need to be around her until my anger subsided. But my absence was only making her more pissed.

Then there was Heaven, who was pissing me off the most. I had already felt some type of way that Ross had come back in town and fucked shit up. It was like as soon as she got that text, things changed with her. That day, she had gone from looking at me as a friend to looking at me like I was the man. Then she looked at me like I was a mistake as soon as she heard that Ross was coming back in town.

The fantasy was over that fucking fast.

When I shot the dice and kissed her, I didn't know we were going to fuck too, but it went there, and I was good with knowing that, even if nothing else ever happened, we would still be cool. I had no idea that making her cum harder than she ever had in her life would make her never talk to me again. I had been blowing her phone up with calls, text messages, and Facetime attempts. She hadn't answered one fucking attempt to communicate with her. She was treating me like a peon. She was treating me like *I* was the one that was cheating on her. That connection we had had for two years was over, and no matter how hard I tried not to, it was all I could think about.

That pussy... Fuck, I could still smell it on my face. I had fulfilled my fantasy. I had felt that pussy, but I still wanted her. I wanted to relive that day over and over again, put that smile on her face over and over again. My feelings for her hadn't been fake. This shit was real...*too* real.

"Fuck," I groaned and punched the steering wheel when I saw

Teyanna sitting on the stoop in front of my apartment building on 80th and Morgan.

I parked and got out of my ride, telling myself not to whoop this girl's ass. The last thing I wanted on top of the bullshit was to end up in the county jail that night.

"What's up?" As she spoke to me, I peeped that she was calm, surprisingly.

"What up?" I spoke back dryly as I stood in front of her with my arms folded.

She just sat there looking at me with this dead look in her eyes. I had never seen her looking this defeated.

"So, you love her that much?"

My eyes bucked as I stared at her. *How does she know?*

Watching the guilty look on my face, she chuckled sarcastically and shook her head as tears filled her eyes. "I knew it. I knew you loved that bitch. If you love her so much, just be with her! She's your baby mama, so you might as well!"

I lowered my head so she wouldn't see me sighing with relief. Then I shook my head at myself. Heaven was on my mind so much that I hadn't even thought that Teyanna could be referring to anyone but her.

But did that mean that I loved Heaven?

"I don't want to be with her," I told her Teyanna.

She hissed. "I can't tell because—"

I cut her off with a blow. "And I don't wanna be with you no more."

Her eyes bucked. "*What?*"

"I can't fuck with nobody that acts like you. I didn't come home for this shit. You following me around, embarrassing me in front of my people, and fighting my baby mama in front of my son. You do too much. I'm done."

I walked away from her stare. She couldn't believe it. After all the kicking, screaming, and fighting she had done, I had never just walked away like this. And to be honest, me walking away wasn't all about her. She thought it was about Paris. She felt I was in love with my baby mama. Teyanna was knocking on the wrong door, though. Paris didn't have my heart. *Heaven* did.

"So, I was right?" I heard the tears in her eyes as I keyed into the building. I turned around against my will and saw her staring at me with tears streaming down her face. "I was right. You *do* love her! Fuck you!" Her crazy ass tossed her phone at me so fast that I barely had the chance to duck. It just missed my head before it crashed against the security door. Just as I stood upright and looked at her, she walked away.

"Yeah, you right," I spoke low as I watched her walk away. "I *do* love her."

❧ 12 ❧

TREASURE

A s I took the coke and dissolved it in a few milliliters of water, Damo walked past me and smacked my bare ass that was swallowing my thong. A smooth smirk spread on my face. This was what I liked about Damo the most. Damo let me be his Bonnie; cooking crack in his kitchen after we'd just fucked the shit out of each other.

I filled a small baby food jar with water and then put it in a pan on the stove that was filled with water. I put the vial filled with the coke and water in the baby food jar. Then I allowed the solution to heat until it was hot but not so hot that it would burn to put my finger in it.

"It's time for you to start dropping the ammonia in there," Damo told me as he kissed my neck.

"I knooow," I popped slick, and he smacked my ass again. "When you done, you wanna take a ride with me?"

I could feel his dick on my ass as he stood so close behind me. Just the mere feeling of that phat monster had my pussy leaking.

"Where we goin'?" I asked damn near in a purr.

"I got a few drops to make in the burbs. May take me a few hours. Your man gon' come looking for you."

I turned from the stove and slipped my arms around his chiseled abs. "I guess he's gonna be looking for me then." Then I sucked on his bottom lip.

With it still in my mouth, he told me, "You gon' make me put this dick back up in you."

Just the sound of his deep-ass voice made my sweet crevice seep. He must have known that I was leaking. He obviously smelled my syrupy stench, because he reached into my panties and moaned. "Damn, my pussy so wet for me."

My eyes rolled to the back of my head as he started to make circular motions on my clit.

I ignored that "my pussy" comment and moaned, "Mmmm."

"Bring that ass here."

Before I could say a word or knew what was happening, Damo spun me around, bent me over the stove, and drove his dick into my pussy.

Then he started to murder this motherfucker.

"Ugh! Fuck! Oh my God."

Holding me around the waist, he drove into this pussy long, deep, and wide.

"Fuuuuck, yes, Damo. Fuck meeeeee."

Giving me what I wanted, he grabbed my thigh, lifted it and rested my foot on the kitchen counter, causing his dick to sink in deeper.

HEAVEN

"Heaven, I'm gone."

My eyes rolled as I lay with my back to Ross. "Okay."

"You still mad at me, huh?" he had the nerve to ask. There was a smugness in his voice that made my fucking skin crawl.

I forced myself to sound as unbothered as possible. "Mad at you for what?" The last thing I needed on top of everything else was an argument with his ass.

"Shit, *you* tell *me*," he spat.

I could have told him that I was pissed because he hadn't even had the respect for me to pretend like he wasn't out of town with another woman, by actually acting like a husband while he was out of town. But that would have only led to a big-ass argument and him still walking out of the house to go lay up with the next bitch. So, I just bit my tongue.

I heard him suck his teeth. "Fine. Whatever, man."

Then I listened to him leave out of the bedroom. I soon heard him going down the stairs. The further his footsteps got, the more I felt like I could breathe. That headache was gone, but the original headache was still fucking there.

I threw the covers back over my head and fought the sick feeling in my stomach.

It had now been a week and a half since Mello had fucked up my world. We still hadn't spoken. I just couldn't bring myself to do it. I didn't have the heart to tell him that, after taking it upon himself to show me such a good time that day, after showing me what I deserved, I could never be with him like that again because I respected my ain't-shit husband way more than he respected me.

Still in all, I really missed Mello. His presence in my life was so noticeably missing since I hadn't talked to him. For two years, there were regular conversations that made up a lot of my boring days as I sat in the house doing nothing. We used to talk often and intimately. We'd had way more intimate moments between us than me and Ross had. Now, I realized everything that he had been to me over the last two years. Maybe we *were* more than just friends.

"Heaven?"

I turned over in bed and pushed the covers back from over my face. Ross was gone and Esperanza, who had peeped my mood, had taken Sunshine to the park. So, I had been sulking in bed all day. Esperanza, Ross, and Divine thought my mood was because Ross had disappeared during his last trip. Yes, it was obvious to me that Ross had been with another woman. I wasn't fazed, though. I was used to his shit. Mello was what and who had me shook to my soul

"Yeah?" I asked Divine as I watched her standing in my doorway.

I didn't like the look in her eyes. Not at all. She looked scared and nervous.

"You up?"

Barely... "Yeah."

"Okay. I need to talk to you." Walking into the room, she took a deep breath. I watched her cautiously as she sat at the foot of the bed. I sat up when it looked like she was about to cry.

"What's wrong, Divine?"

"I...I'm..." The stuttering frustrated her, so she paused and took another long, deep breath. "I'm pregnant, Heaven."

My heart sank. The last thing I wanted for my sister was for her to have a baby early like I had.

"What?" I breathed. "What the fuck, Divine? I thought you were on the pill."

She shrugged, finally looking as young as she really was, despite the weave, makeup, and curves that made her look twenty instead of seventeen.

"I fucked up," she admitted.

Clearly.

"You're pregnant by who? Who is the father?" I didn't even know Divine had a boyfriend. I knew she was dating and probably fucking, but she hadn't claimed to like or be involved with one particular dude.

When she said, "Damo," I was outdone.

I gasped. "What?! Oh my God! Divine, he works with Ross!"

"I knoooow," she whined.

"Ross is going to kill him."

"I know. That's why you can't tell him."

Everything about Damo started to play before my eyes. He never acted like he was talking to anyone special. He stayed with a different chick every other time I saw him. And... "He's like twenty-five." I frowned at the realization. "He's too fucking old for you. I know. How dare I? But me and Ross were different. He ain't shit, but at least when he met me, everyone knew I was his. I wasn't a damn secret."

Now, tears were running down her face, but they looked more like tears of relief than shame, like she was relieved now that she had finally said something.

I asked, "How long have you been fucking him?"

"We've been dating for a few months."

My eyes bucked. *"Dating?"*

"Yeah."

"Does that consist of more than fucking and Netflix and chill?"

Divine sucked her teeth. "Yeah."

I rolled my eyes to the ceiling. I knew that was a lie. She was only seventeen. What the hell kinda dates was he taking her on?

I took a deep breath, trying to stay calm. By the look on her face, I knew that she already felt bad. I remembered how I felt when I was sixteen and pregnant. Back then, I didn't want to be made to feel worse, so I didn't want to do that to her either.

"What you wanna do?" I asked her.

"I wanna keep it."

I cringed. She looked like an immature little girl who thought a baby would keep a dude. Even though Damo and Divine had been keeping this a secret, Damo didn't act like a dude who was seriously dating anyone. Divine was ready to have this man's baby when she wasn't even sure if he wanted *her*.

There was so much regret in Divine's eyes as she saw my anger grow the more I thought about this.

She begged, "Please don't tell Ross."

"If you wanna keep it, how long do you think we can keep this from him?"

"Until Damo finds a new supplier. Once Ross finds out, he is going to want to end their business relationship."

That was the least of it. Ross felt like Divine was one of his daughters. He was going to kill Damo.

"Promise me, Heaven. You cannot tell Ross anything until I tell Damo and he and I can figure things out."

I chuckled. *He and I? Poor girl.*

Despite me knowing better, I just told her, "Okay, Divine. I promise."

I didn't have the heart to burst her bubble.

⚬⚬⚬

For about an hour, Divine sat on my bed trying to convince me that having her baby would be the right decision. Luckily, when Esperanza came back with Sunshine, she stayed downstairs, cooking lunch. Even though I wasn't arguing with her, she felt the need to convince me that having Damo's body was right. That right there should have told her that she wasn't making the right decision, but I feared she wouldn't know that until she was a single mother, wishing Damo was around to help her more because he was off doing his own thing. But Divine felt like since she was about to be a senior in high school, she could do this. After the hard life she had lived as a young girl with my mother, she felt like she had been taking care of others since she was little, so having this baby wouldn't be any different.

I didn't have the heart to tell her that she was wrong. I didn't have the heart to tell her that since Damo had kept her a secret that he would want to keep her baby a secret too. I couldn't tell her that since he wasn't ready to commit to claiming her, he probably wasn't ready to commit to having a baby with her.

Luckily, the doorbell eventually rang and interrupted us.

Divine's eyes instantly bucked. "Is that Ross?"

I chuckled at how scared she was.

But she think she had enough to have a baby, huh?

"He wouldn't have to ring the bell, Divine," I said as I got out of the bed. Whoever it was had come over uninvited, and we rarely had people come over without calling. So, I was getting out of bed for the first time that day to see who the hell was at the door.

"Heaveeeeen!" Esperanza shouted from the first floor. "Mello is here to see you."

Now, my eyes were bucking as I paused right in the middle of slipping on my house shoes.

"Heaven, promise me you won't say nothing to anybody, not even Treasure. She might tell Vegas and he will tell Ross."

"I'm not going to say anything," I insisted, feeling the butterflies in my stomach.

What is he doing here?

My heart was beating a mile a minute. I was so nervous. Was what I had been fearful of about to happen? Was having sex with Mello about to be thrown in my face? Because what the hell was he doing there? Especially without calling first?

I picked up my phone to see if he had called or texted, and he hadn't. He hadn't even been over since the day we went to the zoo. So, why was he showing up now? My guilty conscience was eating at me so much that I barely heard what my sister was saying. I slipped on my house shoes and made my way out of the bedroom.

I couldn't believe it when I started to fix my hair and adjust the PINK tank and shorts I had on. I cared how I looked for him... Wow.

I felt like I was floating down the stairs. I just knew Mello was about to act out. He had every right to. Considering the friendship that we'd had over the last two years, ignoring him was rude as hell of me. But I just didn't know what else to do. I hoped I would be able to calmly explain everything to him without Esperanza or my sister catching on to what had happened between him and me.

However, all of that hope was shattered when I finally noticed Mello standing in the foyer below with some bitch! He was standing next to this beautiful, slim-thick, dark skin chick who was *not* Teyanna. He was wearing a facial expression that I couldn't read. He just looked normal as if nothing had happened between us, which made me jealous as fuck.

"What up, Heaven?" he asked simply as if he hadn't eaten my pussy until my soul left my body and I wanted to have his babies. He looked past me as if he hadn't given me the best dick of my life like he wanted to give it to me forever or like I was the only woman he had ever touched... but then showed up with *this* beautiful bitch.

I tried to swallow the jealousy, which I was so surprised I felt. "H-hello," I forced out.

But then this motherfucker had the nerve to ignore me like fuck what I had to say! "Is my pops here?"

The nonchalant tone in his voice felt like a knife to my chest. The way she leaned into him was like the knife being driven in deeper and twisted. For the life of me, I couldn't understand why I suddenly felt this way. I hadn't even thought of Mello in this way before he took me out that day, but now, I was jealous because he was standing in front of me with another woman? I couldn't understand if it was the dick that had me feeling this way or if I had grown feelings for the man that had taken my breath away in just one day.

Maybe it was both.

I forced back the jealousy, the memories of his lips on my pussy, and the urge to smack this bitch. "No. Did you call him?" Fuck that. No matter what, he wasn't going to see me hurt or jealous because clearly, he had done this on purpose. He didn't even fucking like his father most of the time and he damn sure didn't just pop up.

"Yeah, I called him, but he won't answer."

I leaned against the railing of the stairway with my hand on my hip.

I wanted him to see these hips and curves. He wasn't the only one who could play games. "Is it an emergency? Is everything okay?"

"Everything is cool. I was in the neighborhood, so I stopped by to say what's up to him."

My lips pressed into a thin line as I shrugged. "Weeeelp, he isn't here."

"I see that." He was still dry...real dry. He was acting nothing like how he used to treat me. I would have at least felt better if he still treated me like a friend. But he was just talking to me like I was some chick he had never met before. That adoring look he gave me the last time I'd seen him was gone. Now, he was looking right through me. I don't know what hurt worse; that I had clearly hurt him so much or that he wasn't fucking with me.

"Hey, Mello!" Divine shouted, coming down the stairs. We all looked at her and watched as she stopped mid-stride when she saw the girl with Mello. "Oooo! Who is this?" she teased with a smile.

For the first time since I'd laid eyes on Mello, he smiled. "What's up, Divine? This is my friend, Diamond."

Diamond? Stripper. She was definitely a stripper.

Standing on the stair, Divine folded her arms with a smirk. "Where's your crazy-ass bitch at?"

Diamond and Mello's eyes bucked, but they both laughed as he asked, "Really, Divine?"

Divine shrugged. "I'm just saying. I'm happy to see you with some-body else."

Mello and Divine were still laughing as he said, "Well, I'm happy she knows about my crazy ass *ex-bitch*."

My heart started racing. *Ex-bitch?*

Divine pressed, "Ex? Y'all broke up?"

He shrugged. Clearly, he didn't feel a damn thing while I was currently on an emotional rollercoaster.

"Yeah, I left her alone," he said.

He was single now. It was something about that that I didn't like. I think it was the instant thought of him spending days with this bitch and a whole bunch of other hoes like the one he had spent with me.

"Whaaaat?" Divine sang with bucked eyes as she flew down the stairs past me. She had no idea...no fucking idea how I was cringing inside. "'Bout fucking time!" Divine beamed as she walked up on them.

With a smile, Mello told her, "Yeah, Teyanna's outta there, and Diamond is working on taking her place."

Fuck this. Mello was playing games. I was already dealing with one ignorant motherfucker; Mello could play these games all by himself.

"Mello, let me know if you find your father." I turned away, and before he could reply, I told his stripper-bitch, "It was nice meeting you, Diamond."

I was headed back upstairs before she could say, "Nice meeting you too."

I didn't like how I felt. I didn't like the jealousy. I didn't like the urge I was feeling to cry. I had gotten in my feelings about somebody who I was not married to and who was my husband's son at that. I didn't like this shit at all. As I walked up the stairs and into my room, I knew these feelings could not keep growing. I needed to move on from that short fairytale that Mello and I had lived. It was over. The story had begun and ended just that fast.

13

HEAVEN

However, telling myself that Mello and I were over that fast was easier said than done. For a week, I tried to act like I wasn't fazed by the fact that he had stopped calling me. There were no more unanswered text messages. He hadn't even popped up unexpectedly again. He had disappeared as fast as he had popped up and fucked my head up even more.

For the next week, I tried my best to act like things were normal when Mello was on my mind more than my own husband. I hadn't thought about how Ross had damn near killed me in the bathtub. I hadn't thought about whoever he had spent that week with when he was out of town. All I could focus on was Mello. He was consuming me. The realization that I had been married to somebody for so long and never experienced what Mello had shown me in one day, was stomach-turning for me. I wondered how it would be to spend every day like that, especially with that connection, chemistry, and passion. I was possessed with thoughts of how it would be to spend my days with someone who I could enjoy and laugh with instead of wondering if he was cheating on me or when he would hit me next.

"Fuck!" I cursed as I felt a sudden gnawing pain in my toe. "Ow!" Looking down, I saw that I had stubbed my toe on the same suitcase that had been on the other side of our bedroom doorway since Ross got back in town.

I groaned and cursed as I pushed it on its side and unzipped it. That bag had been in the same spot because Ross' smug ass had been waiting for either me or Esperanza to get rid of it. I think Esperanza was more irritated with Ross than I was. Her subliminal pettiness was at an all-time high. That's why that suitcase was still sitting there. Ross was still very much on my shit list too. That's why I hadn't moved it either or fucked him or said more than a few words to him. And the more that went on, the more I was super convinced that he was in his head about something else. Usually, Ross would never let me get away with how I was acting, so it was clear that his mind was on something or *someone* else.

As I started to sort out the clothes in his suitcase, I got proof of exactly *who* had been on his mind.

"This motherfucker!" I snapped as I held up the satin thong that was balled up in the corner of his suitcase. Looking at it, I knew it wasn't mine. It was way too small.

I took off downstairs. The sickening feeling I'd had in my stomach for two and a half weeks had now turned to anger. I had been unable to let my guard for a man who was trying to put me on a pedestal, because I had respect for someone who clearly didn't give a fuck about giving me an ounce of respect.

Once inside of the den where Ross was watching TV, I threw the thong in his face. He looked at me like I had lost my mind. Then he looked down on his lap, where the thong had landed. He scooped it up, not realizing what it was until I snapped, "That was in your suitcase, motherfucker!"

He immediately denied it. "No, it wasn't!"

"Yes, it was! And you probably didn't know because the slick-ass bitch most likely slipped it in your suitcase to catch your ass up, dummy!"

Ross shot to his feet, barking, "Who the fuck you talkin' to?!"

I was too mad to worry about what was about to happen as he marched towards me. I was just so pissed off that I had walked away from perfection for this bullshit. I knew I could never be with Mello.

But I could have at least enjoyed the rest of the night he had offered if I was going to come home to this shit. Maybe then we would at least still be friends. But even knowing that now, I still didn't have the nerve to do it. Knowing that this motherfucker was cheating on me while putting his hands on me, I *still* didn't have the nerve to take my ass back upstairs, get my phone, and call Mello. I *still* had too much respect for his ass, and that made me blind with rage. I was seeing red, but what I wasn't seeing was Ross reaching back to smack the shit out of me.

"Ah!" I screamed as his hand landed on the side of my face so hard that I hit the floor on my knees.

I wasn't surprised that he had hit me. These were the exact moments he put his hands on me; when he was trying to beat me into believing that he wasn't cheating on me, when there was a threat of me becoming the exact person that he was.

But I *was* surprised when I jumped to my feet and started to swing back on his ass. There was so much force in every blow. I had never hit Ross back. If you could see hatred, it was all around me, illuminating me in red. I had never fought back. I was always too scared of losing all that he had given me. But now, I was so mad about what he had taken from me and what he had never given me. All of this— the house, the car, not having to pay any bills—had been an investment towards him being able to play me while ensuring that I would look away. I had looked away so much that I had never had the chance to know what real happiness was. He had never even bothered to show me what it was. I was stupid and naïve when we met and he'd kept me in that mind frame just so he could disrespect me and take advantage of me. And because of him, I'd missed beautiful summer days at the zoo. I'd missed walks downtown. I'd missed the passion and the chemistry. So, I just kept swinging on his ass. I wanted my licks back.

"Aye! Yo'! What the fuck?!"

I heard Vegas' voice as Ross and I tussled against the wall.

I felt his body leave from on top of mine. I stood upright and glared at him like a pit bull in a dogfight ready to attack.

As Vegas held him back, Ross gave me a look that I had never seen before. He looked as if he was scared of me. He looked at me as if he didn't know who I was.

"What the fuck has gotten into you?!" he asked.

I just glared at him, feeling the stinging pain on the side of my face that was way too familiar to me. But what wasn't familiar to me was what Mello had made me feel in just a few hours. It was foreign as fuck to me. But this fighting and arguing, I knew like the back of my hand.

I didn't have a response. He didn't want to know the answer. I had been bold enough to fight back but not bold enough to give him the answer. I just glared at Ross. He shook his head and snatched away from Vegas. I got ready for another fight, but he just shook his head, stared at me as if he was taking in this new person that I had become, and then walked out.

I knew that his frustration in not knowing what had changed me would have him out of the house for hours. And I was happy with that because it would take him forever to figure this out. He didn't have a clue, because instead of asking me *what* had gotten into me, he should've asked *who*.

⚝

I HADN'T EVEN NOTICED THAT TREASURE WAS WITH VEGAS UNTIL I stormed upstairs. She was right behind me on my heels.

"Girl, what the fuck happened? I can't believe you were hitting him back. Finally! Good for you!"

I didn't have anything to say. I was still feeling too many confusing and mixed emotions. I was still pissed off. I just continued on into my bedroom. I immediately saw the suitcase that had started all this shit.

Treasure was looking at me the same way Ross had. "What happened?" she asked.

"This motherfucker was out of town with some trifling-ass bitch that had the nerve to put her thong in his suitcase, and I found it." I plopped down on the bed, expression still filled with fury.

"Woooow," Treasure replied.

"Then he had the nerve to hit me."

Treasure sucked her teeth. "Of course."

"I got so fucking mad." I took a deep breath, trying to calm down.

"Girl, you look pissed the fuck off. What is wrong with you? It's not just Ross. He acts like this all the time and I've never seen you this pissed off."

I looked at her, wanting to tell her what happened between me and Mello. She had been the first person I wanted to tell about that good dick and incredible head. More importantly, I wanted to tell her about the date that we'd had that wasn't even supposed to be a date but definitely felt like the best that I had ever been on.

But I couldn't tell her. I wasn't ready to say it out loud. I felt like such a slut, even though I had just caught my husband cheating. But I was sure that his mistress wasn't my family member or friend. She was a stranger. I couldn't say the same and it still embarrassed me.

So instead, I told her, "Divine is pregnant."

Treasure's eyes rolled. "Damn. For real?"

"Right. I know that a lot of girls are having babies who are way younger than Divine. In this day and age, I can't believe she didn't get pregnant before now."

Treasure chuckled with a nod. "True."

I sighed and told her, "And she wanna keep it."

"Who is the baby's daddy? She doesn't even have a boyfriend."

I laughed sarcastically. "That's exactly what I was thinking when she told me. Girl, you would never believe who she's been fucking with."

Treasure inched closer to me and sat on the bed with this look of potential good tea in her eyes. I knew Divine had told me not to say anything, but it was too late. It was easy to tell her secret over mine, and I wasn't ready to tell mine yet.

"Spill the tea, bitch. Who she fucking with?" she anxiously asked me.

"Damo."

I was waiting for her dramatic-ass response or a gasp to drop from her mouth or something. But there was nothing. She just sat there looking at me with this sick look that slowly came over her. I sat there staring curiously at how suddenly so serious she had become.

After a few seconds, "Oh my God," finally left her lips in a whisper. And then tears came to her eyes and I was so confused.

"Why are you crying?" I asked. I watched her with both sympathy and confusion in my eyes. "It's not that serious, girl. I mean I don't want her to have the baby either," I started to ramble. "But she will be okay. Clearly, she's way more into him than he is into her, but—"

"Oh God!" she suddenly snapped and threw her hands over her face.

I watched in disbelief as she broke down. Treasure was a strong-ass chick. I hadn't seen her cry since we were in high school.

"Oh my God, oh my God, oh my God," she started to chant in tears as she started to rock back and forth, pacing.

Now, I was starting to get scared, so I put my hand on her shoulder and asked, "Treasure, what's wrong?"

When she looked up, I had never seen such fear on her face.

"I... I..." she stuttered. "I've been fucking Damo."

What the fuck? I jumped to my feet with my hands clasping my mouth. Confusion and shock were pouring from my eyes as I gawked at her. "*What*?!"

"Ssshhhh!" she insisted.

No one had heard me, though. Vegas had walked out of the house, chasing after Ross. Divine was gone with her friends and Esperanza was out grocery shopping. Surprisingly, all the chaos Ross and I had caused downstairs hadn't awaken Sunshine from her nap.

"You've been what?!" I snapped.

"I knoooow." She cringed as she held her forehead. "I fucked up."

"How long has this been going on?" I asked as I sat back down next to her.

She answered with reluctance laced in her voice, "A few months."

My mouth dropped. "What?! And you never told me?!"

"I know. And I'm so sorry. I just...I knew I was wrong and I was too ashamed to tell you." Her own words made her shake her head. "That sounds fucked up because I wasn't ashamed to do it. I can't explain it. I was just being my usual ain't-shit self. It had been so long since I had something new. And Damo lets me into his world. You know I love that shit. He treats me like his Bonnie. That's why I have been letting it go on so long."

I had to agree. "Right. You never fuck a dude for months."

"I know. I liked Damo. I thought he liked me. But he was a fraud." She cringed. "I have been risking my relationship for this motherfucker, and he has been fucking your sister the whole time?!"

I shook my head. The feeling of disbelief couldn't even describe what I was feeling. I felt like I was in the fucking Twilight Zone today. "I gotta tell Divine."

Treasure's eyes bucked. "Noooo!"

"I *have to,* Treasure. She wants to have his baby. She needs to know."

Treasure winced and gave up, "You're right."

"She won't say anything."

"I know."

I sighed and shook my head. "You gotta stop fucking with him."

She pouted, laying her head on my shoulder. "I know."

✲ 14 ✲

ROSS

"**A**rgh!" I fussed as I swatted at April's hand.

She sucked her teeth, saying, "Be still, Ross."

My face balled up as April applied the cotton swab of alcohol on my face. "That shit burns!"

April had the nerve to chuckle. "Are you serious?"

I ignored that smart-ass comment and sat still as April cleaned up the scratch on my face that Heaven had left.

"I can't believe she fucking hit me," I fussed.

The first time I ever hit Heaven, she looked up at me with these big doe eyes full of tears. I was scared she was gonna leave me. I had been putting my hands on women for years. I saw my father do it. I saw him keep my hoe-ass mama in line that way after she cheated on him. I started doing it to show a woman to never fucking think about cheating on me. But I had never been scared that a woman would leave me for putting my hands on her until that first time I hit Heaven. That's when I knew I loved her. That's when I knew I could never let her do to me what my mama had done to my daddy. And when she didn't leave me for doing it the first time, I ran with it. She had never fought back.

But now, suddenly, she was. Something was up with that.

"This was her *first* time hitting you back?"

Since April and I had been knowing each other for so long, she knew me well. She knew how my hands worked because she had felt them a time or two.

Even though I didn't have much of a relationship with my son, his mama stayed on my dick. April was too busy pressing me to have a relationship with her to make me have one with Mello. As long as I was sending money to Florida and fucking her every time she came to Chicago, she was cool. When she moved back to Chicago, I stayed dicking her down on the low. She didn't even make me stop when I got married. She knew I would never want to be with her and she was cool with the time and dick she got.

"Yeah. She's been in this weird-ass mood all week. I don't know what's gotten into her."

"I know what's gotten into her," April mumbled under her breath. When I whipped my head towards her, she swatted my shoulder. "Be still."

"Fuck you mean you know what's gotten into Heaven?"

"I mean, nothing makes a woman stand up to her man more than...*another man.*"

I frowned, hoping she wasn't saying what I thought she was saying. "Huh?"

"She's probably cheating on you."

Just the suggestion made my chest swell up with rage. "Shut the fuck up. You don't know what you talkin' about."

April smacked her lips. "I'm a woman so I know."

I grimaced in disagreement, but my mind started racing. My ego was too big to say it out loud to April, but she had hit the nail right on the head. For two years, Heaven hadn't been anything but loving and submissive. Even when I acted a fool, put my hands on her, and denied cheating on her, she remained the same sweet, loyal girl I had met a few years back. I knew it was because I had taken her from nothing and given her something. If she had left me, she would have nowhere to go.

Yet, over the last two weeks, I had seen that helpless girl turn into a woman who didn't give two fucks. It was clear that Heaven's mind was on something else. Something was changing her. And I knew nine times out of ten that *something* was another man.

April looked at me with her eyebrows curled as I jumped up from her bed.

"Where you goin'?"

"I gotta go." I marched towards her bedroom door and she swiftly followed me.

"Why?" she nagged.

"I got some shit to do."

"Wait. You said it was me and you today." She grabbed my arm, trying to pull me back. I flinched when I felt her nails clawing at my elbow. "Ross, stop!"

I snatched my arm back, drew back, and tried to knock her ass out.

"Ahhh!" she screamed when my fist connected with her jaw. Her head whipped to the side so fast that I thought the sudden movement had broken her damn neck. She held her face and went flying to the floor, crying.

I gruffed and continued towards the door.

"Ross, waaaaait!" I could hear her crying.

I grimaced and kept it the fuck moving. Fuck her. I needed to get to the crib. I had been so busy under other bitches that another man was possibly under *my* bitch. If he hadn't already been under her, considering the way that she was acting, he soon would be.

As I let myself out the front door, I still heard April's tears and begging. But fuck April. She would be here...right fucking here whenever I decided to come back. But my baby, Heaven, I wasn't so sure... not anymore.

TREASURE

I bit my lip and groaned as my phone started ringing. Flying down the e-way, I hit the answer button on my steering wheel and Vegas' voice came through the car.

"Babe?"

I cringed. Now that I knew what Damo was really on, the guilt was killing me. "Yeah?"

"Heaven good?"

I tried my best to sound like I wasn't falling apart. "Yeah. Where that stupid motherfucker at?"

"We got something to eat, and then he split."

"Oh." That was all that I could muster up the strength to say. I was literally sick to my stomach. What had I done? What the fuck had I done?

"I can't believe Heaven was hitting his ass back," Vegas said.

I tried to make my laughter sound sincere. "Right. I hope he doesn't try to make her feel that shit when he gets back to the crib."

"He looked too blown to have any strength to fight. That motherfucka scared."

Now, my laugh was authentic as hell. "Scared? Ross scared? What he scared of?"

"He's scared that Heaven is stepping out on him. He said she's been acting different since he got back from his trip."

"Oh, so he's been cheating on her for years, but now he's scared she's fucking around?"

"Aye, when a woman cheats on her man, it's different."

"How?" I wanted to know that for personal reasons.

"For men who cheat, it's okay for them to, but it's not okay when their woman does it. Men cheat for the pussy. But when a woman cheats on her man, he knows it's a wrap because women cheat for deeper reasons. That shit fucks with our ego."

I became silent in my guilt. I got quiet because I couldn't talk *and* keep my food down at the same time. I couldn't believe that Damo had been playing me all of this time. He'd had no right to play me. I had been honest with him from day one. He knew my situation. I wasn't stupid enough to think that he wasn't fucking somebody else nor did I give a fuck if he was. But my best friend's little sister? That was on a whole other level. Now, knowing how low he could be, I realized what I had risked my relationship for. Damo's slimy ass wasn't worth me losing Vegas over.

"It took everything in me to stunt with Ross," Vegas said with a growl.

"But you have to until—"

"I know. I just hate this shit. I hate being around his ass pretending to be cool, knowing that he is playing the shit outta me."

"It will be over soon," I assured him.

As I got off the expressway, I heard him groan. "You should have just let me kill his ass."

"You can't, babe."

"Why not? I done killed motherfuckers for less...*way* less."

"I know, but we gotta think about Heaven and Divine. I can't be a part of hurting them like that."

"You right."

"The plan we came up with will work."

"I know."

"But make sure my friend and her sister aren't involved at all, Vegas."

"I got you. You think it's gonna work?"

"Yeah. Trust me." I cringed as soon as I'd said those words. This was the wrong time to for me to ask for his trust.

This was definitely bad timing because just as I pulled up in front of Damo's house, Vegas said, "I trust you, baby."

Tears instantly pooled in my eyes. I quickly wiped them away and swallowed my cries.

"I love you." I hadn't said that with such deep meaning in so long. But if I didn't know it before, I definitely knew now that I loved Vegas so much that I was done fucking around. Heaven was dealing with a dog-ass Ike Turner and had never even thought about betraying him. Vegas was far from a Ross-type of guy. He wasn't even a person like me. He was rare. He was a unicorn. But I was out here treating him like he was dispensable. What the fuck was I thinking?

"Love yo' fine ass too, bae. You cookin' tonight?"

"Fa sho. Just text me what you wanna eat, and I'll stop at the grocery store on my way home."

"Gotchu. See you in a few."

I cringed again as I hung up. I was kicking my own ass as I got out of the car. Damo wasn't expecting me, so I walked up to his crib and knocked like I was the police.

"Open the fucking door, Damo!" I shouted as I pounded my foot against the door.

Since his BMW was in the driveway, I knew his slime-ball ass was at home.

"*Open the fucking door!*" I kicked the door so hard that it sounded like the house was shaking. Within seconds, Damo was swinging the door open, looking at me like *I* was the one playing *him*.

"What's wrong? Why you bangin' on my door like that?" he asked with his bushy eyebrows curled.

As I simply said, "Don't ever talk to me again," I never knew there could be so much anger in a voice so calm.

His eyes bucked. I had caught him all the way off guard with that. "Huh?" he asked. "You serious?"

"Serious *as fuck!*"

As I spazzed, his eyes bucked and he asked, "What I do?"

My mouth formed into a psychotic smile. "What did you do?" My arms folded tightly across my chest as he waited for me to go on. "You got Divine pregnant!"

"Oh, *that?*" He waved his hand dismissively, leaning on the door-frame. "That ain't shit."

My eyes bulged out of my head as I stood in front of him. I couldn't believe how he actually said that like it was no big deal at all. He acted like Divine was just some regular bitch off the street. And that pissed me off even more. Heaven was like a sister to me, so Divine was definitely like my little sister.

Niggas...

I no longer gave a fuck about getting dicked down or getting the excitement I was missing; I couldn't fuck with a dude like this and I couldn't believe that I had risked my reputation and relationship by idiotically doing so all this time.

My head tilted to the side as it shook slowly and disgustedly at him. "I am done wit' yo' ass."

His eyes bucked. "Because of Divine? C'mon now. She doesn't mean anything to me."

I was disgusted. "What the fuck did you just say?"

He had the nerve to shrug. "She doesn't. Me and Divine fucked around a few times, but—"

"But what? But you think it's okay to fuck my best friend's little sister and me at the same time?"

He shrugged again. "You been fuckin' me and my friend at the same time."

My mouth dropped to the concrete underneath my feet. "*So!*" I snapped. "You knew what the fuck was up when you started fucking me. You knew! I never kept anything from you. But you played me and somebody who is like family to me!"

"You think Vegas ain't family to me?!"

"You had a choice, though! You had a fucking choice! You knew what it was! But you didn't tell me or Divine shit! You playin' a real dangerous game! This shit ain't cool! That girl wanna have your baby."

Suddenly, Damo became humble. "That ain't got shit to do with me. I was just doing something." I frowned with disgust as he went on.

This was what I had played my man for? I was disgusted more with myself than him.

"But I fucks with you," Damo tried to assure me. "I fucks with you the long way. You know that."

My eyes squinted as I tried to find an ounce of humor in his expression. But there was none. He really was serious.

"What?" I asked unbelievably.

"You're with that motherfucker all in my face all the time. How you think that shit makes me feel?"

"You sound crazy." I tried to turn away from him, but he reached and grabbed me by my belt loop.

"How is that crazy? We vibe, we kick it, and we got good sex. Then I gotta watch you be in a relationship? Hell yeah, I fucked Divine. I don't want her, though. I want *you*."

I pushed away from him, but there was no use. He was using all his strength to hold me right there in front of him, keeping us face to face.

Irritated, I brought my face so close to his that we were now nose to nose. "You can't have me," I said through gritted teeth.

I didn't like how he was looking at me. After all of this, he was still gazing at me with this longing look in his eyes as he told me, "I already have you."

"Well, you can't have me no more!" I spat, getting further in his face until our noses grazed, flesh to flesh.

And he got right back in mine. "So, it's like that?"

"Fuck yeah. This shit couldn't last forever no way. I got a man that I love at the crib."

His eyebrow cocked. "Oh, you *love* him?"

"Yes. Did you think I didn't?"

Clearly, when all the times that he'd said this was his pussy, he thought it was true.

I gotta stop gassing these dudes up.

He bit his bottom lip, seemingly trying to contain himself. "So, what was you doing here with me?"

"Making a big-ass, motherfucking mistake."

I had fucked his head up so much with that one. He was clearly taken aback. He'd lost all strength in his grasp on me. Finally, I was able to push him so hard that he let go of me.

He hit the doorway, but he bounced right back in my face, shouting, "Bullshit! That's *my* pussy!"

"Get the fuck away from me!" I pushed him away as I backed away from the doorway. "Don't call me no more. I'm done wit' yo' ass!"

I was damn near running towards my car as I heard him say, "You can't leave me alone, shorty."

Damo was making my guilt turn into fear. He was acting out, but he wasn't crazy. He knew who my man was at the end of the day. He thought that could keep me, but hell no. I was done as I said over my shoulder, "Watch me."

15

ROSS

I was flying to the crib...*flying*. April's words kept ringing in my head. *Nothing makes a woman stand up to her man more than another man.* I had been too busy trying to make sure that I wasn't on the police's radar for Tisha's murder to pay attention to the fact that somebody was encouraging my woman to pop off. Fighting back was only the first of the bullshit. If she now thought that she was big and bad enough to pop off, she would soon start thinking she was big and bad enough to leave me and flaunt that other nigga in my face like my mother did my father. Fuck that.

I grimaced as my cell started to ring. I looked at it and saw that it was one of my homeboys, Charles. Charles was a smarter man than I was. He was married with kids and way more committed to that lifestyle than I ever had been. I was glad that he was calling because I hoped that he could tell me how to stop what seemed to be happening in my marriage. Usually, I had a lot of bite in me. I thought I could fix any issue with my hands. But hitting Heaven now would only push her further away. And that was the last thing I wanted...for the next man to make her happy and smile. I needed Charles to tell me how to fix this shit.

"Hello?"

"Ross..."

When he said my name, I heard agony in his voice that told me this conversation was about to be about his bullshit and not mine.

"Bro, what up? You cryin', dawg?" I asked in disbelief.

"My wife..." he croaked, his tears causing his usual deep voice to come out in a high pitch. "My wife..." His tears overcame him. He couldn't even speak. His tears alone were fucking me up. I had never heard a grown man cry like this.

I pulled over on the side of 87th street and King Drive and threw my car in park. "Charles," I called his name, trying to get him to come back to the conversation and tell me what was going on. "*Charles.*"

I heard him take a deep breath and then say lowly, "My wife....she...she died."

My eyes bucked. I sat up as if that would make me hear something else. "She...she died?"

"Yeah," he cried.

"What happened to her?"

"She had a stroke," he said as if he was still in shock.

"A stroke? What the fuck? She was only—"

"Thirty-two. She was only thirty-fucking-two! Why the fuck is this happening to me, bro?"

I cringed, not having an answer for him.

"I only had five years with my baby. *Five years.* And now she's gone. I won't ever get her back. I won't ever get to touch her again. Won't ever get to love on her again, man. What the fuck?"

My heart went out to my dawg. Like I said, he was a good dude. Look up the words faithful, committed, or good man in the dictionary, you would see a big-ass picture of Charles. He loved his wife more than he loved himself, it seemed. He was a dedicated family man. He was a great father to his kids and spared no moment to love on his wife.

"Gaaaaawd," he wailed. I had never heard a man wail with so much suffering. It was stomach-turning. "What am I going to do without her? I love that woman so much. I feel like I'm fuckin' dead. She was a big piece of me, and now it's gone."

He spared no moment to love on his woman. He showed her how

much he loved her every day. He had always said she was his Godsend and that he had prayed for a wife just like her. But now she was gone. Yet, I had been taking full advantage of my loving woman...full-fucking-advantage. I had been acting as if Heaven would be there whenever I chose to act right.

As Charles kept explaining to me how he had come home from work to find his wife of five years on the couch dead, I pulled off. Now, more than anything, more than I wanted to when I left April's crib, I wanted to be with my wife.

HEAVEN

"Fuck." I pouted as I hung up the phone. Then I hit the end button and dialed Mello's number again. *Again,* my call went straight to voicemail. I hung up with an even bigger pout this time.

Fighting the urge to call him again, I forced myself not to. There was no use. It was clear that he had put me on the block list.

"Shit," I cursed as I lay back on the bed. I was being selfish. Mello had been trying to talk to me for weeks, but I had ignored him. But now that I'd had a shitty day, I wanted nothing more than to talk to him.

I figured that he was done with me once his calls stopped after he had popped up at my house with that chick. But for the past week, I had been hoping that eventually, we could get back to where we were before we slept together. Now, that hope was gone. I felt like an idiot. I knew that even though Ross was a hoe, I could never be with Mello, no matter how much I had enjoyed how he made me feel emotionally and physically. And regardless of the fact that the sight of him with that stripper bitch had been on mind all week, giving me a sick, jealous feeling in my stomach, I knew being with Mello wasn't an option. But I still felt guilty for playing him for a jerk who was taking full advantage of every fucking chance he got to play me. Ever since Mello had come back to Chicago, he had shown me so much. The experience had opened my eyes to so many things. I had once thought that Ross was a blessing because he had given me this life for free, but clearly, he was making me pay an expensive price for it after all.

And the price that he was making me pay was way more than the trouble was worth.

I wanted to apologize to Mello for dodging his calls and for being stupid. I also wanted to beg for my friend back, but something was telling me that after all that had happened, I wasn't going to get that. For some reason, it felt like me and Mello would never be the same again.

"Heaven..."

I looked up when I heard Divine's voice in the doorway. I ran my hand over my face to hide my disappointment that she was here. I had forgotten that fast that I had sent her a text message telling her that I needed to talk to her. Forget whatever I was going through at the time. I had to set that shit aside to put myself in the middle of some more bullshit.

I forced myself to keep a straight face as I spoke to her. "Hey, Divine."

I watched as she leaned against the doorway. She watched my face, and despite me fronting, she still saw that something was wrong with me. "What's wrong?" she asked.

I took a deep breath and let my fucked up expression back out, and she immediately looked concerned and pissed. "What happened?" she asked as she walked in the room. "Did Ross hit you again?"

Even though he had, I tabled that fucked up conversation for a later date.

"Come here. I gotta talk to you."

She now looked even more concerned as she walked up to the side of the bed where I was sitting. As she sat down, I moved my phone out the way. I knew that Mello had my head gone because, despite knowing that he had blocked me, I checked my notifications for a call or text from him. I was heartbroken when I didn't see either one.

What I did see was a text message from Ross. As I opened the text inbox to read it, my heart broke some more, remembering that he had

had the audacity to hit me again because *he* was being a hoe. I was proud of myself for fighting him back this time, but I had been fighting him for the wrong reasons. Finally swinging on him had nothing to do with me defending myself. I had fought him for not being shit in the process of never showing me in three years what Mello had shown me in a few days. Opening the message, I saw that it simply read: *I love you. Please don't leave me.*

That messed my head up more than anything had that day. He had never asked me not to leave him. He had demanded it with his fists, but he had never begged me to stay.

"Heaven?"

I jumped a little when I heard Divine's voice. "Huh?"

"What you gotta talk to me about?"

"Oh yeah," I said as I put the phone down. "Sorry."

"What's up?"

With a long deep breath, I turned to face her. "I gotta tell you something. It's about Damo."

Instantly, Divine rolled her eyes to the back of her head. "I know you don't think he fuck with me like that, but—"

I cut her off. "He's fucking with Treasure."

Her eyes fell out of her face. "What?"

"She told me today when I told her that you were pregnant."

"W-what? How? But..."

She had so many questions that she couldn't get one out before the next tried to come after it. So, I just stopped her and tried to answer what I knew she wanted to know. "They have been fucking around for a few months—"

She cringed... and she looked sick. "*A few months?*"

"Yeah. Eight." When tears started to flow from her eyes, I told her, "I'm sorry, boo."

She covered her face. "Oh my gawd. Treasure? My sister's best friend? What the fuck?" She stared off with wide eyes as if realization after realization was hitting her. "He's been playing me this whole time."

My lips pressed into a thin line. "Yeah, he has."

"I-I can't have this baby. I don't wanna raise a baby by myself. I thought he was gonna be there for me." She was rambling and talking so fast as her nose ran while she cried. "I feel so stupiiiid."

As she fell apart, I threw my arms around her. "It's gonna be okay. You're not the first woman to be played and you won't be the last. Just learn from this and keep it moving. The only way you can get his ass back is by keeping it the fuck moving. Show him that what he has done to you didn't stop you from doing a damn thing. Stunt on him." I had to stop talking when tears came to my own eyes.

How was I telling her this shit when I had never taken my own advice?

❋

Thirty minutes later, I was in the living room trying to force myself to get my shit together. Divine had gone into her room and slammed the door. We were both in funks over men who had been playing us.

I had been living in this heartbroken-ass fairytale in my head with Mello for the last two weeks. My mind had been so wrapped up in him that I had forgotten that I needed to figure out how and when to leave Ross.

For the last three years, I had been ignoring the cheating while condoning and defending his physical abuse. I didn't see any of it. I had been living in this appreciative cloud for the last three years. Now, I saw everything so clearly. Ross was willing to damn near kill me before he let me turn into a woman that I had never even met. He was so scared that I would play him like his mother had played his father that he was going to beat me into submission and commitment. No matter how loyal and committed I was to him, he had done everything to me but put me in the grave. I needed to leave him. I just needed a place to stay first, which meant getting a job, which was impossible because Ross didn't want to give me access to other men for eight hours out of the day. I could have just left him and then got a job, but the thought of that felt impossible as well because I hadn't even worked since I was seventeen years old. I didn't have the education or the experience to get a good enough job to afford a place to stay and a means to take care of Sunshine and Divine.

So, I was back to square one, where I always ended up whenever I got so mad at Ross' cheating that I was ready to leave.

"Babe..."

I got sick to my stomach when I heard his voice. Fuck that sweet-ass text he had sent me. Seeing Divine's tears and heartbreak reminded me of how a man's words could be coated with genuineness but filled with motherfucking lies.

But when I looked up at and saw Ross coming towards the couch where I was sitting, I saw a look on his face that I had never seen before—*terror*.

"Why didn't you reply to my text message?" he asked.

I shrugged as he sat close to me. "I didn't have anything to say."

So much hurt filled his chocolate eyes as he asked, "You didn't?"

"No." Ross was visually surprised at of how much bite my honesty had in it. Usually, I approached him with love and appreciation, even when he had fucked up. "You left town and ignored me for a fucking week because you were with another woman. Then you hit me because I caught your ass! What was I supposed to say to that shit?"

He looked at me like he had no idea who I was anymore. "You could have said that you love me too." I just looked at him. I had no response. The longer it took me to say something, his eyes bucked. "You don't love me no more?"

Irritation swam over my face. "Why are you asking me that, Ross?"

The shock was still in his eyes as he replied, "Because you're acting different."

"I'm just fed up. I'm sick of you putting your hands on me because you're scared that I'm going to treat you exactly how you've been treating me."

"I'm sorry." He tried to hold my hand, but I pulled it away.

I got scared, expecting his sadness and shock to turn back into Ike Turner at any moment like it usually did. But I quickly stopped caring. If he wanted to continue the fight from earlier, I was completely with the shit.

"I don't wanna hear that, Ross," I told him. "You're always sorry."

He turned towards me even more so that I couldn't avoid his eyes.

"I know. I fucked up. I been fucking up. But I don't wanna lose you. I'll do what I gotta do to fix it."

"Fix it how, Ross?"

His eyes bucked. "So, what you sayin'? You think it can't be fixed?"

I shrugged. "I don't know."

His eyes grew even bigger. I knew that this was a first for him. I had always been the one willing to stay in the relationship and fix it no matter what because he meant so much to me. But I had gotten to the point that I was tired of fighting for somebody who was not fighting for me. Instead of fighting *for* me, he was beating my ass, and I was over that shit.

"You don't know? Wow..." He genuinely looked confused and hurt. He had never looked so humble before. I don't think he'd looked so meek since he'd gotten my number three years ago.

He scooted closer to me and held my hand softly. "Babe, let's talk. Have a drink with me and let's talk about it. I don't wanna lose you."

Seeing the sincerity in his eyes made my heart melt. However, my mind hadn't changed. I could no longer put up with his shit, but if my one night with Mello had turned me into the person that Ross now felt forced to respect, then maybe I wouldn't have to.

For my sister and my daughter, I hoped so.

MELLO

"Ma?"

My mother jumped and tried to wipe her face, but it was too late. I had already heard her crying.

"Mello? What you doin' here? I didn't know you were coming over." Her back was still to me as she failed like a motherfucker at hiding her tears. I walked towards her as she sat on the floor in front of the loveseat in the living room.

"You a'ight?" I stood in front of her, examining her. She tried to smile through her pain, but that didn't work. I could see the sadness all over her brown face.

"Yeah, baby. I'm good." She stood up, hugged me real quick, and then kissed me on the cheek. "How you doin'? What's going on?"

"Ma, stop playing," I said, ignoring her bogus attempts to front.

"I'm okay," she insisted.

When I rolled my eyes, they caught a glimpse of a watch sitting on the accent table next to the couch. I recognized that watch. It was the same watch that my father had had on at my welcome home party." I had eyed it the whole time he chopped it up with me because I wondered how much he had spent on it.

I looked at my mother with eyes narrowed into slits. "My father been over here?"

She had the nerve to look at me like I was the one full of shit. "No. Why would you—"

She stopped when I flew towards the accent table, scooped up the watch, and held it up. She cringed with guilt.

"So, he ain't been here?" I asked.

Her shoulders slumped in defeat.

I didn't mean to look at my mother the way I did, but she was acting like a little-ass girl. I knew that she had still been after my father over these years. Before he married Heaven, I caught my mother lying about coming to Chicago and being with him a few times. It blew me how she was so in love with him that she didn't give a fuck if he was being a father to me or not. As long as he was dicking her down, she was cool. I was grown now, so it was no sweat off my back. But she was still that immature little girl with a crush on a man who didn't want her.

"You fucking with him again?" I asked. "Don't tell me you willing to be his side bitch after he chose another woman over you."

"No," she insisted. "I haven't slept with your daddy in years, Mello."

"Then why you gotta lie about him being here?"

"Because I know you don't particularly care for your father."

"I got a right not to care about his ass!" I snapped. I hated when she took up for him.

"Well, we have been in each other's lives for years. We're friends. And he came over here to talk to me about Heaven."

I froze. Just hearing her name did something to me. Even after she had turned her back on me after I took that chance, I still felt like a bitch when I heard her name.

"Heaven?" I asked. "What about her?"

"He...he..." She shook her head. "Never mind."

I stepped closer and pressed, "Tell me."

"No. You and Heaven are friends. I don't want you repeating anything."

"Mama," I growled. "I won't say anything. You're my friend first."

She was. We had practically grown up together. She was the homie.

She sighed. I could see the reluctance in her eyes as she told me, "He thinks she's cheating on him."

I sent a prayer to the Man Upstairs, begging Him to not let my mother see the guilt on my face. "Why?"

"Because she's been at home acting up, getting outside her body, and shit like that."

Umph. I guessed I wasn't the only one Heaven was tripping on. I forced myself not to think too long about her, though. I had to move on from shorty. She wasn't giving me a choice.

"Well, why you have to lie about that?"

She shrugged and put her hand lovingly on my shoulder. "Because, sweetie, I know how you get about your father."

"Because he's selfish than a motherfucker. All he thinks about is himself. He don't fuck with me and he don't fuck with you. He's using you. He's stashing his guns and shit over here. You could go to jail, Mama...*you*, not him. He's not stashing his shit at his crib where he lays his head, where his family at, is he? Now, he wanna run over here when he needs someone to talk to? Fuck him. That ain't no friend, Mama."

"*Okay*, sweetie."

I shook my head, but I didn't say anything else because I knew that what I was saying was going in one ear and out of the other. When it came to talking to my mother about Ross, she was a child and I was an adult. But I guess I couldn't blame her. Clearly, he was good at what he did. Maybe instead of hating my father, I needed to try to be more like him, because, by the looks of it, he was winning.

❊❊❊

I chopped it up with my mama for like an hour before I jetted. I barely remembered the conversation we had while I was there checking up on her. Hearing Heaven's name had me right back where I was a week ago when I decided to leave her alone.

My mind had been so consumed with Heaven that I finally took this chick, Diamond, up on all of her thirsty-ass advances and hung out with her. Between Heaven ignoring me and Teyanna blowing my phone up trying to get me back, I needed to take my mind off of the bullshit.

Diamond was a great distraction. I had met her at the shop when Mo was cutting her son's hair. I had never really given her any play because I was with Teyanna at the time. But after Heaven continued to dodge my calls and texts, I hung out with her that day that I showed up at my pops crib with her.

Yeah, that was petty for me to do, but I was being petty on purpose. It pissed me the fuck off that after telling that girl what she meant to me that she went ghost on me. Did I expect her to leave her husband after one day and some dick? Fuck no. But I did expect her to be the friend that she had always been by at least acknowledging me. And when she didn't, that killed my ego. I felt the need to show her that I wasn't fazed, even though I most definitely was... even though I continued to lick my lips besides having washed my face countless times, just hoping that the taste of her pussy was still there so I could remember how sweet that motherfucker was.

That bullshit move had been a fail, though. I still hadn't gotten a reaction from Heaven, so I was done chasing her ass. I was now feeling like I had fucked up. Before, when I was crushing on her from afar, at least she was in my life. But now that I had finally fulfilled my fantasy, she was gone.

"Uuuuh, fuuuuck! Yes, Mello! Shit! Give me that dick."

I looked down on Diamond as her face contorted into ugly expressions as she forced herself to take all of this dick. She was a fucking champ too. I was pissed at myself for ruining what Heaven and I had, so I was taking my frustrations out all on that pussy, and she was letting me.

Since the day we'd hung out, Diamond had been on my dick, thinking she had her one. But after Teyanna and Heaven, I wasn't 'bout falling for nan nother bitch. Now, I was wearing my heart on my sleeve and these bitches were tank tops.

❧ 16 ❧

TREASURE

When I was leaving Damo's house that day, I had a right to be scared. He wasn't trying to take no for an answer. The moment I got in my car and peeled off, he started blowing my phone up to the point that I had to turn it off when I was around Vegas. He was sending me text message after text message, asking was I seriously done with him. The things that he was saying were scaring me even more. He was acting as if what he and I had been doing for the last couple of months was a real thing to him, not just the fun that it was supposed to have been.

And then a few days later, on a Wednesday morning, I woke up and could've sworn I heard Damo's voice in my house.

I lay in bed completely still on my back staring up at the ceiling, making sure not to make a noise. I wanted to be sure that I was hearing what I thought I had in my sleep.

"Man, I swear to God."

I sat straight up as I gasped. I jumped out of the bed, cursing, "Fuck, fuck, fuck!"

Since Damo and Vegas were friends, he had been in my house a few times. But he had been acting so erratic that I didn't trust him being here now.

I ran towards the basket in the corner. I dug inside, throwing clothes everywhere until I found something I could throw on. Finally, I came across some joggers and one of Vegas' white tees. I threw them on and sprinted out of the bedroom door. Once in the hallway, I slowed down, took a deep breath and tried to appear as calm as I could as I strolled into the dining room. Damo was sitting comfortably at my dining room table, rolling a blunt.

Sitting across from him, Vegas looked up at me with his gorgeous smile. "Morning, babe."

I looked at him and tried to make my smile look genuine. Not for him, but for Damo's petty ass. "Morning."

Then Damo had the nerve to smile at me behind Vegas' back. "Morning, babe," he had the nerve to say.

I immediately cut my eyes at Damo just as Vegas looked at him, laughing. "This motherfucka funny."

I forced myself to smile as I walked towards the dining room table. "Yeah, you full jokes this morning, Damo. What you doin' over here so early?"

"Came to smoke a blunt with my homie. You gon' cook us break-fast?" I hated the way he was looking at me. He was doing the most. Before, he would have never been looking at me like this with Vegas in the room. Now, he was smiling, licking his lips, and playing games.

Vegas didn't peep anything, however. "Yeah, baby, what's up with some pancakes and salmon croquettes?"

I looked at Vegas and smiled. "I got you, baby."

And Damo kept on fucking with me. "What about me?"

"She got you too, fool," Vegas replied while scrolling through his phone.

"Aye, man, you lucky as hell to have a woman like Treasure."

Vegas looked at Damo and then at me with a loving smile that made the guilt gnaw at me from the inside out.

"Yeah, I know," Vegas said as he gazed lovingly at me.

"You got a real one, dawg."

Now, Vegas was looking suspiciously at Damo as Damo stared at me. I suddenly felt really faint. The longer Vegas watched Damo stare at me, the fainter I felt. It felt like the time crawling by was hours, but it was probably only seconds before Damo broke our eye contact and looked at Vegas.

When he then said, "Bitches ain't shit, man," in this suddenly serious and dry tone, I felt the world moving under my feet.

Vegas' eyes squinted with curiosity. "Why you say that?"

I couldn't stand there and listen to Damo's reply. "Uhh, babe," I said to Vegas before Damo could answer him. "Let me go brush my teeth and what not before I start breakfast."

The guilt and shame made me turn around and head back to the bedroom before Vegas could even respond. I scurried down the hallway. As soon as I got inside of my bedroom, it felt like God had returned my air supply. I could finally breathe. I took big, long breathes as I bent down and rested my hands on my knees. I was breathing so loud that I could hardly hear what was being said in the dining room. All I could hear were the deep rumbles of Damo and Vegas' voices underneath the deathly afraid thoughts in my head that were as loud as thunder. I couldn't think. Despite feeling the air in my lungs, I felt like I was suffocating.

"Treasure..."

I jumped out of my skin, spinning around to face the doorway. When I saw Damo's face, I raced towards him and started swinging on him. He was easily able to grab me, holding my arms in a tight grip. I couldn't move as he walked me into the room.

"Stop playin' with me," he threatened lowly in my ear.

"Where is Vegas? What did you say to him?" I asked frantically.

"I didn't say shit. He went to the car to get his weed." He saw my relief and laughed like he was watching All Def Comedy Jam. "I told him I was talking about some bitch I was fucking with that wasn't shit. Didn't bother to tell him that it was *you*."

My eyes narrowed at him, but before I could say anything, he walked out. I felt the urge to chase after him and curse his crazy ass out, but I soon heard the chirp of our alarm, indicating that Vegas had returned.

HEAVEN

"Ooooh, Goooood." I moaned as I held my stomach and rocked back and forth slowly in the bed.

I could feel the cold towel that Treasure was pressing against my forehead.

"Thank you, friend," I managed to say through the sharp pains shooting through my stomach.

"It's okay," she assured me. "I was happy to get the hell out of my house. Damo was over there."

The nausea and dizziness were so strong that I just knew I was dying. But I still managed to cut my eyes at Treasure.

"I know, right?" she asked. "I told you he been on bullshit ever since I stopped messing with him. I fucked up with that one, girl. I was sexing him too long. Now, he thinks he owns the pussy for real. I was supposed to stick and move—"

"Urrrgh." Just then, I felt a sudden wave of nausea come over me. I groaned, interrupting Treasure's venting.

Treasure eyes suddenly filled with so much sympathy. She started to dab the cold towel on my forehead as I tried my best to keep myself from throwing up. At this point, it hurt to throw up because I had been doing it so much and there was nothing left in my stomach to come up. It had now gotten to the point that I was just gagging violently.

"I'm sorry, friend," Treasure comforted me as she dabbed my forehead. "I'm over here talking about his dumb-ass while you feel like crap. You don't wanna hear about my bullshit."

I went to shake my head to stop her, but then stopped because even head movements made my stomach swim. "It's okay. I wanna hear about it. I've been in this bed bored as hell for days because I can't move without having to throw up."

"Did Sunshine give you a virus or something?"

I swallowed slowly. My throat was so dry that it felt thick and like sandpaper. "No, she isn't sick. I think I got alcohol poisoning or some shit. I've been like this since I woke up three days ago."

"That day you and Ross were fighting?"

"Yeah. He came in that day really apologetic. I never saw him so sincerely sorry before."

Treasure's eyes rolled to the ceiling. "And you believed that shit?" she asked me.

"I don't know," I mumbled and continued, weakly, "But I stopped arguing with him when he told me that Charles' wife died."

Treasure removed the towel and looked at me with disbelief. "His homeboy from school?"

"Yeah."

She sighed. "Damn. For real?"

"Yeah. It fucked Ross' head up. So, we drank the whole night. I haven't been feeling right ever since. Now, I'm dying."

Treasure chuckled. "You are not dying, girl."

Groaning, I whined, "I feel like I am."

Then Treasure looked at me skeptically. "Are you knocked up too?"

"Hell no."

"You know that shit comes in threes."

"And?" I asked, immediately dismissing her. "I'm not pregnant."

"Well, lucky for you, I brought a test over here with me to make sure."

"Lucky for *me*? I'm not the one who thinks I'm pregnant!"

She sucked her teeth as she sat up on the bed and bent down on the floor. I could then hear her going through her purse. Then there was suddenly a Clear Blue Easy box in my face.

My eyebrow rose. That was the only movement that I could make without feeling sick to my stomach. "You just walk around with that?"

"Nah. I stopped at the drugstore on the way over here since you said you've been so nauseous." My eyes rolled as she asked me, "Can you make it to the bathroom?"

"Fuck no. But you can use the bedpan under the bed."

She was repulsed, with her dramatic ass. "Ewwwww!"

"What? I haven't been able to move in days."

Treasure laughed and shook her head as she opened the box. As she took the test out, I started to think how ridiculous she was being. Pregnancy never entered my mind because Ross and I had barely been having sex.

But then...

"Oh shit," I mumbled.

"What?" Treasure asked curiously.

Treasure was too busy on the floor sticking the test into the bedpan to see my face. So, I replied, "Nothing."

But, on the inside, I was freaking out! It had dawned on me that Mello and I had had unprotected sex. This was the last thing I needed; for me *and* my sister to be in the fucking abortion clinic. I was already having a hard time trying to figure out how to sneak Divine in for her appointment without Ross finding out. How the fuck was I going to make it there? Because I couldn't shoot the dice and have a baby that was possibly by him *or* his son! Just thinking about it was making my stomach turn more than it had been for the last three days. I was *really* sick now.

"Okay," Treasure said as she stood upright looking at the test. "It should tell us any minute now."

I wanted to disappear. I couldn't even hide how anxious I was. I sat there biting my lip. Looking at the ceiling, I could feel Treasure looking at me.

For the past few days, I had been so sick that I really couldn't do anything but lie in bed, watch TV, and look at my phone. Of course, I was all over Mello's social media, watching him kick it and live life as if he hadn't turned my world upside down. He was out on the streets with Diamond and his friends, kicking it while he had possibly just completely ruined everything for me. He'd claimed he was feeling me, but he couldn't have been feeling me that much if he had disappeared so easily. Yeah, I hadn't been answering his calls at first, but considering the circumstances, I thought he would've understood.

I guess those feelings he'd had, had suddenly disappeared. I had to stop calling since he had me on the block list. In the back of my mind, I hoped that he would show up at some point. I missed my friend and I wanted to him back, but I definitely didn't want him to be my baby's daddy.

"It's negative."

Man, I felt so relieved that I damn near didn't feel how sick I was anymore.

"Thank God," I sighed out loud.

It was so quiet in the room that I looked over at Treasure, who was staring at me curiously.

"What?" I asked her. "Why are you looking at me like that?"

She didn't answer. She just looked at me with this weird glare on her face.

"What?" I pressed.

"Why are you so relieved?" she asked.

I frowned. Damn. I didn't know she had peeped that. "Huh?"

She leaned against the dresser and folded her arms. "What would be the big deal if you were pregnant by your husband?"

"Because, Treasure..." I paused. I was considering lying to my best friend or finally telling her the truth and getting this off of my chest. I was tired of talking to myself about this anyway.

Fuck it, I thought. Then I admitted, "Because, if I was pregnant, it might not have been Ross' baby."

The look on Treasure's face was fucking priceless. If I could have taken a picture so I could've laughed at that shit later when I had the strength, I would have.

"Biiiiiiiitch," she sang as she slid dramatically towards the bed. She kneeled down on the floor next to me and stared at me with wild, wide eyes. "You fucked somebody?" She was still whispering, even though Ross had crept out of the house an hour ago.

"Yeah."

"When? Who? What the fuck, bitch? Why didn't you tell me you were feeling somebody?"

My eyes narrowed at her as I held the cold towel on my head myself now. "Did you tell me about Damo?"

She waved her hand. "That's different. I've been a hoe. That's nothing new. You've never been a hoe, though, and you most definitely ain't neva stepped out on Ross. Bitch, we besties! And you ain't tell me?"

I pouted. "I was ashamed."

"Why? Fuck Ross! You ain't got shit to be ashamed of. You should have *been* stepped out on his ass. No wonder you started fighting his ass back. You must have gotten dick whipped." Before I could even say anything, her eyes got even bigger. "Oooh! You *did* get dick whipped! Who is he?" Every time I opened my mouth, she kept rambling, "Where you meet him at? What's his name? He got some friends? Wait. No, I need to put this pussy up. She has been making wrong decisions lately—"

"Treasure!" I forced out. Yelling made my stomach move, so I cringed and held it.

Treasure's pout sympathized with me. "Sorry. *Tell me.*"

I looked at the ceiling and swallowed my embarrassment. Even that taste gave me the sudden urge to vomit.

I heard Treasure suck her teeth. "Who—"

"Mello," I spit out. Then it got so eerily quiet that I got scared, thinking the bitch had passed out. I slowly turned my head, hoping that I didn't have to peel myself out of this bed to bring her ass back to life. Instead, I saw her sprawled out on the floor, kicking and punching the air with a big-ass smile on her face.

"Yaaaaaaaassss, bitch!" she finally let out as she jumped to her feet. "Yes!"

"Treasure..."

"Mello, bitch? *Mello?* That tall, sexy, big-dick motherfucka?" I nodded, and her smile got even bigger. "Yaaaaaaaaaaaaaaaassss!"

I stared at the ceiling still. Treasure was loving this shit, but that quick pregnancy scare had just reminded me how much of a mistake Mello had been.

She could be as happy as she wanted to be, but it was for nothing because me and Mello would and could never happen again. It was best for both of us.

✳ 17 ✳

MELLO

I grunted as I hit the ignore button, put my phone back in my pocket, and hit the blunt.

Mo laughed at me as he stared into the street. The party was crackin' on his block. It was damn near two in the morning, and people were still pulling up. This block party looked like a festival. It had to be at least five hundred people in the middle of the street getting it to DJ PJ, smoking and shit.

"Ain't shit funny," I fussed after exhaling and watching as the light cloud of loud left my lungs.

This motherfucker was *still* laughing as he took the blunt from me. "Man, she's been blowing your phone up all night."

I didn't even say anything. I wasn't about to entertain him. I didn't want to talk about Diamond. She had been a straight-up stalker. Ever since she'd gotten the dick, she acted like she didn't know how to breathe without being next to me. If she wasn't calling my phone, Teyanna was. The more they called me, the more I got frustrated that I could get any bitch to be on my dick except for the one I wanted. No matter how hard I tried not to think about her, she was still on my mind. Putting my dick in Diamond hadn't fixed a goddamn thing.

This summer wasn't going how I had planned it at all. I had just gotten a degree. I was damn near a genius. I was supposed to be downtown at a cushy-ass job, chilling with my bitch. Instead, I was sitting around dudes that were getting more money than I was, when they hadn't even finished fucking high school. And instead of chilling with my bitch, I was in the middle of a bunch of bullshit with every piece of pussy I had been in since I touched down in Chicago.

This was all so whack. I was starting to think that I should have stayed my ass in Florida.

"Aye, fam," I heard Mo say as I felt him nudge me in my side.

"What up?" I looked over at him slowly. Mo and I were working on our third blunt. I was high as fuck and moving slow.

Mo's eyes were on the middle of the street. "There go yo' baby mama."

His head tilted towards a sea of hundreds of people who were in the middle of the street. But I could still see my baby mama sticking out like a sore thumb with her fine ass.

For a long time, it was easy for me to ignore how fine my baby mama was because she had been such a lying-ass bitch. At sixteen, when I found out she'd had a boyfriend the whole time she was fucking me, when I looked at her, all I saw was a hoe. Now that I had gotten over that and was much older, I could appreciate her beauty. And all the other dudes on the block were appreciating it too. She had on another pair of little shorts like her booty wasn't too big for them. She had never been my woman, but I instantly stood up, ready to go get her out of the fangs of these thirsty-ass dudes. She wasn't my girl, but she was definitely my baby mama, so motherfuckers had to respect her.

But before I could even take a step down, shots started to ring out.

"Shit!" I spat as I immediately ducked.

Everything started to happen so fast. While lying on the concrete step, I peered up to see where the shots were coming from. I saw a car barreling its way up the street, despite the fact that it was full of people. Everybody was screaming while running to get out of the way as the car drove through the crowd, firing shots. It was mayhem. The screams were deafening. The gunshots sounded like thunder. The music had suddenly stopped. The block party went from the sound-track of the Migos and Jay Z to a soundtrack that resembled a horror film.

My eyes darted everywhere, trying to find my baby mama. Finally, I found her. She was running toward the corner. I looked back towards the car and saw the shots firing from the passenger's side window as it came speeding down the street towards the house where I was. I jumped to my feet, jumped down the concrete steps and ducked down in the alley. I was wondering whether I should shoot the dice and run to make sure Paris got out of there. Peering over the house that I was hiding behind, I looked towards the corner and saw Paris nearing the corner. Once she disappeared around the corner, I was relieved.

And then, just that fast, the gunshots stopped and were replaced with the sound of screeching tires. We all stood up slowly and looked around to try to measure the casualties. Bodies were laid out in the street and on the sidewalk. When we should have run to ensure our own safety, we just stayed.

This was nothing new. This was summertime Chi. Screams started to ring out as people started to discover bodies that were laid out suffering from gunshot wounds or dead. Just that fast, things had gone from sugar to shit, but most of us had little reaction because we were used to it. We had been raised in this shit. I looked down the street and saw my baby mama jumping in her car. I didn't bother to call her because I didn't want her to come back looking for me.

One thing was for certain, I definitely shouldn't have brought my ass back to Chicago. I was starting to think that I needed to go back to boring-ass Florida.

I stood in the gangway, looking around in awe. My heart was still beating fast because it was like my life had just flashed before my eyes. Looking at this mayhem made me appreciate life and the people who were in it. I thought about my mama and then I thought about Heaven. What if I had gotten shot? What if I had died tonight? She had been in my life for two years. She didn't even know the effect she had been having on me all of this time and what she meant to me. I could have died tonight without us even speaking.

I knew I could never have her like I wanted her. I knew the feelings I had for her would never be reciprocated. I could never give her what my father had given her. We were in a no-win situation. There was nothing I could do but try to repair our friendship. But I didn't know what to say. So, all that I could do was text her three simple words: *I miss you.*

HEAVEN

The next day, I wasn't feeling better at all. The weakness, dizziness, and vomiting wouldn't stop. I was sure that I *had* to be pregnant. I was so sure that I had taken another pregnancy test that morning, but it had the same negative result.

"Let me take you to the emergency room, Heaven," Esperanza begged as she sat on the bed next to me. She was looking down on me as I assumed a mother would when her child was sick.

Ross was sitting on the bed next to me as I lay on my back watching as they also looked down on me with faces that appeared to be staring down in a damn coffin.

They are so fucking dramatic.

"I don't feel like it," I complained.

I just wanted to lay there. Moving would just make it worse.

Divine smacked her lips as she stood about fifteen feet away in my bedroom doorway holding Sunshine. I had refused to have her around me until I was better.

"It's just the stomach flu or something," I told them both. "I'll be fine in a few days."

Esperanza scowled. "But you're dehydrated. You haven't drank or eaten anything in two days."

"I ate some of the soup Ross brought me this morning, but I got worse. I couldn't finish it. I just want to lie down."

Esperanza was sucking her teeth now. "Fine, but if you aren't better by morning, I am taking your ass to the emergency room myself. Understood?"

Ross chuckled and shook his head at her bossy ass. I nodded, and she lightly tapped my thigh before standing up to leave. "I'm going to get you some medicine."

"I took some already."

"Yeah, it isn't working," Ross added.

"Well, I'm going to figure out what will work." She disappeared out of the doorway, and Divine followed her.

I felt sorrier for Divine than I did for myself. The look on her face since I told her about Damo reflected how I was feeling on the inside. Too bad she had no clue that this wouldn't be the last time she would be played by an ain't-shit nigga. This was only the first time of many to come.

As I felt Ross' hand run softly over my cheek, I looked up at him. Ever since Charles' wife died, he had been so attentive and sweet. Had I known that nutting up would make him act right, I would have done it a long time ago.

"I gotta go make some moves, babe." He bent down and kissed my cheek. "Call me if you need me. I'll be back soon. I won't be out too late."

I said, "Okay," but I looked at him strangely behind his back as he got out of bed. He had been acting like the picture-perfect husband for the past two days. During the talk we had after Charles' wife died, he made promises that he would change. It was hard to believe, considering his bullshit ways, though. However, it was like his bullshit ways had vanished just that fast. I wanted to believe that it was because he was really trying to change. But I could only hope that it was the case and wait to see if he would break bad yet again.

In the meantime, I had been too fucking sick to even think about if I wanted to wait around to see if he would or not.

"See you, bae. Love you," Ross said. He looked at me while standing in the doorway, waiting for my reply. As we looked into each other's eyes, I actually felt like I was looking at the sweet, loving Superman that I had met at the club that night three years ago.

When he smiled, I did too. "Love you too, baby."

He walked out, and I lay there looking at the ceiling wondering if Mello had actually fixed my marriage. I had stood up for myself because of what he had shown me. And now, it seemed like things were better. But even though things seemed like they were better, I was still missing something. And if I were to be honest with myself, I knew that what I was missing was *Mello*. I wondered if his phone calls over the years had actually meant more, but I didn't see it because I was too far up Ross' ass. I wondered if Mello had actually been to me what I had been missing from my husband this whole time.

As I looked at my phone, I realized I hadn't checked it since the night before because I had been so sick. I started to go through my notifications and saw that I had some unread text messages. My heart skipped a beat when I saw Mello's name. I had yet to even read what the message said; just knowing that there was something there from him, fixed everything. Butterflies flew intensely through my stomach. My world smiled so big.

But then I instantly felt so much shame because I had no business feeling this way for him.

I opened his text message and read a simple: *I miss you.*

I was shocked when tears slid out of my eyes and down my face onto the pillow that I was lying on. I couldn't believe I was crying tears of joy. I couldn't believe I felt so much relief and happiness that he had sent those words. But I was still so frustrated. Those tears were also of anger because I knew I couldn't have Mello, no matter what.

It had been weeks since we'd slept together, and my feelings for him were only multiplying. I had wanted my friend back. But, because of the emotions swimming through me, it was obvious that our friendship would never be platonic again. And since we could never be more than friends, he could never know that I missed him too.

ROSS

I took a deep breath and forced myself to get out of my ride. I couldn't believe it, but I actually felt guilty for sneaking and doing this. I had been lying to Heaven for years without feeling any remorse, but now, I felt bad for going back on my word. When I told her that I was going to change and fix us, I was being genuine. Watching Charles mourn his wife and seeing that I was losing Heaven had me ready to change my ways for real. These hoes weren't worth Heaven.

But I didn't know how to change. Not on my own.

I hated keeping this from Heaven, but I was too embarrassed to tell her about this. I walked towards the building with a heavy heart, feeling like she should be the one here with me.

18

HEAVEN

"So, is this his bitch or nah?" Treasure sat next to me at the island in the kitchen looking down at my phone, frowning just like I was.

I sighed, shrugged, and tossed the phone down on the island. "I don't know."

On the screen was a picture of Diamond and Mello that Diamond had posted on her Instagram. Leave it up to Treasure to find Diamond's Instagram account. It's not like Diamond and Mello weren't booed up in the picture. It was a picture of him, her, and some other guys, whom I didn't recognize. They appeared to be at the club from the night before. But the fact that he was still kicking it with this chick and was all out with her on social media had me feeling some type of way. This bitch was out with him probably enjoying nights out like the one he had given me while I was at home dealing with the bullshit.

I felt the heat of jealousy rising under my skin as I stirred the grits in front of me with my fork.

Today, I was feeling ten times better. I was still a bit weak, but the dizziness had stopped, and I was actually able to keep something down.

"You gonna ask him?" Treasure eyed me as she stuffed her mouth with the omelet that Esperanza had made us along with the grits. Sunshine was next to us, eating the bits of a pancake that I had cut up. She was using a fork like a big girl. My baby was growing up so fast.

"No."

"Why not?" I was glad she had lowered her voice as she said, "He said he's feeling you, and you feeling him."

My eyes rolled. "I never said I was feeling him."

"Girl, please. You think about him all the time, you miss him, and you're jealous that this bitch keeps posting up with him on Instagram... *You're feeling him.*"

Fuck it. There was no need to deny it because she was right.

I told her, "There isn't a reason to ask him. What's the point? It's not like I can be the one with him."

"True... But so? I know you can never really be with him. I mean, even if you do leave Ross, he would *never* let that happen. But that doesn't mean that you can't fuck with him." She ended with a slick smile.

I shook my head, saying, "Treasure, I'm not like you."

She dramatically clutched her chest with her eyes bucked. "Excuse muah?!"

I slightly rolled my eyes. "I didn't mean it like that."

"I know. I know you're not like me. You are better than me and way more committed to your man than I am... I mean, *was...* because I'm done being a hoe. But, *anyway,* you a better person than what I used to be, but in this case, you don't have to be. Ross ain't shit. He doesn't deserve you."

I hated that she was right. The day before, when Ross left, I called him because I had actually started to feel a little bit better. I was actually hungry. I called him for a whole hour, and he didn't answer the phone. And when he finally answered, I didn't like the fucking answer that he was giving me. Just that fast, he was turning back into his regular self in just two days. Just that fast, he was back to lying to me, and he was probably back fucking the next bitch. He was also working out every day all of a sudden. He had never worked out. Not once since

I had met him. Now, he was hitting the gym every day. Who the fuck was he trying to look good for? For a week, I had been eyeing him sideways. He hadn't disappeared again since, but I still had a sick feeling he was still the same ol', ain't-shit-ass Ross.

"You should at least reply to his text."

"Saying what?" I asked Treasure.

She looked at me as if I should have known. "That you miss him too. Duh!"

'That was a week ago. He doesn't want to hear what I gotta say now."

"So—" Just then, Ross walked into the kitchen, so Treasure's conversation stopped immediately.

"Babe, I'm out."

I hate this nigga.

"Where you goin'?"

Why did I even bother asking? Because his reply was just, "To take care of some business."

He kissed my cheek while Treasure eyed me from behind him. On his way out of the kitchen, he kissed Sunshine on the cheek as well. "See ya'll."

"Bye," Treasure and I mumbled.

Once he was out of earshot, I asked Treasure, "See what I'm saying?" I felt my anger boiling into rage. "Where the fuck he goin' this early?"

Treasure shrugged. "You're right."

"It was the same shit last week and on the same day. Whatever bitch he hanging with must be off on Thursdays."

Just then, we heard the door close. I picked up my phone and unlocked it. The picture of Mello and Diamond was still on the screen. I was so pissed that tears were coming to my eyes. I had lost Mello's friendship all because I was so busy being a submissive fool for Ross. It wasn't fair.

My fingers started dialing Mello's number before I knew it. I wanted my friend back. I wanted the chance to grovel and tell him that I was so sorry. That one night I had spent with him had me feeling him in the worst way. But I treasured his company and his friendship more than anything. And since that was all I could have of him, I wanted it.

But my call went straight to voicemail. I hung up and called again, and again... and again. Each time, my call was met with the automated voicemail message. I gave up and guessed after he'd texted me again, he had put me back on the block list since I never replied.

Suddenly, I stood up from the stool. "I'm 'bout to go over there."

I could feel Treasure eyeing me. "Where?"

"To Mello's house."

Treasure grinned from ear to ear. "Yas, bitch!"

"Divine!" I called for my sister as I helped Sunshine down off of the stool.

I heard Treasure's stool scrape against the floor as she scooted it back, hopped down, and followed me out of the kitchen. Divine was at the bottom of the stairs with the same sadness that she'd had last week. It had only gotten worse after she and Treasure compared notes on Damo. Her abortion was scheduled, but there was no termination scheduled to take away the hurt that her heart was pregnant with.

I told Sunshine, "Baby, go play with your toys."

"Okay, mommy!" As she ran off in the direction of the living room, I told Divine, "I'll be back. Watch Sunshine for me. Esperanza went to the grocery store."

"Where you goin'?" she asked.

"Uh..." I paused, trying to think of something fast. "I'm going to the ER."

"I thought you were feeling better?"

Shit. "I got a little nauseous when I tried to eat breakfast," I came up with. "So I'm gonna go see what's wrong with me."

"Want me to go with you?"

Gawd damn it. "No, Treasure will."

Finally, she slowly nodded and stopped giving me the third degree. "Okay."

Divine headed to the living room. Treasure was on my heels as I went into the living room to get my purse.

"What am I supposed to tell Vegas?" she asked.

I shrugged. "I don't know. Think of something. You're good at lying to him."

She cut her eyes at me. "Okay, bitch, that's your second time shading me today."

"I'm just sayin," I said as I rushed towards the door.

She laughed. "You know I got you."

ROSS

Miranda crossed her legs as she sat in the loveseat. She looked over some sexy-ass black, cat-eye glasses at me as I sat on the couch. I felt intimidated as fuck sitting across from her. Miranda was a beautiful biracial woman. Her skin was dark, but it was obvious that she was mixed with something like Indian, because her dark hair was long, down to her ass, and wavy. She often swung it over her shoulder because it kept falling into her slim face, covering her exotic eyes. What made her beauty even more intimidating was the fact that she was so intelligent and was not intimidated by my terrifying stance and natural scowl at all.

"So, what did you do to manage your anger this week?" she asked me.

I leaned back on the couch, adjusting my jeans and getting comfortable. "Worked out, played some basketball... shit like that."

She nodded slowly and smiled. "That's good," she told me through her grin. Then she jotted something down in her notebook.

I smiled proudly. "Thank you."

"Have you had any episodes of lashing out this week?"

"No," I told her proudly.

"No?" she confirmed. "No one you work with or your wife?"

"No."

Miranda had another satisfied grin on her face. "So, the things that we talked about last week were helpful."

"Most definitely. I mean, I figured the way that I treated Heaven had a lot to do with the shit I went through when I was a shorty, but I guess it just took someone else to tell me, ya know?"

She nodded again as she asked, "Have you tried opening up to Heaven?"

I rested back on the couch, making myself more comfortable. "I told you she knows what my mother did to my father already."

Just then, my phone rang, and Miranda glared at me.

"I know," I insisted as I saw that it was Heaven. Then I turned my phone off. "No phones on in your therapy sessions. My bad. I turned it off."

"Thank you." Then Miranda went on, "Have you been honest with her about how it makes you feel, how it hurt you when you were a child?"

I frowned. "No."

"Why not?"

I shrugged, getting frustrated that she was bringing up my past. Even though I knew what I was there for, I still didn't like talking about the things that I had gone through as a kid. I had watched my father hurt my mother with the men she was giving herself to. I watched him whoop her ass because he loved her too much to leave her, even though she was making a fool out of him. All of that had me feeling like a scared and confused little boy back then. I hated rehashing those memories because I never wanted to feel like that little boy again.

"I don't know," I replied. I felt the frustration showing on my face. I was probably looking like the little boy that she was referring to.

"Put your ego to the side, Roosevelt—"

"*Ross*," I corrected, cutting her off.

She smiled her apology. "*Ross*... Heaven needs to see a side of you other than anger. She needs to see why infidelity is such an issue for you. If she understands your fear and how it hurt you as a child, she will see why you lash out the moment you see a possibility of her cheating."

"She won't get that because while I am scared to death of her doing it to me, I am still doing it to her."

Miranda sat her pen down between the pages of the notebook. "And you are doing it to her because you are trying to hurt her before she can hurt you. You saw your mother do it, so you think that every woman will. You want the upper hand because you are expecting her to cheat any day now."

I shrugged, running my hand over my beard. "I guess you right."

Ever since I had started seeing Miranda, my therapist, last week, I was learning a lot of things about myself. I had never known anything about getting therapy. I always fixed my issues with alcohol, a blunt, or taking my frustrations out on somebody. But I had surprised myself when I purposely made Heaven sick all last week just to make sure that she didn't leave me. The day that she found Tisha's thong in my luggage, I was convinced that she would leave me, especially when I came back home and she was treating me the way that she was. Heaven had never stood up for herself with no apology. She had never told me about myself and stood on that shit.

I was scared to leave the house because I felt like when I came back, she would be gone. So, I put Visine in her drink that night and continued to put it in her food just to keep her with me, until she got the point that I was willing to change for her.

I knew then that I had some real fucked up issues that I needed to fix if I didn't want to lose my woman by killing her or pushing her away for good. So, I found Miranda online. This was my second session with her.

I knew I should have told Heaven that I was going to therapy, especially since disappearing during the day was making her think I was still cheating. But I was just too much of a man to tell her that I needed this much help.

"You're punishing her for something another woman did to you," Miranda went on. "Your mother hurt you and your father, not Heaven. She hasn't done anything to make you think that she is cheating."

"You're right," I admitted. "Well... she hasn't done anything to make me think that she was cheating...not until *recently*."

"What did she do?" Miranda asked. She then picked up her pen again.

"Her attitude changed. In the past, no matter what I did, she never left me. She never got mad at me. I would get caught cheating I would hit her, but she would still be her loving self. Now, I can tell that she has suddenly had enough. She treats me as if I have one foot out the door."

"Maybe that is simply because she is tired of you treating her the way you have."

"She can only be tired if she knows there's someone out there that will treat her better. I was all that Heaven had, all that she knew. If she now knows that there is something better, it is because some man done showed her."

"So, you put a tracker on her car, instead of just talking to her?"

I frowned at the judgmental smirk that she was giving me.

I knew I should have never told her that shit.

"Yeah," I answered boldly. I wasn't ashamed of what I'd done. "I don't wanna just talk to her. I wanna know who the nigga is that got her turning on me."

Just saying that shit out loud was leaving a fucked up taste in my mouth. I knew I had put Heaven through some shit. Obviously, all of my wrongdoing had turned her into my mother. But I wasn't going to be my father; taking that shit lying down. I was going to find out what the fuck was going on and dead it, once and for all. That's why I had put the tracker on her car a few days ago. Heaven hadn't left me yet. But it was clear that, though her body was physically in my bed, her mind was somewhere else. And I was about to find out where.

HEAVEN

♫ *You say you got a girl*
And how you want me
How you want me when you got a girl?
The feelin' is wreckless
Of knowin' you're selfish
Knowin' I'm desperate
Gettin' all in your love
Fallin' all over love, like
Do it to last, last ♫

I was zooming through the city heading towards Mello's crib. To keep myself from feeling guilty, I kept calling Ross. Every time I called, just like I thought, my call went straight to voicemail. So, I felt better about going to see Mello, even though I had no fucking idea what was about to happen when I got there.

♫ *Hanging out the back, all up in your lap*
Like is you comin' home?
Is you out with her?

I don't care long as you're here by 10:30
No later than, drop them drawers
Give me what I want ♫

I turned the radio up and started to sing loud as hell along with Sza. *"My man is my man is your man. Her, this her man too. My man is my man is your man. Her, that's her man. Tuesday and Wednesday, Thursday and Friday. I just keep him satisfied through the weekeeeeend!"*

I shook my head as I continued to sing, feeling the meaning of each word down deep in my soul. The only thing was, I didn't know if I was the main bitch or side bitch in my marriage because Ross gave these bitches all of his time—Monday, Tuesday, Wednesday, Thursday, Friday, the weekend, the holidays, nine-to-five; these hoes were getting *all* of his time. I felt like even more of a fool than I had been. After pouring out his heart to me for a week, he was right back doing the same shit.

"Oh shit!" I screamed as the pickup truck in front of me suddenly came to an abrupt stop. "Shit, shit, shit!" I chanted as I hit the brakes. But I had been flying down Cottage Grove, going about sixty miles an hour, so my car wasn't stopping fast enough. I quickly looked to the left of me. There was a car in that lane. In the lane on the right of me was the Cottage Grove bus. I couldn't do anything but brace myself and mash the breaks. Thank God, the truck stopped centimeters away from the truck, but the car behind me wasn't so lucky.

⚘

"Ma'am, are you sure you don't need medical attention?"

"I'm fine," I quickly told the officer. I just wanted him to get the hell away from here. Even though Ross had people that made our vehicle registration come up legit, I was still nervous. Thank God none of the drivers had been hurt, but my truck and the Neon that had rear-ended me were fucked up. My truck wasn't in driving condition. I had pulled my car over on the side of the road and called Treasure. The driver that had hit me was very apologetic as she gave me all of her insurance information. I took it, knowing that Ross would just get the boys at the chop shop to get me another car.

"Okay," the officer told me. "Take this card. Wait twenty-four hours and then go to this website so that you can download the police report for the insurance company."

I nodded. "Okay. Thank you." Then I just walked away from him with Treasure next to me.

"I need you to take me to Mello's house," I told her.

I should have taken all of this as a sign to take my ass home. Ross still wasn't answering the phone, though. I had gotten in an accident and couldn't depend on my husband to come to my assistance. I'd had to call Treasure instead. So, *fuck* Ross; I needed to go get my friend back.

"Okay. How are you going to get home?" Treasure asked.

I groaned. All of this chaos and deceit was weighing down on me.

"I don't even care." At this point, nothing even mattered to me anymore.

⚬⚬⚬

"Whose car is that in the driveway?"

Treasure and I sat in her car parked in front of Mello's house. We were staring at the PT Cruiser parked next to Mello's Jeep in his driveway.

I squinted to see if I saw what I thought I did. I sighed when I realized that I had. "A bitch's car, considering the car seat in the back."

Treasure smacked her lips. "Damn, so he has company."

"I guess so," I said as I opened the door.

Treasure looked at me with a slick grin on her face. "You still goin' in?"

"Yep."

She laughed, sticking her tongue out. "Aaaaahhh!" she sang. "I heard that shit, bitch! Go get your dick."

I shook my head as I got out. This wasn't about dick. It was so much more than that... and that's exactly what should have told me to get back in Treasure's car and go the hell home.

I cared too much.

But I didn't pay attention to all of the signs that were showing me that I shouldn't have been there.

Bending down to look into the car, I told Treasure. "We are at the emergency room. Don't forget."

"Okay. It's cool. Vegas has been handling business all day. But don't take all day. You got two hours."

"Okay."

I closed the door and instantly got nervous. But I kept walking through Mello's lawn because this was something that I had to do. I couldn't take it anymore. I missed him. I wanted my friend back. I wanted him to know that he hadn't deserved how I had been treating him.

The only two people wrong in this triangle were me and Ross. The only thing that made me worse than Ross was that Mello was his son. But Angel had always told me that karma was a bitch and you got it back worse than how you gave it. So, I didn't feel bad for fucking his son. I only felt bad for me and Mello because we were stuck in these feelings that we couldn't do anything with.

As I knocked on the door, I was scared that he wouldn't answer. A few seconds went by before I heard the locks turning on the other side of the door. I looked back and waved at Treasure, letting her know that she could leave. Once the door opened, I heard Treasure pulling off as Mello appeared on the other side of the door. His face was contorted with confusion, but he looked so damn good. Looking at him made me wonder how I had missed how he felt about me all of these years.

"What up?" He was so nonchalant in his greeting that it hurt. He had never been so dismissive. "What you doin' here?"

My heart was pounding so hard that I could hardly catch my breath. I was feeling so many emotions; confusion, guilt, ... lust... a lot of lust.

Mello stood in the doorway, taking it up with his massive body. His exposed chest was screaming at me. Memories of me running my fingernails over it as he fucked the shit out of me clouded my memory.

"You blocked me," I forced out.

"I know," he confirmed.

I pouted. The way that he was being so dismissive was unbearable. "Can we talk?" I was almost begging.

His mouth opened but a noise behind him stopped his words from flowing. When he turned to look behind him, I peeked in too. Diamond was sitting on his couch looking comfortable as hell. My heart exploded. Yeah, I had only had him for one night and had completely dismissed him afterward. But I was feeling territorial as fuck over his generosity and kindness. He had given that to *me*. That was for me. She couldn't have it.

Something came over me. I was already sharing one man who was supposed to care about me; I didn't feel like sharing this one too. Not today.

I made my way into his house, brushing past him. He watched me in disbelief.

"How you doin'?" I asked Diamond, shortly.

This bitch had the nerve to smile. "Hi. Heaven, right?"

"Yeah." Then I looked at Mello. "I need to talk you." When he kept staring at me, I pressed. "It's *important*."

He just kept fucking staring. It was a stare off! He was silently asking me was I serious. I was glaring at him, silently telling me that this wasn't a fucking game.

This was not a damn drill.

"Really?" he finally asked. And the depth and tone of his voice had me. Even though it was laced with irritation, I loved hearing it again because I had missed it so much.

"Yes, really," I insisted.

He sighed and looked at Diamond. "Aye, I need to holla at her. This family. I'll get up with you later."

I could tell that Diamond was terribly confused. But she got on up anyway. As she collected her things, I felt some type of way about him calling me *family*. Three weeks ago, he was whispering sweet nothings in my ear, now I was family?

As he walked her to the door, I sat on the couch. I nervously adjusted the T-shirt dress that I had flown out of the house in. I raked my fingers through my barrel curls, which had fallen into beach weaves because of the heat.

Mello said something to Diamond lowly that I couldn't make out. Then he let her out. Now that it was just him and me, the tension and feelings between us could be felt so much that the air around us was smothering.

When he just stood in the middle of the floor looking at me, I cringed with embarrassment. I had never seen so much disappoint on his face when he looked at me.

"I'm sorry," I whined.

"Maaaan..." He groaned. "You know you bogus as fuck."

I shot up on my feet and went towards him. "I knoooow. And I am so sorry. I didn't know what to say!"

"You could have said something!"

Walking up on him, I lightly grabbed his hands and looked up into his eyes. He tried to look away, but I stubbornly followed his eyes. "What? What was I supposed to say?"

"Something! Anything! I told you how I felt about you, and you dipped."

"I had to!"

His facial expression went from disappointment to irritation. "Why? To run to Ross? He ain't shit!"

"He's my husband."

Mello frowned as he snatched his hands out of my grasp. "Yeah, he's your husband who don't give a fuck about you enough to treat you right. Hell, he don't treat anybody right! I ain't sayin' I expect you to leave him. That's your husband. I get that. But you could have at least said *something* to me. You dipped and then ignored me like I'm some pussy—"

"I know and I'm s—"

"I been the one here for you, Heaven! Me!" he snapped.

The hurt was all over his face. I hated that I was the one responsible for putting it there. He had done nothing but put a smile on my face and made me see my worth. How dare I?

"Who you been talking to for two years? Who you been venting to?" Mello badgered me, making me feel even worse. "Who you been lying up on Facetime with for hours at night because he was out fucking somebody else, huh? Who?!"

I held my forehead, feeling the stupidity swim over me. I was constantly cringing from the sense that he was making. He was right. He had been the one who had been there for me. Besides Treasure, he had been the one who filled my days with meaningful conversation. He listened to me vent. Without even knowing the details of what I was going through, he made me feel so much better about myself. I hadn't told him all of my secrets, so he didn't even know that his conversations had helped me through missing my sister and dealing with Ross' cheating and abuse.

"I didn't see it like that!" I swore. "I didn't know!"

"But you knew that I was your friend. You knew how we had been rocking for two years, but when I told you how I felt about you, as soon as that nigga called, you ran to him but cut me off! *Me*! Of all people!"

Pain overflowed from his eyes. I rushed towards him and wrapped my arms around him so tight that he didn't have a choice but to let me hold him. He tried to push me away, but he didn't have the strength to do so. That's when I knew that maybe he really didn't want to. He was mad at me, but he wanted me at the same time. That made my heart go out to him even more. That was unconditional; still wanting someone even after they had hurt you. That's what I had given to Ross for the past three years. He cared for me like I cared for my husband. That realization was so eye-opening and heart-melting.

Now seeing even more how Mello felt about me, I held him tighter. I wanted him so close to my heart that he could feel it beating for him. I let him go only to grab the sides of his face, feeling the softness of his beard between my fingers. I made him look at me. The passion in our eyes for one another was so intense. Even though I hadn't seen how he felt about me for the last two years, it was impossible for me to ignore what was between us now.

As we stared into one another's eyes, I realized that coming over here was a mistake. I was finally seeing the signs. The people standing in that living room could never be friends again. It was too late. We were already so much more. I couldn't deny it anymore. Not even if I wanted to.

Yet, the power in our passion was drawing me to him anyway. I just needed to feel this intensity inside of me. It was something that I had missed just as much as I had missed his friendship. So, I kissed him. I hadn't come over for this, but as our lips connected, I forgot about preserving our friendship. When I could taste him on my tongue, I forgot all of the reasons why I shouldn't have come here. I easily forgot that I could never really be with him. I just enjoyed temporarily having him. I enjoyed being with someone who I did not have to worry about respecting me or loving me right.

Suddenly, his frustration was replaced with aggression. He bent down and picked me up. He raced towards the nearest wall and pressed me against it. I held onto his neck tightly as he took my mouth with his. Then he grabbed my neck and forced me to look up towards the ceiling. He started to molest my neck with his tongue as he held me tightly around his waist with one arm. Through his jersey shorts, I felt his dick hardening against my pussy, which was leaking through my panties. The passion between us was so electrifying that it caused tears to fill my eyes.

His nails grazed me as he pulled at my thong, pushing it aside. He continued to kiss me as he pulled his dick out of his shorts. I had no time to prepare myself before he thrust himself inside of me. I gasped as he reached behind me to hold on to the stair rail to support his weight as he drilled into my pussy over and over again. His ability to hold me up against the wall with one arm was making my pussy push out waves of my juice all over him.

The dick was so fucking exceptionally good. I wanted to tell him how good it was. I wanted to sing his praises. But every time I opened my mouth, no words could come out. The passion was strangling me. And, as my mouth opened, he just took it and started fucking it with his anyway.

My arms were hooked tightly around his neck as I bit my lips, trying to take every punishing stroke. His thrusts were so relentless, filling me up so completely. He was fucking me hard as if he was trying to fuck me into never doing this to him again.

✥ 19 ✥

HEAVEN

♫ *I like it when you lose it*
I like it when you go there
I like the way you use it
I like that you don't play fair
Recipe for a disaster
When I'm just try'na take my time
Stroke is gettin' deep and faster
You're screamin' like I'm outta line ♫

Mello had had a point to prove, and he was going over and beyond to prove it.

"Aaaaaaah! Oh my Goooood!" I was in tears as he gave me the complete and utter business in his bed.

After I had cum the first time downstairs against the wall, he carried me upstairs into his bedroom. He turned off the lights and closed the curtains. Then his sexy ass lit a candle and turned to some music on his phone that started to play through a speaker in his room. Then he lay me down and continued to unselfishly fuck the shit out of me.

It had been an hour, and he still hadn't even cum yet. While he delivered stroke after stroke, he watched me so intently. I didn't know what that look meant. I had never seen it in any man's eyes. That look scared the shit out of me, but it made me cum over and over again at the same time.

I cried over Tank's voice that I could still hear over my moans. "Mmmm. Uh huh. Yes, Mello."

He was taking over my body in a way that I had never experienced. I had never had a man give me the dick with such unselfishness. He was so quiet and focused, as if his sole purpose in this moment was to make sure that I never had the nerve to ignore him again.

> ♫ *You love it when I lose it*
> *You love it when I go there*
> *You love the way I use it*
> *You love that I don't play fair*
> *You end up callin' me master (master)*
> *Say this universe is mine*
> *When we're done it's a disaster*
> *End up like this every time* ♫

"Mello..." My moan was filled with much passion.

He bent over, placing his hands under me and gripping my ass. He was holding me right where he wanted me as he moaned into my ear, "Yes, baby?"

That was enough. That was all it took to send me over the edge. I was cumming for him again. My body was trembling under him. He was torturing the fuck out of me, kissing my neck while moving inside of me like a beast and filling me up to the rim.

"Ahhhh!" I moaned load as the pressure finally exploded all over his dick.

"That's it. Just like that. Cum for me, baby."

> ♫ *Who came to make sweet love? Not me*
> *Who came to kiss and hug? Not me*

Who came to beat it up? Rocky
And Imma use those hands to put up that gate and stop me
When we fuck
When we fuck ♫

ROSS

"What?"

I grimaced. I knew that April was going to act dramatic as fuck about this. Something had told me to just have this conversation over the phone so I could hang up on her when she started being extra. But I at least wanted to give her the decency of saying this to her face. So, I had come over to her crib after my therapy session to tell her that it was over.

"I can't fuck with you anymore," I repeated.

I stood in front of her, watching her go through all different types of emotions as she sat on the couch. She was going back and forth between confused, hurt, and pissed. She looked up at me with the most confused look on her face. I could understand why she was confused. We had been doing this off and on for twenty years. I had never told her that she couldn't have me. I just disappeared and reappeared.

"Are you serious?" she asked me.

I nodded. "Yeah."

Her mouth was stuck open as she continued to stare at me in disbelief. "Ross, we've been together for years."

I looked at the ceiling, trying to bite my tongue. "We haven't been together, April. We've been fucking each other for years, but now I'm done."

"Why?"

"Because I'm married."

She slapped her thighs and shrugged. "And?"

"*And* because I want to do right. What's the purpose in us fucking anyway? It ain't goin' nowhere."

Her eyes narrowed. "So that's it? You're done? Because of that young bitch?"

My chest heaved. "Don't call her that."

"Wow." Then she hissed, "Get out!"

I simply nodded. "No problem." I turned to walk towards the door.

"You bet' not call my phone asking me for shit either! Especially when that young-ass girl turns bad on you, Roosevelt!"

I ignored her attempts to get me mad. That's what she wanted; more attention, even if it was me beating her ass for talking shit to me about my wife. But I was intent on being a better man. It was past time for that. So, I opened her front door, let myself out, and closed it shut. I hoped to God that she didn't come outside with her bullshit.

She didn't. The front door never opened. But I could hear loud thuds and things crashing inside of the house. April was spazzing out. We both knew it was best for her that she spazz out on her furniture than on me.

On my way to my ride, I realized I hadn't heard from Heaven all day. I took my phone out and realized that I hadn't turned it back on after leaving therapy. Turning it back on, I got in my ride, turned the engine, and waited for my phone to power back on. That insecure little boy in me was ready to check the tracker app to see where Heaven had gone that day. But as soon as I was about to open the app, the overwhelming sight of red and blue lights behind me accompanied the sound of sirens.

"What the fuck?" I looked in my rearview mirror. Three squad cars swooped down on me in front of April's crib. "I know this bitch didn't."

"*Roosevelt Morris*, get out of the car with your hands up!"

Before I could react, I heard April's voice suddenly. "Ross!" she shrieked as she ran out of the house.

She was running towards my car, barefoot through the lawn. But she stopped suddenly when an officer shouted, "Ma'am, stay back!"

I rolled my passenger's window down and spat at her, "What the fuck did you do?! You that mad?! You called the fucking cops?!"

"Get out of the car with your hands where I can see them!" an officer barked.

"Ross, I swear, I didn't do anything!" April cried as she stood on the lawn. "I didn't call them. I swear to God! I wouldn't do that to you!"

Biting my lip, I griped. I slowly opened the car door and got out with my hands first. As I slowly got down on my knees, I was able to see just how many squad cars there were. There was even a SWAT team preparing to raid April's house.

April was right. She hadn't done this. These motherfuckers had come prepared. They were looking for something and knew that it was in that house.

I had been set up.

MELLO

"I never want you to think that I don't respect what you said to me that day. It took my breath away. That was why I was willing to go home with you that night. But when it comes to Ross, even though I know that he ain't shit, when I say that he saved me, he really did. That's why I respect him more than he deserves."

I just looked up at the ceiling as Heaven lay on my chest. I appreciated what she was saying, but I honestly still didn't get it.

"Saved you how?" I asked her. "Because he pays your bills? Because you don't have to work?"

"It's not that simple, Mello." She stopped and sat up. She took a deep breath. Suddenly, she looked nervous. She placed her hand on my chest that was still sweating from the work out that I had just had, trying to show her how good this dick could be if she would just take it. "My... um... Divine and I had it real bad when we were younger. You know my mother is schizophrenic and my father left us, right?" I nodded, and she went on. "Well, when my father left, my big sister left too."

My eyes tightened. "Big sister? You have another sister?"

"Yeah."

"Why haven't you ever told me about her?"

"Because she's dead." My heart went out to the sadness in her eyes when she said that. I rubbed her thigh as she sat Indian style next to me. I looked up at her as her hair fell into her face. Her sadness pierced through the waves that it was in. "But before she died, she had run away when my father left. She was tired of my mama spazzing out and acting crazy. She was tired of us not having enough money to eat. She was only sixteen. She was living on the streets, but she was trying to get herself together so she could come get us. Eventually, she met this dude that let her move in with him. He took me and Divine in too. Life was perfect then."

Even as she thought about it, she smiled like she was still living in that perfect past.

"Divine and I had food to eat and new clothes. I could finally be a teenager, except for being a mother to Divine. And then..." Tears came to her eyes. These weren't the same tears that she was shedding when I was dicking her down. These tears were full of anger and pain. "Then..." She wiped away the tears, but only more slid down in place of them. "She and her boyfriend got killed. They were killed in a drive-by on the expressway. I was pregnant at the time. And you already know about Sunshine's father, so he couldn't help us. So, Divine and I had to go back to my mother. And it was terrible. I had to beg on the streets for money just to feed me and Divine because I was selling my mother's food stamps to get the lights back on. She still wouldn't take her meds, so she was having all these delusions. She always thought I was an intruder trying to kill her. She fought me constantly. But I took all of that bullshit to ensure that Divine and Sunshine were okay. At seventeen, I had three kids that I was taking care of: Sunshine, Divine, and my mama. That's when I met Ross. And when he let us live with him, everything was perfect again just like when Angel and Caesar were alive."

My eyes narrowed. She saw that and asked me, "What?"

"Who is Angel and Caesar?"

"My sister and her boyfriend."

Shit. Luckily, just then, a notification on her phone went off. She reached for it on the nightstand, so she couldn't see me trying to look like what she'd just said hadn't fucked my head up. She looked at the phone, put it down, and just kept talking. "When they were alive, I didn't have to worry about how me and Divine would eat. I didn't have to worry about anybody from my school seeing me beg on the corner. So when Ross started to cheat, I figured I had taken way worse than that just to keep a roof over my head."

I forced myself to focus back on her. "So, that's why you let him cheat?"

Her eyes darted at me like that had offended her. "I don't *let* him cheat."

"He knows that you know he's cheating and still willing to be with him. That's *letting* him cheat." Yeah, I had feelings for her, but I also didn't like how, despite how much sense she had, she was letting somebody do her like this. I had seen how priceless she was without even meeting her physically, so why couldn't she see it?

"It's not that easy."

Before I could say anything, her phone started to ring this time. She reached for it, and her eyes bucked when she saw who was calling. She answered immediately, so I thought it was Ross. But she answered, "Hey Vegas... What?!" She jumped out of bed and started to throw her clothes on. "Okay... *Okay*! I'm on my way."

When she hung up, I asked, "What happened?"

But she was too busy calling somebody else. After a few seconds, she said into the phone, "Hey, Treasure, you outside yet?.... Okay, good. Vegas just called me. Ross got locked up... I know. I'm on my way out now."

She hung up and was breathing sporadically as she threw the phone on the bed and started to throw her dress on.

I laid there watching her in total disbelief. When she saw the look on my face, she looked apologetic as she told me, "I *have* to go."

I shook my head, wondering why she ran like a puppy every time this motherfucker called for her. "You're there way more for him than he is for you."

Her eyes bucked a little, as she stepped into her panties. She was shocked at how I was talking to her. But she needed to hear this real shit instead of the fake shit she had been feeding herself to persuade herself to stay with Ross.

She stood next to my bed looking at the doorway like she was really ready to hit it up outta there. "What you expect me to do? Stay here with you?'

I didn't get why that was so unrealistic. "Why not?"

Don't get me wrong; I wasn't some sap that expected her to pack up her shit and leave her husband for his broke ass son. But, gawd damn, I did expect for her to give herself the happiness that she felt when she was with me... even when it was only when she could sneak and get it.

"Because we can't be together!"

"But you can fuck me?"

She cringed while pouting. "I didn't come over here for that. I have feelings for you too. I didn't expect this. I love how you make me feel, I can't lie, but we can't do this. You're his son. It's wrong on so many levels."

"Does he consider you when he is laying up with those other bitch-es?" Fuck this. I had been doing alright. She had played me after I told her how I felt, but I had taken that L and kept it moving. She had brought her ass over to my crib as if she was wanted this. Now, she was back running away again? Nah, fuck that.

Her shoulders shrank as she watched the irritation flow over my face. Then she tore her eyes away from mine and shook her head. "This was a mistake."

I chuckled sarcastically. "Oh, now, it was a mistake because you ain't cumming no more?"

Heaven's eyes bucked and she sneered. "*No*, it's a mistake if you expect me to choose you over him. Are you gonna take me and my family in? Are you going to take care of us? He is all that I have. I have nothing else!"

Still laying there calm as fuck, I told her, "You're confused."

Heaven inhaled sharply. "*Confused?!*"

"Yeah. You wanna respect your husband but fuck his son."

That was it. She'd had it then. "Fuck you!" she snapped. "You don't know what the fuck you're talking about! You don't know what I go through at home!"

I shrugged. I didn't give a fuck about her feelings being hurt. Shit, she didn't give two fucks about playing with mine. "Obviously, whatever you're going through is good enough to make you fuck your husband's son, but not leave him."

Shaking her head again, she said lowly, "This was a mistake," as if she was talking to herself.

Now, I was a mistake? "No, shorty, your life is a big-ass mistake. You have been in one fucked situation after the next. You don't even know what the hell real love is."

She winced. Tears instantly filled her eyes. I should have felt some type of remorse for what I'd said once I saw a tear slowly roll down her face. But I didn't. I was sick of going back and forth with her. She was so busy thinking about herself and Ross that she wasn't considering me at all.

She stepped into her flip flops saying nothing. Then she grabbed her phone off of the bed and walked towards the door. I was good with her leaving. I wasn't with the drama. As she left out, I didn't even watch. I wanted this to be the last time that I saw shorty. She was right. This had been a mistake, and it hadn't even been worth making.

I was done, but I guess she wasn't. Once you she stepped into the hallway, I heard her say, "You're more like your father than you realize."

That shit burned me up, but I let shorty have the last word if that was what she needed to make herself feel better about running away from a good man to an ain't-shit nigga.

Besides, I'd known ten minutes ago that I had to let her go. I just didn't want to. But it was for the best. I had my reasons, and Ross was far from one of them.

20

ROSS

"Hello? Ross?"

I was relieved when April answered. I hadn't known that when she told me not to call her for shit that I would have to call her this damn fast. But in order to keep Heaven from being able to leave whenever she got ready, I hadn't given her access to my stash. April had it.

"I need you to come to court tomorrow to bail me out. Do you still have my money?"

Since we were on the jail phones, I couldn't come right out and ask her had the police gotten to my safe. My lawyer had already told me that they'd found the stash of weapons.

When April answered, "Yeah," relief flooded my body.

"Ross," April called my name with a sigh.

I groaned, thinking she was about to be on that bullshit that we had left off on. I had just caught a case. The last thing I wanted to do was argue with a bitch about me fucking her again.

But instead, she surprised me when she said, "I think Mello did this."

I looked at the phone, hoping that I had heard her wrong. "Huh?"

"I think Mello did this. He was pissed the other day when he left here. He saw your watch and knew you had been here. I think he knew you had upset me, even though I tried to tell him that you hadn't. He is the only person who knew where things were. How else would the police know to—"

"*Okay*," I snapped, cutting her off. Her dumb ass was saying way too much over the phone. "I'll holla at him when I get out. Be at court tomorrow."

VEGAS

"You ready?" I asked Treasure.

She didn't look ready. She was standing in front of the door of the mansion in Lincoln Park. She was nervously fidgeting with her clothes. Her voice was shaky as she said, "Yeah."

I couldn't remember the last time that I had seen Treasure look unsure of herself. She was most definitely out of her element, but I was making moves to ensure that this would end up being my baby's permanent element real soon.

As I heard the locks on the other side of the door turning, I grabbed Treasure's hand so she could calm down.

The door opened. Sam appeared in the doorway with a slight smile.

"Mr. Rossi," the butler acknowledged me with a nod.

"What's up, Sam?" I greeted him as I shook his hand. "This is my girlfriend, Treasure."

He smiled and extended his hand to shake hers. She shook it, nervousness still in her smile as she told him, "Hi."

"C'mon in. The *other* Mr. Rossi is waiting." Sam chuckled at his own lame joke as he led me and Treasure into the fourteen-thousand-square-foot estate.

Leaning into me as we walked through the foyer, Treasure whispered, "Why the butler gotta be *black*?"

I chuckled and just shook my head.

"I'm just sayin'," Treasure whispered just as we entered my Uncle Vinny's office.

"Vegas, my boy!" he greeted me with a cigar in the corner of his mouth. He stood up from his desk and rounded it. We met in the middle of the office and hugged just as Sam closed the door, leaving us inside.

Releasing me from his embrace, Uncle Vinny stood smiling at Treasure. "And this must be Treasure, your beautiful girlfriend."

Looking at her, I couldn't help but look at her in admiration too. My baby *was* beautiful. The sun had been baking her light skin all summer. Now, she had this sexy-ass exotic tan that made her look like she was glowing from the inside out. "She is. This my baby."

"Hi, love. It's nice to you meet. She's gorgeous, Vegas."

"Thank you," Treasure blushed as he bent down and hugged her.

He let her go, giving her a final once over and then told us, "Please, sit," as he motioned towards the leather chairs facing his desk.

Treasure and I sat down and then Unc got right down to business. "I called you here because after hearing about Ross' arrest, some changes need to be made."

I smiled inwardly. I knew it. I was right and as Treasure reached over and grabbed my hand, I knew she was happy that I was right too. The plan had worked. A few weeks ago when Treasure first suggested that I kill his pockets instead of him, it hit me. I knew if heat was brought to Ross, my uncle would want to sever his ties with him. That's why I had set him up.

Ross had never told me where he kept his stash, but any idiot would assume he had it at April's crib. That's why she always felt tied to him no matter how much he fucked her and then went home to his wife. She had something on his ass, and that *something* was his product and his money.

Now, I would be the only major gun supplier in the Midwest. Ross may have stolen from me, but he was about to lose way more than a hundred G's.

꧁꧂

"I told you, bae!" A shit-eating grin was spread across my face as I took long, satisfied strides towards my ride. Treasure was next to me, damn near jogging in order to keep up with me, but she was smiling too.

"Yeah, you did. I feel so much better." She let out a deep sigh that was laced with her pleased smile.

"I know you feel better with me making this move. I know you didn't want me to hurt Heaven like that."

As we approached my ride, she leaned against it and looked up at me. I liked the admiration for her man that she had in her eyes as she stared at me.

"She's lost so much in her life," Treasure told me. "I don't think she would have survived losing Ross if you'd killed him."

I bent down and kissed her forehead. "You right."

"You can get your revenge now that you have the gun business all to yourself. You've taken away over fifty percent of his income. Your uncle is the only gun connect in the Midwest. Ross would never be able to re-up, especially after word gets around in the game that he got arrested."

I nodded, agreeing with everything she'd said. "And when I take over his chop shop, it'll be a wrap for his ass."

Treasure looked pleasantly surprised. "You're taking over the shop?"

"Hell yeah. He met most of his major clientele through my family. He don't know the people with the type of bread to afford putting down thirty or fifty G's on a ride. But *I* do. And once I get those buyers on board with me, along with some of the guys who work at the shop, I will start my own setup."

Treasure slipped her arms around my waist. As she stared at my uncle's mansion, I told her, "This is what I want for us."

Her head whipped towards me with wide eyes like Bambi's.

"I do," I assured her. "You deserve a mansion like this with real foreign cars in the driveway, not that stolen shit we're riding in. You deserve legit foreign cars that are sitting on acres of land in front of a mansion like this with ten bedrooms that I fuck you in on a different day of the week." I pressed my dick against her. It had gotten hard just thinking about this. She felt how stiff my joint was, and she giggled lustfully. "And I'm gonna get it for you. Just hold on and keep rocking with me. Can you do that for me?"

She teared up, and it surprised me. "Yeah, baby. I can do that for you."

❁

"Come on in, man."

Mello walked slowly into my crib. He looked curious, and he should have been. I had called him over once Treasure and I got back home. She had left to go check on Heaven, who had been losing her mind since Ross had gotten locked up.

Once we were in the living room, I told him, "Have a seat. Want a drink?"

Mello shook his head as he sat down on the couch. "Nah. I'm good."

"Okay, well, let's get right to it." I sat across from him in my recliner. I rested my elbows on my knees so that we were eye to eye. I needed him to know how serious I was. "I need you, man."

His eyebrow curled. "For what? What's up?"

"I need to tell you something that you have to keep between me and you."

Mello replied cautiously, "Okay..."

I nodded and went on. "Your father doesn't know it, but I am severing our partnership."

As expected, Mello looked shocked. "Word?"

I nodded in confirmation. "Word."

"Why?"

"He's been stealing from me."

He was shocked at that too. "Damn. For real?"

"Yeah. I have proof. And with his recent arrest, my uncle wants to sever ties with him too."

Mello nodded slowly. "Okay. What's this got to do with *me*?"

"You're a smart kid, Mello. Real smart. I know you got out the streets, and I want you to stay on this path that you're on. *But* I need you to work with me." Instantly, I saw rejection on his face, so I started to persuade him. "Look, man, I need somebody I can trust, and you're like a nephew to me. I plan on taking over the chop shop business too. So, I need you to help convince your guys to come with me. I also need somebody intelligent to move these guns. I know you wanna be legit, but it's gonna take some time for you to get where you wanna be financially going that route. So, until you get there, let's make this paper."

Mello stared at nothing in particular for a few seconds. He was thinking, and I was good with that as long as he wasn't telling me no off bat.

Since he had been home, I had been watching Mello hustle to be a good man. He was a businessman. College had taught him well. That was obvious. He didn't look right cutting hair in a barbershop, though. He was smart and deserved to be put on.

Besides, what better revenge could I get on Ross than grooming his son to take his place?

"I'm down," he finally said.

A slow grin spread across our beards at the same time.

"Word?" I asked.

"Word."

I sat back, feeling the satisfaction of my plan coming into smooth fruition.

"Look, nephew," I addressed Mello. "I don't want you to think I'm some grimy motherfucker for doing this. But your pops played me. And even after I found out he had played me, it still took me a while to do this to him because he's my brotha. But I gotta do what I gotta do because he's been doing that shit all his life—"

Mello's laughter cut me off. The way he chuckled was full of hatred for his pops. "You ain't lyin'."

'That motherfucka is for self and self only. No matter how much anybody fucks with him, he ain't loyal. I should have known that shit when I saw how he treated Heaven. That girl loves the shit outta him, but all he does is cheat on her and beat the shit out of her."

Mello's head whipped towards me so fast that I thought he was going to break his fucking neck. "He be putting his hands on her?"

"Yeah, man. You didn't know? She didn't tell you?"

He looked off in space, slowly shaking his head.

"Umph. Maybe she didn't want you to know. So, don't say shit. But, yeah, he done whooped her ass a few times, knowing that girl wouldn't leave him because she ain't got nowhere else to go. I don't see how she deals with his ass. That motherfucka ain't right."

Mello nodded and cleared something imaginary out of his throat. "Yeah, well... Like I said, I'm down." Then with a deep breath, he told me. "I'll take that drink now."

21

HEAVEN

"**W**hat if he gets some time? What am I gonna do?" I held my head, trying to catch my breath and calm down. I was having a fucking panic attack. I had been spazzing out since Ross got locked up on Friday. All weekend, I had been losing my mind.

God was getting me back for what I had done. He had to be. This was the ultimate punishment. Because if Ross winded up doing time, it was over for me.

God didn't even need to punish me, though. I had been punished enough at Mello's house that day. His words had hurt worse than anytime Ross had hit me or cheated. That let me know my feelings for Mello had gotten way too deep. When I walked out of his house, I knew I had walked out of his life for good this time. Mello and I had treaded on very thin ice that had broken and caused our special friendship to drown.

The sex was fascinating. How he made me feel was marvelously overwhelming. How he had come to Chicago and showed me so much in so little time was beyond amazing. But now, we had no friendship, and Mello had been so butthurt that he had set Ross up.

When the summer started, I never knew it would end like this.

Those two days that I had spent with Mello were incredible, but I wouldn't have done it had I known it would end up driving me to this point with no friendship with Mello or no husband.

"I got you," Treasure assured me. She was sitting next to me on the couch watching my sadness with so much sympathy. "Vegas and I got you. You know that."

I smacked my lips, frowning. "I am grown with a child. I should be able to have myself," I groaned. "Fuck this! I don't care what Ross says. I need to go to school, get a job, or something."

"*Well,*" Treasure sang sadly. Her eyes drifted away from mine as if she couldn't bear to look at me. "I gotta to tell you something that you need to know."

"What?" I asked cautiously.

"I hate to tell you this because it is only going to make you feel worse. But you're my girl, and I want you to be prepared because Ross is going to flip out—"

"What? Tell me," I urged.

"Uncle Vinny doesn't want to work with Ross anymore."

I groaned. "Fuuuuck."

"He said Ross has too much heat on him."

"Shit!" I sighed and rested my head back on the couch.

Things were falling apart uncontrollably. I thought that dealing with Ross' cheating was heartbreaking, but no, *this* was heartbreaking. This felt like my life was going backwards like I would end up back on the streets begging for food and loose change.

"So, he's only going to work solely with Vegas?" I asked.

She nodded slowly as if she was scared to answer me. "Yeah."

"Well, that's good for you. Means your man is going to be making more money." I managed a smile.

Treasure was blushing. "He actually took me to Vinny's mansion with him."

My smile got wider. "Whaaaat?"

Treasure smiled from ear to ear. I knew this was like a dream come true for her. Treasure wasn't the housewife-type of chick. She was the cook the coke and bag it type of ride or die female. She loved that gangsta shit.

"You should have heard the things he told me that night." She looked off into space with a glow that told me she was reliving the moment. "He wants so much for us, and I almost fucked that all up over that dumb-ass."

"So, you done fucking around?"

"Yeah." When I looked at her as if I didn't believe her, she decided to be real with me and her damn self. "Well, I wanna be. Shit, if I'm gonna fuck around on my man with somebody, it should at least be an *upgrade*. I definitely ain't on shit right now, though. These dudes ain't worth what my man is offering me." I flinched, and she instantly told me, "Sorry, girl."

"No, you right. They aren't worth it."

She looked so sad for me. She was pouting and everything. "Heaven, Mello's feelings were just hurt. He didn't mean what he said."

"But he still lashed out and said it. Just like when Ross lashes out and hits me. Clearly, I come off as a punk-ass bitch to these dudes." I was getting teary-eyed. God, I couldn't believe Mello had said those things to me. He had made me feel so stupid and naïve. I expected that type of treatment from Ross, but I never expected it from Mello. That was because he was my friend. We had a different connection. But I guess my radar was off, because he didn't care about me enough to think about me when he was calling the police on Ross.

"I think he set Ross up."

Treasure's eyes bucked, and she just stared at me. The way she was looking at me was odd, as if she didn't know what to say. But I could understand her confusion. I would have never thought that Mello was that type of person either.

"I know; crazy, right?" I said.

"Yeeeeah. That's crazy," Treasure said slowly. "What makes you think something like that?"

"When I finally talked to Ross Friday, he told me Mello had to be the one who had set him up. No one knew that he was keeping his stash at April's house, not even me. Then he called me right after he got bailed out and told me that April said that Mello was just there upset that his mother was still associating herself with Ross and his business. I mean..." I sighed deeply before I went on. "He *was* pissed at me for ignoring him, and he damn near hates Ross. He was so mad that I had run back to Ross that day that he told me how he felt about me. You think he would do something like that?"

Treasure just shrugged like she was speechless.

Right then, my phone rang. I leaned over to look at it on the end table. Seeing who it was, I groaned, "Speak of the devil."

I didn't know whether I should answer or not. Like a fool, I was hoping that he was calling to apologize and beg for us to be friends again. But now that I knew that he had snitched on Ross, we definitely would never get back the friendship we had.

"You gonna answer?" I hadn't even realized that Treasure had leaned over to see who I was staring at calling me.

"Fuck no. He set Ross up. He's petty as hell."

Treasure sucked her teeth, frowning in frustration. "You don't know that for sure. He might have hated Ross, but he wouldn't do you like that."

I groaned again before I answered and put it on speaker. I didn't feel like repeating our conversation to Treasure.

"Hello?" I answered dryly. I was not trying to hide how irritated and pissed off I was.

"What's up?" He wasn't trying to hide how irritated he was either.

"You tell me," I said with more attitude rising in my voice.

With a long sigh, he told me, "I just wanted to apologize for the things I said to you. I was wrong. I have no idea what you go through at the crib and I should have been smart enough to know it had to be some shit if you ended up fucking with me. You *were* wrong about one thing, though. I'm nothing like my father." I rolled my eyes. He was fucking obsessed with Ross. "I rock with you unconditionally. It's been that way for two years now. When I said I was feeling you, that wasn't just to get the pussy. But since I care about you so much, I shouldn't have said those things to you regardless."

Treasure's eyes bucked at me when I was quiet for too long. I rolled my eyes to the ceiling and asked him, "So, that's why you set your father up?"

I watched as Treasure's eyes fell out of her face.

"What?" Ross spat. "What the fuck are you talking about?"

"Don't play stupid. Ross told me that you were mad at your mother about him keeping his stash at her crib. You were that mad at me for ignoring you that you would send your father to jail? You phony as hell; laying up with me, knowing you were setting him up. He could be locked up for a long time. That charge can give him twenty years."

Treasure sat next to me with her head in hands, just shaking it. I didn't care how she felt, though. I wasn't about to let him sit on this phone being phony with me.

Mello's voice was calm as he said, "Wow, shorty... You ain't gotta worry about me no more. I'm outta your life, Heaven. I'm done. Take care, sweetheart," and then the line went dead.

MELLO

I had known the day Heaven left my house that I had to be done with her. But after Vegas told me that Ross had been whooping her ass, I felt like shit for the things I had said to her. I then knew the meaning behind her tears. I just wanted to apologize to shorty and move on. But after she accused me of being a snitch, I knew it was a definite wrap for us. Heaven was too far gone in the head for Ross to see a real man or a real friend when she saw one.

Now, she was dead to me.

This hadn't been a part of my fantasy at all, all the times I daydreamed about her.

A day later, after hanging up on her, I was still boiling with anger. And to add to the bullshit, now, this nigga was at my door.

"What's up?" I quickly assessed the situation, looking at his hands to see if he had a gun or not.

Ross looked surprised at my demeanor and attitude towards him as he said, "I need to talk to you."

"About?" I hadn't moved to let him in. I stood my ground and put my hands in my pockets. He might have donated his sperm to make me, but this motherfucker had never treated me like his son. So, there was no telling what he was on since he thought I'd set him up.

Ross stood on the stoop glaring at me with this questioning squint in his eyes. He was sizing me up, and I was sizing his ass up too. If this motherfucka wanted to scrap, I was more than ready. I had years of pent-up anger to take out on his ass.

Finally, he asked, "You hate me that much?"

"I don't know what type of goofy shit you and my mother on, but I ain't no fucking snitch. I don't even care about you enough to give a fuck if you in jail or not. I ain't no snake like you."

"*Snake?* Everything thing I did and every move I made took care of you and your mother, boy."

"Yeah? Including killing Heaven's sister?"

His face balled up, looking at me like I was talking none sense. "Fuck is you talkin' 'bout, boy? Divine is—"

"I ain't talking about Divine. I'm talking about Angel, *Caesar's* woman." I leaned against the doorframe and watched with a little humor as he tried to figure this all out.

At first, Ross was lost. I could see him thinking back, trying to put two and two together. So, I helped him out. "You know how close I am to Heaven. She mentioned her sister, Angel, the other day. She got killed along with her boyfriend, Caesar, on the e-way in a drive-by."

I didn't like my father for how he treated me, but I most definitely didn't like myself for being so thirsty for a father when I was young that I jumped the few times that he called for me. One night a few years ago, I was riding with him. I heard him and his man talking about finding somebody named Caesar. They rode around looking for him all night. I was in the backseat on my phone, just happy that I was spending time with my father. I was starting to get in the streets myself, so I knew what it was, and I wasn't scared of what might take place once they found this Caesar dude.

They did eventually find him. They rode right up on him leaving his crib with his girl. They followed his ride until they hit the e-way. I saw the gun when my father grabbed it from under his seat. I didn't even close my eyes as he leaned out of the passenger's side and started to light that truck up.

I watched as the realization finally hit Ross. All that tough shit was out the door when he realized he had killed his wife's sister.

I laughed, sarcastically, happy to fuck his head up. "Don't worry, Pops. Your secret is safe with me." Then I stepped back and slammed the door in his face.

TWO MONTHS LATER...

❧ 22 ❧

MELLO

"Daddy, I like these!"

I grabbed the Jordan Barons from TJ with a frown. "These old, man."

"But I like them, Daddyyyyy," he whined.

I smiled at the pout on his face. "A'ight, man," I told him, playfully muffing him. "Stop whining like a girl. You know I don't like that shit—"

"But you gonna get 'em for him anyway," Paris muttered through her teeth with a smile.

"Yeah, I am," I said, laughing and Paris just shook her head. "You gettin' these 13's, too, though, dude," I told TJ. "They slick."

"Okay!" he told me happily. Then he took off, looking at the other gym shoes along the walls at the Kid's Foot Locker.

I followed Paris as she walked over to the women's gym shoes. "When are y'all heading back to Chicago?"

I was in Gainesville, Florida now. I had left the Chi two months ago. That month and a half I had spent in Chicago had shown me exactly why I had left in the first place. There was just too much drama there for me. Teyanna was bugging. I had seen people shot to death and mowed down right in front of me at that block party. Then, there was the back and forth with Heaven. Chicago hadn't been shit but a headache. So, I brought my ass back to Florida and enrolled in school for the computer sciences master's program.

Paris had brought TJ down to Florida about a week ago. She usually only stayed for the weekend. When she had arrived last Friday, I peeped how much luggage she had, but I didn't think anything of it. But now it was Friday again, and she hadn't said anything about needing to get to the airport.

"I... um..." She looked off as if she was too nervous to answer. "I was actually thinking about staying here."

My head whipped towards her. "Word? Like for good? You wanna move to Florida?"

"I think so. I like it here. The weather is beautiful. I don't hear any gunshots and sirens at night. I don't have to worry about TJ's safety while he's outside playing. It's so nice here. Every time I think about going back to Chicago, I get depressed. I haven't been outside since that block party. I'm too scared to even take TJ to the park. It seems like every day somebody I know gets killed. I'm tired of that city, and I can't afford to move to a safer neighborhood. Plus, every time I talk about going home, TJ gets sad. He likes being around you all the time."

I nodded slowly as I considered Paris moving down here.

She went on, trying to convince me. "I was thinking about looking for a job down here and maybe even starting school too."

I definitely didn't mind being around my son fulltime. That would make living in Florida even better. The separation from my son had been the only downside to living down here.

"What do you think about that?" she asked. She looked up at me with so much hope in her eyes.

It was a light in her eyes as she stared into mine that I had been seeing the whole time she was in Florida. The first few times I saw it, I thought it was flirtation. But I'd talked myself out of believing that since she and I hadn't had any action like that between us since before I knew TJ even existed. Teyanna had always assumed that Paris wanted me, but she had always been nothing but respectful of my relationship and a co-parent. So, I figured she was just happy about being out of town and having a good time. But, now, the longer she gave me this flirtatious look, I was starting to think she was feeling me.

I bit my lip while looking down at her, and her stance became even friskier.

"Why you keep looking at me like that?" I asked her.

She shrugged with this bashful look on her face. "Maybe I like what I see."

My thick eyebrow raised. "Oh yeah?"

"Yeah," she said with a more playful shrug this time. Then she just walked away.

I had never been one to deny how fine my baby mama was, but considering our past, I hadn't looked at her like I was now in a long time. When I left Chicago, I left all my potential pussy there too. It had been two months since I'd busted a nut. Watching the sway of Paris' hips as she strolled through the store, my dick was getting rock hard.

But I told my dick to listen to my common sense. After all the shenanigans that had unfolded in Chicago, I wasn't trying to be in a relationship. Paris and I shared a past that would make us more than just fuck buddies if I put my dick in her. Fuck buddies were all I was on at the moment, however. That short-lived love affair with Heaven had left me ready to stay clear of feelings for a long time. I needed to focus on getting this money, not getting in a relationship.

I hadn't spoken to Heaven since the day she accused me of snitching on my father. I was never going to speak to her again either. I couldn't be her friend knowing that her husband had killed her sister. That would be some phony-ass shit. And, even though she had pissed me the fuck off, I could never hurt her by telling her the truth, that her husband had killed her precious Angel. That would only put her in an even more fucked position. No matter what—the cheating, the abuse, the fact that he had killed Angel and Caesar—leaving Ross would put her, Sunshine, and Divine out on their asses. Had she left Ross when I was confessing my feelings for her, I could not have given her what he had. I was a broke, young dude with a fresh degree, looking for a job. There was no way I could take care of myself, let alone Heaven, her sister, and her child.

That was then, though. Even though Heaven and I were unfixable at this point, I was making moves to ensure that the next chick never had to choose another man over me because I couldn't take care of her. I had taken Vegas up on his offer and started to work with him as he built his organization separate from Ross. Even though I was in Florida now, it worked out perfect for Vegas because there was a port here where many of his gun shipments came into. I was in control of these shipments and the distribution of the guns to various states. I saved my first couple of payments from Vegas and then got some work from a drug connect through Uncle Vinny. I never wanted to be back in the streets, but selling drugs to these college white boys was nothing like serving in Chicago. I didn't have to deal with crack heads and stick-up boys that wanted to stick me for my money. I was just selling party drugs to these white boys, and shit that helped them cram all night while studying. I was getting this money so I wouldn't have to depend on another motherfucker for anything, while finally taking care of my family the way I've always wanted to.

HEAVEN

"That went well," I told Ross, trying to sound encouraging.

Ross shrugged. He was still frowning as we walked out of the Cook County Building. So, I guess I hadn't been encouraging enough.

"I guess," he mumbled.

He grabbed my hand and led me down the concrete steps. I asked him, "What you mean, you guess? Your lawyer said he can possibly suppress the evidence. That would force the prosecution to drop the charges."

"It's a shot in the dark. I mean it works in my favor that April never told them the guns were mine. But since I own the house that she lives in, they have pretty much tied me to it anyway."

After Ross' arrest, we found out that the police had received an anonymous tip that guns were being sold out of April's house. They had sat on the house and gotten surveillance of Ross going in and out. They had also searched Ross' vehicle that day and found a substantial amount of weapons in the trunk. The prosecution tried to get Ross to turn on his distributor, but he refused to do it. He was facing up to thirty years if convicted.

Ross groaned. He had been doing that a lot since we'd arrived for his hearing that morning. "I'm just so tired of this court shit already, and it's only the beginning."

"I know, baby."

When he sighed, I looked up at him and saw him smiling down on me.

"Thank you for coming with me," he said so sweetly.

I blushed. "You don't have to thank me. Where else would I be? You're my husband."

As we walked, he bent down and kissed my forehead. "That's why you my baby."

The last two months had humbled my husband so much that I barely even recognized him. The old Ross who used to disappear for hours without calling was gone. He was no longer coming in the house at five in the morning. He hadn't put his hands on me, except in a loving way. He had proven to me that he was being truthful when he told me that he was going to change. It was a shame that we'd had to go through so much for him to make that change, but I had no complaints. Ross did, however.

" I'm just still so salty about Vinny turning on me the way he did. How the fuck he gon' take money out of my pockets because the next motherfucker wanted to be a snitch? I can't blame him for watching his own back, but I most definitely blame Vegas for turning his back on me."

I discreetly cringed. I was so sick of hearing about this beef he had with Vegas.

"That is his family, Ross—"

"Fuck that! I was his family too!"

"You're right. You were, but you couldn't expect him to choose you over his uncle and getting more money, though. You didn't have another gun dealer, so what was he supposed to do? Vegas did what he had to do for his family, and you are doing what you have to do for yours."

He just grimaced, which was what he always did whenever we had this conversation. Ross was so stubborn that he refused to be cool with Vegas again. It made it awkward when Treasure came around because she was still my best friend. Ross and Vegas' beef wasn't going to change that. At this point, she rarely came around Ross, though. We just met up outside of my house away from our men so we could kick it without the bullshit. Vegas wanted to still be cool with Ross, but Ross wasn't fucking with him. It was to the point that they couldn't even be in the same room with each other without Ross trying to whoop his ass. In retaliation, Vegas went and started his own chop shop. He even took some of Ross' employees and clients. That only made their beef worse. Now, they just stayed away from each other because they still had too much love for one another to kill each other like they wanted to. But I felt that love slipping away every day. It scared me. They both were beasts. It was tossin' the air who would win that fight if it were to ever go down.

I looked up at Ross, smiling at the way his face was balled up. I leaned over and nudged him lightly with my shoulder. "Babe, you have money. You're fine. You still have the chop shop."

"Yeah, I know. I just hate that a motherfucker turned bad on me. I wish I could figure out who the fuck it was so I can murk they ass."

As always when he mentioned that, I got sick to my stomach. Two months ago, Ross had come home and told me that Mello wasn't the one who had snitched on him after all. He just didn't think so after going to Mello's house and talking to him.

I felt so stupid. All I could think about was the hurt in Mello's voice when I accused him of being a snitch. I hadn't heard from him ever since and I didn't think I ever would again. Treasure had told me that he had left for Florida soon after he told me that he was out of my life. I knew he had left because of me.

I still missed him desperately. I missed our friendship more than anything, but I definitely missed the brief intimate time that we had spent together. Even though Ross had turned into the picture-perfect husband, I still yearned for Mello. I thought about him every day and I dreamed about him every other night. It had gotten so bad that I really was just so happy to be with my husband because he was a part of Mello. In some horrible, freakish way, I still felt like I had a part of Mello because I was with Ross. It was disgusting and terrible, and I blamed Mello for making me feel this way about him and then leaving.

But every waking moment I lived, I blamed myself for being so stupid that I had pushed him away.

But I also pushed away my feelings for him. At this point, I didn't have a choice. I was married to a good man now, and Mello was gone. There was nothing I could do but move on.

TREASURE

I was lying on my bed, scrolling through Instagram. *He* was once again in my house, so I was hiding out in my bedroom.

"Hello..." I heard Vegas answer his phone in the living room, so I strained to hear his conversation. "Oh, hey, Ma." After the greeting, I heard the balcony door open and then close, telling me he had stepped out to talk to his mother in privacy.

I kept on scrolling through the latest posts on Baller Alert. One caught my eye about some Breakfast Club interview with Cardi B. I pressed the button to make the sound play through my headphones. I was so busy listening that I jumped out of my skin when I felt a smack on my ass.

"Damo, would you stop?!" I sprang up and scooted back on the bed. "That shit is not funny." I was glaring at him, but this goofy-ass nigga was just looking at me with this dumb-ass smile on his face. "Get the fuck out," I hissed as I kicked at him. Unfortunately, he was standing too far away from the bed for my foot to connect. I wished it had, though. I was trying to kick his ass into the mirror he was standing in front of.

"When are you going to come back to me?" he asked with a smile.

My eyes bucked as I told him, "Never!"

"So, you still need some time?"

My head tilted in disbelief of how crazy this motherfucker was. "Time for what?"

"To miss this dick." He licked his lips and that creepy-ass smile returned.

I leaned forward as if it would make him hear me clearer. "How many times do I have to tell you that I don't want to cheat on him anymore?"

"And how many times do I have to tell you that it's not that easy? You're not about to just leave me alone."

My eyes narrowed into evil slits. "You think that because Divine got that abortion that I forgot that you got my best friend's little sister pregnant?"

Damo shrugged. "You think I give a fuck about that shit?"

"Look, I am sick of your bullshit. You playin' games. You wanna tell Vegas, tell him." I didn't mean that. The last thing I wanted him to do was tell Vegas. But I wasn't about to keep allowing him to think he had this to hold over my head.

He just stood there looking at me with this irritating grin on his face. God, I couldn't believe how attracted I used to be to him because now, he just made my damn skin crawl. I wanted to jump out of bed and knock that smile right off his face. But that would have only caused a bigger scene.

Suddenly, I heard the balcony door open, which meant that Vegas was coming back inside the house. I panicked. I got ready to beg Damo to leave, but then he suddenly just charged me. I thought he was about to fight me or something, but then I felt his lips on top of mine as he hovered above me, pressing all of his weight on me. I quietly tried to push him off me. I kicked and punched. My heart was beating frantically. I anticipated the moment that Vegas came into the room and killed us both.

"Yo', Damo, where you at? Let's roll."

I tried to fight harder as I heard Vegas' voice coming closer. But Damo was stronger than me. He lay on top of me trying to force his tongue into my mouth. I could feel it pushing against my teeth as I pressed my mouth tightly closed. I could also feel myself losing my man.

"Yo', Damo!"

At this point, I was crying as I tried to push him away by the shoulders. I heard Vegas' footsteps coming closer and closer towards the bedroom door.

And then suddenly, Damo just... stopped. He stood up, and I glared up at him while frantically wiping my tears away. He had such a menacing look on his face as he looked down on me that it made the hairs on the back of my neck stand straight up.

"Damo..." My heart sank as Vegas' voice could be heard in the doorway of the bedroom. I looked towards the door and there Vegas was looking back and forth between me and Damo with a scowl on his face that I had never seen before.

He looked me over, noticed the panic and barked, "What's wrong?"

He rushed towards me and Damo just stood back, not saying anything.

"I...uh...I fell and hurt myself." I cringed and grabbed my elbow as if it were really hurting. "Thanks, Damo," I said looking up at him. Then I looked at Vegas, still forcing myself to cringe in phony pain. "Damo heard me scream and came to help me. How is your mom doing?" I asked, trying to change the subject.

Vegas was still looking back and forth between me and Damo as if he were unsure of what was really going on. I held my elbow tighter and started to rock back and forth, trying to sell my story. But my heart was still pounding out of my chest because Damo hadn't said a word. I wasn't sure if he would go along with my story or not. Finally, he just walked out, which only looked even more fucking suspicious.

"What's wrong with him? I asked Vegas, getting in front of the bullshit before he could.

Vegas shrugged and just said, "I don't know," with the same perplexed look on his face.

I had been going through this for the last two months with Damo. He had randomly picked different times to test me. I really wanted to tell Vegas to no longer allow him around me, but I didn't have a good reason to explain why. And it seemed like the longer I didn't fuck with

Damo, the closer he got to Vegas. Now that Vegas had his own operations, Damo was especially attached to his hip.

"I asked you how your mother was doing," I reminded him. I was trying to steer Vegas away from following his first mind that was telling him something wasn't right.

"She...uh...she's fine. She said she wants us to come see her one day."

I smiled. "That would be nice. I'd love to go to New York." I smiled harder and leaned into him.

Finally, the puzzled look on his face vanished, and he broke into a smile. "Yeah, whatever. You just wanna go shopping."

As I said, "Well, of course," teasingly, I felt so much relief that it appeared like I had talked my way out of this one. But that relief was also overshadowed by a fear that Damo was going to ruin things for me.

Vegas had seriously come up over the last two months. He had easily replaced what Ross had stolen from him. His money was stacking even more now that he didn't have to split his profit with Ross. His hustle was at an all-time high, and I was finally the Bonnie to his Clyde. Because we shared the secret of him setting Ross up, we instantly became partners in this. I was part of the moves he made and I strategized with him as he built his own little organization.

Yes, I had the urge to go back to my old ways, but I had yet to meet a dude that would be worth me stepping out on Vegas.

I had officially been scared straight right in the nick of time to keep my man and ride with him on his come up.

I could *not* let Damo fuck this up for me.

❧ 23 ❧

MELLO

"You like it?"

With her hands on her hips, Paris looked around the two-bedroom condo that I had rented for her and TJ. It was a cool lil' spot on Forte Clark Boulevard in Gainesville, only nine minutes away from campus. I had given her a week to stay in the hotel that I had put her up in when she first got to town to decide whether she really wanted to make the move. Meanwhile, I had found this place. And once she assured me she definitely wanted to move here, she was able to move right into this pot. I had furnished it during the week that I was waiting for her to decide. It made me feel good to be able to do this for TJ. I had a big-ass smile on my face as I waited for her response.

"I love it." She grinned, staring out of the balcony. "TJ is going to love that pool."

I beamed proudly. "Yeah, he is."

Paris turned around, looking at me in a way she never had before. There was usually always some tension between us that had started when she suddenly reappeared in my life with TJ. But over the last two weeks that she had been in Florida, the tension changed from mistrust to flirtation. It made me wish that she and I had made it a priority to spend this much time alone before. Maybe we could have been something. I was so dedicated to TJ because of the bullshit-ass father figure I'd had. I always wanted to give him everything I could, including being with him full time. But that meant being with his mother, who had started off our relationship showing me I couldn't really trust her.

Paris took a deep breath and broke our eye contact. She paced back and forth in the living room, checking out the grey and ivory furniture that looked really nice against the grey walls.

"You gonna stay here with us?" she asked.

"Huh?" I hadn't seen that coming at all.

"I mean, you live on campus."

"I know. I don't mind. It's free since I got the scholarship."

"I know your smart-ass got a scholarship." I blushed as she inched towards me. "But I'm saying, why not stay here with TJ and me?"

"Y-you...you want me... to stay here?"

She smiled at my shock and stuttering. "Yeah."

"Like me and you staying here... together?"

Paris giggled. "Yeah." Before I knew it, she grabbed the back of my head softly, brought me down to her level and started kissing me. I had no reason to stop her. I'd had my reasons for not smashing her over the last four years, but she had spent the last two weeks in Florida erasing those reasons. She had shown me that she and I were two people who had matured since we'd had TJ. We got along great as co-parents, and I was willing to now shoot the dice to see if my dick could get along with her pussy since it had been so long since it got wet with the juices of a woman.

Once she sucked my tongue and bottom lip, my dick got rock hard. She got down on her knees and started to claw at the belt holding up my jeans. TJ was in his Spider-man bed taking a nap, so I braced myself on the bookshelf next to me and tried my best to muffle my moans as she ate this dick. I didn't have to put it in her mouth. She shoved it down her throat all by herself. She looked hungry for this dick. She was sucking it furiously as if she had been waiting the entire two weeks since arriving in Florida just to taste it. I didn't know where that hunger had come from. I could feel her flirting with me for the last two weeks, but I didn't know that she was on this type of shit. If she called herself trying to thank me for the apartment, a nigga felt appreciated as fuck.

She was force feeding herself the dick. All I had to do was put a palm on the back of her head and she was deep throating it like she had a point to prove.

Against my will, my cum shot right down her throat.

"Arrgh!" My knees buckled as I braced myself on her shoulders while she swallowed me all up, moaning as if it tasted so good to her. "Shit!"

I could feel her throat as she pulled me out of it. It felt like pulling out of a wet pussy, which made my dick stay rock hard.

She guided me towards the couch and lightly pushed me down. She stood in front of me with this satisfied smile on her face as she pulled up her cotton tank shirt dress. My dick got so hard that it hurt when I saw her bare pussy.

I sat there glaring at it, wondering if she had any idea how much better my dick had gotten since I was sixteen. "What you doin' with no panties on?"

"Hoping you would finally get the hint and take this pussy."

My eyes turned into lust-filled slits as she came towards me and straddled me. Taking the dick into her hands and squatting over it, I asked her, "You've been wanting this dick?"

Sliding down on it, her eyes rolled to the back of her head. "You—" As she tried to speak, I took her hips into my hands and forced her down my dramatically long length. She inhaled sharply as she moaned. "Ahhh. You di-didn't notice?"

My dick got even harder as she talked to me and rode this motherfucker at the same time. As she started to bounce on it, we gave each other a confident grin. Yes, we had gotten way better since we were sixteen, and we were about to prove that to each other right now.

HEAVEN

"You gotta do something, Treasure." I tried to speak lowly so that Vegas wouldn't hear me, but he was all the way in the back in their bedroom, sleep.

As soon as I had gotten to Treasure's house that day, we started talking about that stunt that Damo had pulled in her bedroom, just as we had been every day since it happened a week ago.

"I am. He got me fucked up." She rocked back and forth, the memory of the stunt he had pulled making her more and more pissed off.

"He is trying to get you caught up."

"I know! But I got his ass. I'm way crazier than he's *pretending* to be. He thinks this shit is a game when I am with the shit for real."

I shook my head, slowly. I couldn't believe how insane Damo was acting. Dudes always talked about how women couldn't let go, but they were just as bad as us. "You better do something before he fucks around and tells Vegas."

"Exactly."

Just then a phone started to ring on the counter. It must have been Vegas' phone because Treasure's was in her hand.

She picked it up and looked at the Caller ID like she was used to doing it. She then looked at me and gave me this weird stare.

"What?" I asked.

She didn't say anything. Her answer was turning the phone around and putting it in my face. Mello's name flashed back at me as the phone continued to ring.

"Answer it."

"No," I said, swatting the phone away.

She rolled her eyes and hit the answer button. But then she put the phone to my ear. I started to push it away but froze when I heard his voice. "Hello?... Yo', Vegas."

"Say something, bitch," Treasured mouthed.

"Hello?" I heard Mello say again.

"H-hey," I stuttered.

"Who is this?"

"It's..." I cleared my throat. "It's me, Heaven."

Silence! Fucking crickets!

"How are you?" I asked.

His end of the line went so dead that I looked at it to check to see if he was still on the phone... He wasn't. Damn, I felt so stupid. I groaned and pushed the phone away from my ear, like I should have when Treasure first came up with this dumb-ass idea.

"Fuck you, bitch," I fussed.

She didn't care. She waved her hand, asking, "What happened?"

"He hung up on me," I pouted.

Treasure sucked her teeth as her face became long as well. "Damn..."

Why did she have to do that to me? Why did I have to hear his voice? I hated the way that I still felt for him. It was going on three months since I had last seen him and just hearing his voice had brought up memories of us. The recollections gave me goosebumps and chills, like he was still right there with me. I didn't want to like him. I did not want to have feelings for him. I had no reason to now. Ross was the perfect husband.

So, why did I still think about Mello?

I was so confused. Why did I feel this way when I finally had what

I wanted? I was starting to wonder if having exactly what you wanted was good enough if it wasn't from the person you wanted it from.

"He's down there in Florida getting money, girl. He started selling drugs again."

Was this bitch purposely trying to fuck my head up? "Is he?" I tried to sound like I didn't care.

"Yeah."

"Well, good for him."

Treasure had told me that Mello had linked up with Vegas and started hustling. I, of course, had never told Ross that because that would have only added fuel to his fire. But I was disappointed that Ross had gone that route. He had told me so many times that he'd left the streets alone for a reason. Hearing that he was selling drugs again too was disappointing. He was a smart guy, so I figured if he had gone back deeper into the streets it had to be for a good reason. I just hoped that nothing bad would happen to him out there.

As she popped a piece of gum, Treasure then told me, "I heard him say something about his baby mama moving down there with him."

I'm leaving.

I forced myself not to look irritated or jealous. "Really? Like, are they together or something?"

She frowned and shrugged. "I guess. It sounds like it. But I don't trust that shit. He ain't been with that bitch all this time. Now, all of a sudden when he start getting money, she wanna move to Florida? I call bullshit."

She kept rambling, and her voice faded out under my thoughts. I felt like I was dying slowly. I felt so guilty. I wanted my friend back, but from what I was hearing, he wasn't even the same person anymore.

TREASURE

After Heaven left, I told Vegas I had to go to a few stores, hopped in my car, and headed to Damo's house.

The way I had been handling the situation wasn't working. The more I ignored Damo when he was around, the more he came around and the more outrageous his behavior was becoming. There was no way that I was about to let him ruin my good thing. I had to boss up and nip this shit in the bud. I didn't need the constant reminder of my betrayal at my house every day. I was already dealing with the guilt of watching Heaven wonder if she had been the one who had run Mello out of town when she accused him of snitching on Ross.

I was so ashamed that I had been betraying my best friend. Her husband wasn't shit, so I felt no remorse for how Vegas and I had figured out how to push him out of the game. He had stolen from us, so he deserved the way he was falling off. But Heaven didn't deserve to feel that shit while not knowing the truth.

But she was riding with her man, and I definitely had to ride with mine.

Once I turned onto Damo's block, I immediately slowed down when I saw Steve standing in the doorway talking to Damo.

"How do they know each other?" I asked myself as I squinted, as if that would make me see any better. It was definitely Steve, though, and I wondered how in the hell Damo knew the accountant that Vegas had hired to get the proof that Ross was stealing from him. I watched as Steve and Damo shook up. Then Damo handed Steve what looked like a wad of cash. Then Steve walked off to his BMW.

I remained in park a few houses down until Steve pulled off. Damo was going back into the house and closing the door just as I pulled up and hopped out.

I ran up to the door, trying to catch it before Damo was able to lock it, and I did. Turning the knob, I barged my way in, startling Damo. At first, he squared up, ready to defend himself against the unknown person barging into his crib. He relaxed, however, when he saw that it was me. He even smiled as I slammed the front door shut.

"What's up?" I asked him. I eyed him as if that would help me figure out what the fuck was going on.

Still smiling, he licked his lips. "What you doin' here?"

"How do you know Steve?" I wasn't about to play no fucking games with this motherfucker.

"Who?" He tried to play dumb.

"Steve."

"I don't know no fucking Steve."

"The motherfucker that just walked outta here!" I snapped through gritted teeth.

He just stood there with this teasing look on his face. Seeing that he thought this shit was funny, I was now seething.

I was sick of his shit. Reaching into my purse, I pulled out my gun, aimed at his head, and fired.

Pow!

"Arrrgh!" He screamed like a bitch and fell to the floor. As expected, I had only grazed his ear, which I had aimed for. I rushed towards him as he held his ear. I stepped on his neck, pressing only hard enough that he was still able to answer my questions.

"You crazy bitch!"

"Uh huh," I taunted him as I aimed the gun right in his eye. "I am crazy, and you gon' stop fucking with me. Why are you lying about Steve? What you on, motherfucker?"

He was calling me crazy, but he was the psycho one who still had the nerve to smile while his ear was bleeding and a gun was being pointed at his head.

"Are you the motherfucker who told Vegas that Ross was stealing from him?"

His constant laughter was making my trigger finger happy. "Yo', your boyfriend so easy to manipulate, I swear to God."

My heart dropped to my stomach. "And you paid Steve to convince him with bogus information and documents?"

His answer was laughing at me so hard that he looked psychotic.

I suddenly felt so sick. My anger turned into disgust with myself. My pussy had made a really fucked up decision that had cost my man his best friend and right hand.

Damo continued to double over, laughing as I removed my foot from his neck. My movements were so slow as I walked towards the door. Whatever my issues were with being monogamous had fucked with my man's livelihood. Yeah, he was getting more money now, but it was coming at a cost. He and Ross stayed at it. Any day, their beef was going to explode. Knowing that the potentially deadly outcome was my fault left me feeling so heavy that I was only able to inch my way to the door.

"I guess I can be sure that you won't say nothing because telling on me will be telling on yourself."

I couldn't give Damo the satisfaction of looking at him, because my eyes would only tell him that he was right. I just tucked my tail and left, feeling as if my attempts to come here and dead this shit had only opened up a bigger can of worms.

🦗 24 🦗

MELLO

"**B**ae?"

Hearing Paris' voice made me cringe. It had been a few days since she had moved into her apartment and let me hit that. All weekend, I had reunited with that pussy. I had also stayed at the apartment with her and TJ. Every morning, I woke up to breakfast. TJ seemed really happy to see my face when he woke up and every night before he went to bed. Paris was too happy to cook, clean, and suck my dick; anything to keep me from leaving. And she was really comfortable spending my bread too.

By Tuesday, however, I was uncomfortable with the way Paris was acting like I was her man. For four years, she showed no interest in me, and then, *bam*! Suddenly, she was living in Florida, sucking my dick every night, and calling me *Daddy*.

The shit was phony as hell.

"What up?" I finally looked up at her after sending a text message to a customer on campus that was looking to buy some mollies. Even though it was a party drug, a lot of students took mollies to stay up and cram.

"Why didn't you come back last night after class?"

Standing up and grabbing my book bag, I told her, "I had a few customers to serve after class, so I crashed at my apartment on-campus." I adjusted the bag on my shoulders. With it, while walking this neighborhood, I looked like any other college student in Gainesville. This book bag was filled with weed, zans, coke, and mollies, though; not books.

She replaced my seat on the couch and grabbed the remote. "When are you going to get rid of that apartment?"

I shrugged, fishing in my pocket for my keys. "I don't know."

"I thought you were going to move in with TJ and me."

"I never said that. You asked me to, but I didn't get a chance to answer because you started sucking my dick, remember?"

She blushed and bit her lip while looking at me. Her legs crossed. I wondered if she had had to squeeze her legs together because that pussy was throbbing for me.

"You're right," she agreed. "But I thought since you never left afterward, it meant you were living here."

Looking at her smile paint a ray of sunshine all over her face, I didn't have the nerve to tell her the truth. So, I just told her, "Don't worry. I ain't goin' nowhere."

She was happy with that as I left. Being a woman, those words were good enough for her. But the truth was I really wasn't trying to live with Paris.

Paris was a dope chick and great to look at. I was sure that any woman with a kid would want to be with her baby's father if he was getting his master's and hustling. I was like the best of both worlds to her. It should have been an ideal situation for me too. She was the mother of my kid. She was also a beautiful woman who had always shown me that she had sense and was a great mother.

But being with her, I didn't feel like I was with *my* woman. It felt like something was missing, as if we were both pretending. But let some of my older male family members tell it, they pretended every day for the sake of being a good father and having at-home pussy. It didn't feel right to me, but whatever did?

I shook off the constant questions nagging me about what my dick had gotten me into and just flowed with it.

ONCE ON CAMPUS, I TOOK THE MOLLIES FROM MY BAG, STUFFED them in my pocket, and left my ride parked in the student lot. I made my way to the dorm room where my customer was waiting. I had served him before a few times, so I wasn't as worried as I should have been.

Walking towards the hall, I couldn't help but appreciate the weather. It was September and still eighty degrees. The air was nothing like Chicago either. There was something crisp and clean about it that made a hood dude like me appreciate the hell out of it.

I made my way through Buckman Hall saying what's up to a few of the undergrads that knew me as "the dope man." Over the last two months, I had served so many of these white boys that I was like their best friend at this point.

Once I made it to the second floor, I wasn't even paying attention as I approached Mark's room. Had I been, I would have known to turn around and go in the other direction. But it was too late to do that. Once I looked up, I was already two feet away from Mark's room ...and the campus police were approaching me.

"Carmello Young?"

Shit.

I instantly stopped and made an about-face, but I bumped right into my academic advisor, Harold.

"Be cool, Mello," he urged me.

"What the fuck is going on?" I asked him through gritted teeth.

The campus police walked up to me, instantly grabbing me. Each one had an arm on lock. I cringed from the way they were twisting my arms.

Harold could see me getting more and more pissed off by the second. He held his hand up. "I got him." When they didn't let me go, he griped, "Let me take care of this."

At this point, I was starting to become irritated as well because a bunch of students were standing around watching what was going on. As I looked around, I noticed Mark standing in the doorway of his room with this fucked up look on his face.

"Mello..." Harold called my name, but I was too busy threatening Mark's life with my eyes. I didn't know what was about to shake, but I knew he had something to do with it and afterward, I was going beat his ass. "Mello..."

I finally gave Harold my attention. He told me, "C'mon on, son. You have to come with us."

I had too much respect for Harold to snap on him. Plus, in my heart, I knew whatever they were here for, I probably deserved. For the last two months, I had been flooding this campus with drugs. My customers were both students and academic professionals. Shit, I had even served Harold some weed on the weekends. So, I allowed them to escort me back down to the first floor and into the resident assistant's office.

As soon as Harold closed the door, one of the officers told me, "Empty your pockets."

When he came towards me, I squared up, and Harold begged me to comply. "Mello, please do what they ask you to ... Please?"

Fuck that, I wasn't doing shit, but I didn't fight them as both officers went fishing through my pockets. Harold shrank when the one on my left took out the bag of mollies, as if he was hoping they wouldn't find anything.

"Sit down, son," Harold told me sadly.

I sat slowly, watching the officers and wondering when they were going to arrest my ass.

Harold sat across from me and folded his hands in front of him. "A student overdosed last night." My stern expression collapsed instantly. "It was one of Mark's friends."

My head fell into my hands. "Is he okay?"

"Yeah. He'll be okay, but the police know that you have been dealing drugs on campus."

I sat back in the folding chair, defeat all over my face. "So, Mark was setting me up? Wow."

"Not exactly. That wasn't him texting you. That was these fine gentlemen right here," he said sarcastically as he pointed at the officers. "They questioned Jacob, Mark's friend who OD'd, and he told them that Mark had bought the drugs from you. You can't expect them to take the heat for you in this situation."

I sneered at him. "You knew about this and let me walk into this shit?"

Harold sighed, but I could see his nostrils flare in offense at what I had insinuated. "Mello, I pulled all of the strings I could. I'm here, aren't I? They are trying to charge you with drug distribution."

I groaned and recoiled in my seat. "Shit."

"I've talked them out of arresting you. You're a smart kid...too smart. You deserve another chance." At the sound of that, I was relieved. But then he made my relief feel like a fucking fool, "But you won't be able to get that chance here. Unfortunately, you're expelled from this university."

ROSS

♫ As I pour this glass of wine
I hope it helps me express these thoughts of mind
(Noo) I don't think I ever felt the way I feel for you girl
So I'm turning these lights down and I'm telling you right now ♫

As soon as the track started to play, Heaven instantly looked at me with a natural blush on her face that reminded me just how much younger she was than me. She already looked like a baby in the face, but when she blushed like that, it made her look even younger.

I stood up, took her hand, and made her stand up on those five-inch heels that she had put on, knowing damn well that her feet would be hurting by the end of the night. We were out kicking it, just me and her. I had taken her to dinner downtown, and now, we were having drinks at the S2 Ultra Lounge.

"C'mon," I coached her as I pulled her onto the dance floor with a grin on my face. "You know this is our song."

Heaven continued to giggle as I pulled her against me, wrapped my arms around her, and started to sway back and forth. Once she rested her head on my shoulder, I started to sing in her ear. *"I don't think I've eeeever ever really told you how much I neeeeed you. I need you more than my next breath."*

Heaven slightly pulled her face away from my shoulder and looked up at me with this amused grin on her face as I kept singing, off-key as a motherfucker. *"Never would I eeeever leave you cause darling I neeeed you. I need you more then the next breath I breathe."*

She was cracking up, but I was serious. I meant every word that was coming out of my mouth off key. I had been singing that song to her since the first time I fucked up and thought that she was going to leave me. I wasn't a man who knew how to express my emotions very well, so I would play this song in hopes that she would understand how I was feeling. This was the first time in a long time that this song was playing while I wasn't in a fucked up place with her—that she knew of.

For the last two and a half months, I had been trying to wrap my head around the fact that I had killed her sister...the sister she had never even told me about. I was more so concerned with the fact that Heaven had secrets. I had always thought she was open and honest with me. I was supposed to be the one with the secrets and the lies. But she had been hiding a sibling from me and for what reason I didn't know. Apparently, she felt more comfortable telling Mello about Angel than me. That made me feel some kinda way, but I had to face the fact that I hadn't been the husband to her that she felt like she could confide in.

That was in the past, though. Lately, I had been surprising myself with how committed I was to her. Therapy had been helping me manage my anger. I was finally honest with her about me going, even though I still didn't feel like it was necessary for her to come with me just yet. But I could never tell her that I was the one who had killed Angel. That was a secret I was going to have to take to my grave if I never wanted to lose my wife.

Angel had been an innocent bystander. I hated that I was the one who had taken her life. She was guilty by association, however. Caesar had owed me a load of cash, and he had been avoiding me for months. He had taken a shipment of guns and disappeared. Motherfuckas died in the street every day for far less than thirty thousand dollars, and I had given his ass four months to come up with my shit. I was becoming a joke in these streets by letting Caesar walk. I had to do what I had to do. And being the woman of a hustler, Angel knew the possibilities of her life being taken because of the life he lived.

"You so silly, baby," Heaven said when I finally stopped singing. "You know this my shit."

She sighed as she wrapped her arms around my waist and snuggled closer to me. She said, "I know," with a sound in her voice that I didn't like. She had had this melancholy undertone in her conversation all night, but every time I had asked what was wrong, she said she was fine.

I knew she wasn't, though. Something was wrong, and for the first time in forever, I could wholeheartedly say it wasn't me who had her in this mood.

Then a tear slid down her brown face. She quickly wiped it away as I asked, "What's wrong?"

"Nothing," she answered lowly.

"Stop lying to me."

"You... you're just so sweet, babe. That's all."

That was bullshit. I knew it. I could feel it. I was about to call her on it as soon as Vegas and Damo caught my eye. They were coming in the door. My body instantly became so rigid that Heaven obviously felt my tension, looked up at me, and followed my fiery eyes as they watched Vegas and Damo go straight to the bar.

Grabbing my hand, Heaven urged, "C'mon. Let's go."

"Nah, fuck that," I said. I glared at the back of them as they stood ordering drinks at the bar. "We ain't gotta go nowhere."

"Please?" She squeezed my hands, trying to get my attention. When I didn't take my eyes off of them, she stood in front of me trying to look me square in the eyes. It was cute because in those heels she was barely eye to eye with me. "We were having such a good night."

I smiled at her pout. She was right anyway. We had been having a dope-ass night, and I wasn't about to put my baby in the middle of this bullshit.

I took her hand and guided her towards the opposite end of the bar. I was going to be the bigger man, even though I wanted to clear all of Vegas' fronts for the shit he had been pulling. All summer, he had been having something against me, and I had no idea what the fuck it was. And now he had actually become my competition. Shit was crazy. We had gone from bros to enemies just like that.

I threw a couple of five's on the counter and saw Vegas and Damo finally peep that I was in the building. Heaven squeezed my hand again when she saw Vegas and I staring each other down. I looked at her and kissed her forehead. That was my way of letting Vegas know that I was only tucking my tail because my lady's safety was more important than me whooping his ass.

With her hand in mine, I led her towards the door. We walked right passed those motherfuckers. Vegas stayed seated, clutching his drink. But Damo's extra ass stood up with this look on his face that told me that he was on straight bullshit. Vegas must have seen he was on bullshit as well because he turned around in his barstool just in time to hear Damo say to me, "You *better* leave, snake-ass nig—"

Damo couldn't even finish his sentence before I fired on his ass, pushing his face in with my fist. He fell back onto the bar, knocking over glasses as he slid down onto the floor. Still sitting there calmly, Vegas eyeballed me, and my glare dared his punk ass to get up or he would be the next one to get it.

VEGAS

Ross was lucky that he was with his woman. I had mad love for Heaven, and she had nothing to do with this shit. I wasn't trying to piss my woman off by allowing her best friend to get hurt in the middle of my war with Ross. So, I didn't even say intervene as Ross left the club hand in hand with Heaven as Damo picked himself up from the floor. Besides, Damo had been the one on dummy.

"You good, man?" I asked him as he palmed his face. It was already swelling up as he checked himself out in the mirror behind the bar.

"Hell fucking yeah, I'm good. That shit felt like a bee sting." He threw some bills on the bar, threw back his double shot of cognac, and headed for the door.

"Fuck," I cursed as I jumped from the barstool and headed out of the door after him.

By the time I got out of the club, Damo was already jumping to his ride. I had caught a ride with him, so I hit a light jog and jumped into the car just in time for him to throw it in drive and pull off.

That's when everything started to happen so fast. I didn't even see his gun in his hand, until he was aiming out of his open window. By the time I realized he was pulling alongside Ross' car, heading north on

Ashland, I didn't even have time to say shit before he started firing into the Ross' car. The deafening sound of gunshots and shattering glass overshadowed my shouting, "What the fuck?! Yo', what the fuck is you doin'?!"

Ross' car suddenly hit the brakes, and he made a U-turn in the middle of the street. I looked back as he drove the wrong way on the street, ducking and dodging as cars blew their horns at him and hit sharp turns trying to avoid colliding with them.

"Fuck is wrong with you, motherfucker?!" I barked.

"Fuck that nigga! His bitch ass has been on bullshit all summer. He deserved that shit. You should have been got his ass for stealing from you anyway. That's why he walks around this bitch like he runs shit, cuz he got away with that bullshit."

"Man, pullover!" I snapped.

"What?" he asked, scowling.

"I said..." I reached over, grabbed the wheel and yanked that bitch. "Pull the fuck over."

He quickly took control of the wheel and pulled over. I jumped out and slammed the door. Damo peeled off, and I started walking down Ashland. I pulled out my phone and before going to my Uber app, I called Treasure.

"Hello?" I could hear that I had just woke her up.

"Call Heaven and make sure she's okay."

"Why?" She sounded much more awake now. "What happened?"

"Damo just shot up Ross' ride, and she was inside."

Her gasp was as loud and deafening as those gunshots had been. "Oh my God! What the fuck is wrong with y'all?!" she shouted.

I cringed. Now, this dumb-ass motherfucker, Damo, had me in the doghouse with my woman too. "I didn't know he was going to do the shit. Would you just call her?"

"Okay," she rushed.

"Call me back and let me know if she's good."

She hung up on me, and I swung at the air. Anger was boiling over inside me so fast that I almost threw my phone. I had stopped myself, though.

Damo had kicked this shit off in the wrong way and started some shit. But he had been right. This shit wasn't going to be over between Ross and me until I finished it.

A war had officially been started.

HEAVEN

My eyes rolled when I saw that it was Treasure calling. This was the last thing Ross would want at this very moment. "Hello?"

"Oh, thank God! Heaven, are you okay?"

"Yeah," I said on a heavy breath. "What the hell is wrong with them?"

"Fuck them niggas! They dead!" Ross spewed as he sped through the city towards our home.

"What happened?" Treasure asked.

Before I could answer her, Ross spewed, "Treasure, tell your man he a fucking dead man for letting that motherfucker do that shit."

"Oh God," she groaned. "What happened, Heaven?"

"Ross and I were at S2, and Vegas and Damo walked in. Ross and I just decided to leave. As we walked out, Damo stood up and started talking shit. Then Ross knocked his ass out. We had left and were on our way home. Then Damo and Vegas pulled up next to us, Damo just started shooting. Luckily, neither one of us got hit. Vegas is bugging. Ross didn't get arrested on purpose. Somebody set him up. And just because somebody set him up, Vegas is going to turn on him like this? We know he had to get his money, and we didn't expect him not to work with his uncle, but gawd damn! He's going too far. Why the fuck are they beefing with him like this? You know he just kicked shit off, right?"

Treasure groaned long and hard. "I'm so sorry that happened to y'all. But I don't think Vegas would have ever shot at y'all. That had to be all Damo."

My eyes rolled to the ceiling. I had so much to say about that last comment, but since Ross was in the car, I bit my tongue. Instead, I asked her, "You think Ross gives a fuck about that?"

"Man, hang up the phone," Ross barked.

I sighed out in frustration. "Treasure, I have to go. I'll talk to you later."

I hung up with tears in my eyes. I already had been feeling like shit all day. My heart had been heavy since I left Vegas' house that day. Ross had such a big smile on his face as he took me to dinner tonight, but all I could think about was Mello. When he was just singing to me on that dance floor, I got so full of emotions that a tear slid down my face. I was so frustrated that I actually cried. I wanted to lose these feelings for Mello so bad that I would have paid for it. As Ross danced with me, I told God that I would do anything to make Him erase these feelings for Mello that were making it impossible for me to enjoy my "new husband".

And now this. Vegas had only kicked off a never-ending war between him and Ross. This wouldn't stop until one of them was dead, and that would only ignite more and more tragedy amongst the circle. I only hoped that this would be it, but unfortunately, this was only the beginning to the end.

TREASURE

As soon as I heard the alarm chirp, I sprang out of bed. I wiped my tears as I ran barefoot out of the bedroom and down the hall. As I ran up on Vegas, he looked so apologetic. I was too angry to even care about his remorse, however. As soon I was close enough to connect, I started swinging on his ass.

"How could you?!" I snapped as I landed blows on his face and chest.

"It wasn't me!" he told me.

"Why would you let him do that?!"

Blocking his face, he told me, "I didn't know he was gonna do that!"

"Arrrgh!" I was so frustrated that I could only scream.

"Baby!" He ducked and dodged my fists, while trying to block me. "Baby, stop!" Finally, he was able to catch my wrists and hold them tightly. I squirmed, trying to get out of his grasp, but there was no use. "Stop," he insisted. "Please?" When I heard the sincerity in his voice, I finally calmed down and looked up into his eyes. Those ocean blue eyes were filled with so much sadness that I was forced to realize that I was responsible for putting it there.

I weakened with guilt. I burst into tears.

"Baby, I'm so sorry."

I cried even harder. This was not his fault. Hell, even Damo wasn't to blame. It was *my* fault. Mine alone.

"Damo was out of line," he said as he grabbed the back of my head and brought my face to his chest. I could only sob and grip his shirt. I was trying to find the strength to stay on my feet. That's how much the remorse was weighing me down.

"I'm done fucking with that motherfucker. He dead," Vegas assured me. "I even texted Ross and told him that it wasn't me and that I was sorry. I told him I was done with this beef."

I felt some relief, but it wasn't enough to erase the remorse. My pussy had caused all this grief, and as long as I was with Vegas and as long as Treasure and I were friends, I would walk around with it every day.

25

HEAVEN

"What the fuck are *you* doing here?"

My eyes rolled to the ceiling as Ross looked Treasure up and down. His look was so evil as if she were the one who had shot at him. She didn't see it, though. She stayed seated on the stool at the island. Her back was to him as she continued to cut up the eggs for the tuna salad. But I could see the uncomfortable look on her face.

I warned him, "Ross, don't..."

He sucked his teeth, still eyeballing her. "Nah, fuck that. Her man tried to fucking kill us."

Treasure turned to look at him. "That was Damo, not Vegas. And I got in his ass about that. Vegas is pissed that Damo did that shit too. He would have never done that with Heaven in the car."

Ross chuckled sarcastically. "Oh, he just wouldn't have done it with Heaven in the car, huh?"

Treasure looked so sad as she reached for him. "Ross—"

He swatted her outstretched hand away. "Nah, don't worry about it."

"Ross," Treasure called out to him as he walked out, but he kept walking.

Tears welled in Treasure's eyes. I went towards her and wrapped my arms around her. She didn't say a word as her head rested on my shoulder, but I could hear her tears.

I had been able to quickly forgive her for Damo shooting at us a few days ago because she had been this apologetic. Once I had calmed down, I knew that Vegas would have never shot at Ross. I also knew, from what Treasure had been telling me, that Damo was crazy. Vegas definitely hadn't played a part in it.

"He's just mad," I told Treasure as I rubbed her back soothingly.

She left my embrace. She reached for a paper towel that was on the island and dabbed her tears away, trying not to mess up her makeup.

"I'm okay," she insisted. "I just hate that all of this is happening."

"They need to sit down and talk to each other."

"Ross doesn't look like he is trying to let that happen."

"Maybe I can talk him into it."

"Maybe... Anyway, enough of that. Let's get this shit done. The party is about to start."

It was a beautiful Saturday afternoon at the end of September. It was also Sunshine's fourth birthday. I had planned a small party for her and some of the small kids in our circle. The basement was full of balloons, inflated Disney characters, treats, and cakes. The party was set to start in about an hour, so Treasure and I were trying to hurry up and finish the finger foods.

Still hearing Treasure sniffling, I asked, "You sure you okay?"

She was more emotional than I had ever seen her.

"Yeah, I'm okay."

⚜

Two hours later, the basement was full of toddlers. Disney songs were blaring from the surround sound. A clown was entertaining the kids while Treasure and I sat on the couch sipping "adult juice."

"Why did you invite her?"

"Who?"

Treasure was too busy glaring at the basement door to answer. I followed her eyes and saw Paris walking in, holding TJ's hand.

"Oh. I saw that she was in town. She and TJ have played together a bunch of times when April brought him around to see his granddaddy."

Treasure stared at me with an expression that told me that she knew that I was full of shit.

I rolled my eyes with a telling smirk. "Okaaaaay... Yeah, I wanted to get some tea on her and Mello." I giggled, but I was done finding things funny as Mello walked in behind her. My heart fluttered uncontrollably. I was literally shaking. I had to tighten my grip on my cup to keep from dropping it. "I didn't think *he* would come with her, though. I had no idea he was in town."

Luckily, Ross was still so pissed off at Vegas that he refused to come down to the party as long as Treasure was there. Therefore, he couldn't see me eye fucking his son.

Damn, he looked good. He had the nerve to be a little more cut up. He must have been hitting the gym down in Florida. He looked like the money he was making now too. He was draped in labels that made him look tastefully expensive. His beard was full, luscious, and lined to a crisp shape that connected to his sharp lining and ocean waves. He was a tall mountain of chocolate steel. My mouth watered as I tried to pull my eyes away from him.

Treasure sighed long and hard while staring at Mello. He was following Paris like this was the last place that he wanted to be.

Finally, I tore my eyes away from them and gulped down the mixture of rum and pineapple juice. "Well... I guess it's a motherfucking party now."

MELLO

-A few minutes ago-

"Mello, wake up."

I stirred in my sleep. As my eyes opened, I squinted as the sunlight burned my eyes. I sat up in the rental car, yawning and stretching. When I looked around, I realized that we weren't at the hotel.

"Where are..." I stopped mid-sentence when I looked out of the passenger's window and saw my pop's crib. I whipped my head around towards Paris. "What the hell are we doing here?"

She was wearing this unapologetic smirk. She thought this shit was a game. "You said that Vegas won't be ready to meet up with you until later."

"Yeah. And?"

She put the car in park, saying, "So, I figured TJ could come to Sunshine's birthday party." Right away, I groaned. Paris sucked her teeth. "I'd rather him be here playing with other kids than getting on my nerves at that damn hotel."

I snatched my seatbelt off. "Whatever, man. Go on in then."

"You're not coming in?" She had the nerve to sound surprised. I didn't know why, though. I had made it clear to her that I didn't fuck with my pops after the summer I'd spent in Chicago.

"No."

Her lips pursed together. "Are you serious? All because of your father?"

"Man, I told you I was just trying to be in and out this city. All I needed to do was come here and make sure that this shipment and cash got to Vegas. That's it."

She huffed and puffed. "And you said I could see my people too since we're here."

"*Your* people, not mine!" I snapped.

This was why I shouldn't have started dicking her down. She thought she ran shit. But now, I was stuck. I had helped relocate her. It wasn't bad being stuck with a pretty chick with a phat ass. However, this type of shit wasn't worth the nut.

"Just come in for like twenty minutes please," she begged. "I don't want to be stuck here. If you leave, you might be gone forever handling business with Vegas."

I shrugged. "You got an Uber account."

"Mello, please?"

My hands ran over my face with irritation. My reluctance wasn't about my pops, of course. Fuck him. I wasn't for walking into the bullshit with Heaven, though. I was pissed at her for what she had said to me last, but I couldn't lie; these two months apart hadn't erased my feelings for her. I still cared for the girl, but circumstances had forced me to let her go. It was taking longer than I wanted, though. So, I wasn't trying to see her.

But as I recalled our last conversation, I figured fuck it. She had had the nerve to think that I was a snitch. So, why should I even still care? She was still my father's wife. We would have had to see each other again at some point. I needed to man the fuck up, take this L, and act like Heaven and I never happened. So, I got out of the car.

There were pink and silver balloons lining the driveway. I could hear the Disney music coming from inside of the house. There were signs that directed people to enter through the back door, which lead to the basement.

I let Paris and TJ go in first. Once I walked inside, it was like my eyes were drawn straight to Heaven's. She mumbled something to Treasure that I couldn't hear. Then she gulped down whatever was in her red cup.

Then, she smiled at me.

That smile... It was like love winking at me. Right then, no matter the bullshit between us or the time we had spent without seeing each other or speaking, I immediately knew why I hadn't been feeling Paris. No matter how pretty she was, or how submissive she was, or how good the pussy and head was, I wasn't feeling being with that girl. It was the ideal situation, but I still hated it. Looking at Heaven, I knew exactly why. Paris and I were missing the authentic connection and chemistry that Heaven and I had. When Heaven smiled, I saw her soul. When Paris smiled, I didn't believe the happiness in it.

That was the difference.

"Hey, y'all!" Paris walked right up on Heaven and Treasure. It would have been too obvious if I didn't follow, so I did.

Treasure gave me a slow, scowling look that judged me from head to toe. "Hey, y'all." I could hear the messiness all in her tone.

Heaven mumbled a low, "Hey."

"Thanks for the invite, girl," Paris went on. She was clueless to the tension between the rest of us.

Heaven tore her eyes off of me and told Paris, "You're welcome."

"How is Florida?" Treasure asked us both.

"Girl, it's so nice. I just be chilling," Paris rambled. "Enjoying the sunshine and my man."

Why the fuck did she say that? This frantic bitch. Heaven's face and mine dropped. I didn't have the heart to bust Paris out in front of Heaven and Treasure. She and I had never said that we were in a relationship officially. Yeah, I was living with the girl, but I figured we were working towards being committed to each other since it had only been two months.

Paris was still rambling as Heaven sprang to her feet. She mumbled,

"I'll be right back," so fast that I could barely make out what she'd said.

She shot towards the stairs that led to the main floor of the house. As I watched her, I fought the urge to go after her. I wanted to make sure that she was okay. But I had been doing that for two years, and the moment she got the chance to take care of me, she dropped the ball.

Whether I liked it or not, Heaven wasn't my concern anymore.

HEAVEN

Get it together, Heaven. Breathe. Breathe.

I was coaching myself as I paced back and forth in the first-floor bathroom. I had locked myself in there. I couldn't believe that my body and heart were reacting to Mello this way. I knew I still had feelings for him, but *damn*! These feelings were so suffocating that I couldn't breathe. They were so electrifying that I felt like I was having a heart attack.

Okay. Calm down, Heaven. Calm down.

I took long deep breaths until my heart rate finally slowed down. The tears pooling at my eyelids finally dried up. I took another deep breath before opening the bathroom door and returning to the basement.

For the next three hours, I made myself put on a happy face while I partied with my daughter. I tried my best not to even look at Mello, but it was so hard. If our eyes weren't being automatically drawn to one another's, Paris' extraness was drawing my attention to them. If she wasn't sitting on his lap, she was rubbing his waves like he was a fucking pet. But no matter how she tried to maintain his attention on her, his eyes kept drifting past her to me. His stare was the same one that had convinced me to give him my body. It melted my heart. But it was also still laced with the disappointment I had put there. Looking at him, I knew that no matter our feelings for each other or what we had shared, it was over.

That only made me want him, yearn for him, and miss him more.

I was so ready for the party to be over, and luckily, it soon was. I had never cleaned so fast in my life. I damn near kicked everyone out of my house the nicest way that I could. Luckily, Mello and Paris had sneaked out of the basement while I was throwing things away in the kitchen. When I returned downstairs and saw that they were gone, I was both relieved and heartbroken. It was taking everything in me not to break down in front of Treasure, Esperanza, and Divine. But as soon as Divine and Esperanza disappeared to their rooms from exhaustion and Treasure left for home because of the same, I made sure Sunshine was asleep before I ran out of the house to my car.

As soon as I hopped in and slammed the door shut, I burst into tears.

"Oh my Goooood." I had never felt heartbreak like this, not even the times when my husband had cheated on me. That's when I was convinced that I had fallen in love with Mello.

۞

"Oh, hi there, Heaven." The receptionist at the desk at Margaret Manor smiled up at me.

I tried to make a smile meet hers, but it was useless. "I know it's kinda late, Sarah, but can I see my mother?"

She sighed. From the reluctant look on her face, I knew what her answer would be.

"I'm sorry, Heaven. Today is just not a good day for her. She is very manic today."

I nodded slowly. "Okay."

"I'm sorry," she said again.

"Don't be." I smiled and headed for the exit.

I should have known I wouldn't be able to see her. The couple of times I had tried last year, I had been told the same thing.

I just needed to feel something familiar because, at the moment, everything felt so strange. My husband was a different person, and so was I. Our circle had been divided. I was in love with another man. I didn't know who or where I was. I wanted a taste of my old life for the first time ever. For the first time in my life, I preferred to be in that tiny bedroom, sharing a bunk bed with Sunshine and Divine.

Once in the car, I drove towards the apartment that I had once shared with Angel and Caesar. The sun had set by now. I parked in front of it and just stared up at the second floor. The lights were on and I could see the silhouettes of whoever lived inside now.

I leaned back against the headrest and just stared at the unknown residents that were inside. I wondered if they were living as happily as I was when I had lived there.

"I miss you so much, Angel." Tears slid down my face as I wished to God that I could go back in time and stop her from leaving the house with Caesar that night. If I had begged her to stay and continue to watch Netflix and eat pizza with me and Divine, she would still be here. She would still be a mother to me. I wouldn't have ever met Ross and I would have never fallen in love with his son.

"Why did you have to go?" I cried.

Just thinking about Angel, I wondered what she had endured to keep Divine and me fed. I wondered what hoes she had put up with. I wondered what flaws of Caesar's she had looked past. I wondered if there was a man who'd had more of her heart than Caesar. Whatever she had chosen to deal with for our sake, she had died for.

Mello was right. My life had been full of bad decisions... of my own and others.

TREASURE

As soon as I got in the house, I stripped out of the Adidas jogging suit, kicked my shoes off, and hopped in the shower. Luckily, Vegas wasn't home, so I was able to jump in bed and relax from the long day. However, my mind was not relaxing. As it had been since Damo had shot at Ross, my guilt was running a race in my mind.

When I cried in Heaven's kitchen earlier, those were real tears. I felt so guilt-ridden for being the sole person responsible for this beef between Ross and Vegas. I could barely look either one of them in the eye.

The guilt was sitting on my chest. It was raping my brain.

As I tried to fall asleep with the sick feeling of regret swimming in my stomach, I heard a car door slam outside of the window in the parking lot behind our building. I knew my man's alarm when I heard it chirp. I grimaced now knowing that Vegas was home. It had been becoming harder and harder to face him with this shame creeping out of me.

One thing that Damo had taught me other than keeping my fucking legs closed was how desperate I was to keep my man. In the past, it had been so easy to fuck around on Vegas because I didn't see myself losing him. But now, those possibilities were so evident that it...

"Ahhh!" Suddenly, the sound of gunshots rang through the air outside. "Shit!" I rolled out of bed as I heard windows shattering. I crawled frantically towards my bedroom door. Once at the doorway, I didn't even realize that the thunderous sound of bullets were still raining through the condo. All I could think about was getting to Vegas, so I started running towards the back door.

"*Vegas!*"

"Baby, get down!"

I was so relieved to hear his voice that I collapsed. But the shots finally stopped, so I sprang to my feet and bolted down the hall.

"*Vegas!*"

He appeared like a ghost, slithering out of a hall closet. I collapsed into his arms, but he wasn't with the emotional shit at the moment. I could feel his rage as he gripped my elbows and gently pushed me aside. I looked up at him. Anger was smoldering behind those blue eyes.

"Get out of the way."

"Where you goin'?" I followed him so closely that my bare toes were literally scraping the heel of his Timbs. "Vegas!" I tried to pull at him, but it was no use. He had so much strength that he was able to pull away from me with a simple flinch. "What are you about to do?"

He suddenly stopped and spun around. "Kill that motherfucker! What do you think?" I cringed as he continued to spew his rage. "I told that motherfucker that we were good. I told him I didn't do that shit, and he still just tried to kill me!"

"How do you know that it was Ross?"

Vegas' head cocked to the side. A questionable smirk spread across his face. "Who the fuck else would it be?"

When he went into the utility closet, I knew he was going in there for his gun. Not the pistol that he carried with him all the time, but the semi-automatic weapons that would ensure a person's death.

Panicking, I sprang back into the bedroom and called Treasure.

"Hel—"

My anxiety cut her off. "Heaven!"

"What?!" she snapped, hearing the panic in my voice.

"Where is Ross?"

"In the den."

"Are you sure?" I pressed.

"Yeah. I'm outside in the backyard. I see him sitting in there. What's wrong?"

"I gotta go."

"Treasure, —"w-what—"

"I'll call you back." I hung up, threw my phone on the bed, and headed for the doorway. When I saw Vegas marching towards me with his gauge by his side, fear swam through me. It made me so sick that I could feel all of the cake that I had eaten earlier coming up. I turned and ran into the master bathroom. I fell on my knees on the cold tile floor just in time to spill my guts in the toilet.

"Oh gawd," I mumbled after the last it spewed out.

I knew that Damo had done this. He was done playing games.

"Baby?"

I fell back on my butt. I reached for the tissue, tore some off, and wiped my mouth.

"You okay?"

I could feel Vegas standing over me, but I couldn't look up at him as I mumbled, "You can't kill him."

I heard Vegas suck his teeth. "Fuck that. I can't keep letting this motherfucka get away with this shit! You see—"

"It wasn't him!" I screamed so loud that Vegas finally shut up and just stared at me listening. I could feel myself about to throw up again. The remorse and fear was making me physically ill now. I couldn't take it anymore. "It wasn't him, Vegas." I forced myself to look him in the eyes. I had to at least give him enough respect to look him in the eyes. "Ross didn't just try to kill you—"

"Well, he had somebody do it—"

"He didn't steal from you!"

Vegas' eyes slightly rolled to the ceiling. "C'mon on now. I know that's your girl's man, but stop taking up for his ass—"

"HE DIDN'T DO IT!" I screamed.

Tears came to my eyes as Vegas' stare questioned what I was about to say next. Now that I had his attention, I said, calmly but fearfully, "Damo lied to you."

"How do you know?" I could see the fear entering his body. I could see his heart beating so fast that it was making him take short deep breaths.

Tears came to my eyes as I stared into his and told him, "He told me."

He flinched in all the misunderstanding. "Why?" He paused, leaned against the wall, and swallowed hard. "Why would he tell you that?"

I couldn't say it. The words couldn't come out. They were there on the tip of my tongue, but I just couldn't say them and break his heart like this.

I didn't need to, though. He saw the guilt on my face. He shrank with heartbreak. Literally, his large frame cringed. "C'mon, man. Nah..."

"I'm sorry!" I cried and covered my face with my shaky hands. I couldn't look at his heartbreak. I couldn't witness that shit.

"You fucked him?!"

My sobs were my response.

"ARE YOU FUCKING SERIOUS?!" He barked so loudly that I jumped in fear. "C'mon... Tell me you didn't..." I heard his breath get shorth. My heart broke as I heard his breaking into tears that he was fighting. I couldn't look at him as he kept stuttering in disbelief. "Y-you didn't..."

I then heard his footsteps pounding out of the bathroom. I sprang to my feet and followed him into the bedroom. "I'm sorry, Vegas." I tried to grab his hand, but he snatched away so hard that I felt my acrylic nail break. "Please talk to me!"

He didn't say a word. His face was turning red as he rummaged through a drawer. I started to panic because I thought he was getting clothes to leave. I started to hyperventilate and sob like I never had before. "I love yoooou." I collapsed on the bed, weeping.

"Yeah? I love you too." I looked up at him, hopeful, but that washed away when my optimistic eyes met the hurt and anger in his. "I love you so much that I bought you this."

Before I realized it, he hurled a small black box at me. It hit my leg so hard that it pierced my skin and made it bleed. But before I could cry out in pain, I realized what it was as it hit the floor and popped open. A beautiful, diamond ring fell out of it and onto the floor.

I melted in shame as I bent down to pick it up, but Vegas stomped on it before my fingers could grasp it. He started to stomp it over and over again. I cried out, feeling as if that was our relationship he was stomping on. I lunged towards him and gripped his T-shirt. He pushed me away, and I fell to my knees again.

"I'm sorryyyyyyyy." I wanted him to believe me so bad that the need hurt my throat as the words came out.

"I bet you are." He started to walk away, and I went into panic mode.

I crawled swiftly behind him. As soon as I could, I grabbed the first thing that I could, which was his pants leg. "Please, don't leave, Vegas! Please?! I'm so sorry, baby!"

He reached down and pushed me away. I fell back and looked up at him. But I couldn't bear to witness his heartbreak. I shamefully looked away as I heard him say, "I'm done. You can have that bum ass mother-fucker. Fuck you."

PRINCESS

I flopped down on my couch, kicking my shoes off. Damo was avoiding my eyes, because I knew he felt me glaring at his stupid ass.

"You see me looking at you!" I fussed.

Damo grimaced as he sat on the loveseat in the corner of the living room.

"You almost killed him!" I spat.

Damo simply shrugged. "That was the plan."

My eyes rolled as I scowled at him. "Because he don't rock with you no more? You were going to ruin this for us because of that?"

He sat there with his face scrunched up, looking like a bad ass lil' boy.

I shook my head at how stubbornly stupid he was being. "Can you blame Vegas for not fucking with you no more? You've been fucking up."

I loved Damo, but his trigger-happiness was ruining this for us.

"Fucking up how?" he had the nerve to question.

My mouth dramatically dropped. Was he serious?

"First of all, shooting at Ross. Now, you shooting at Vegas. Control your temper. And don't act like you haven't been sloppy. Shit, did you forget that you got Divine pregnant?"

"That was an accident."

My head tilted theatrically. "So, you 'accidentally' fucked her raw?"

His dumb ass didn't have a smart comeback for that. He just laughed.

His crazy ass had been better been glad that I loved him. There was something diabolical and twisted about our relationship that I just couldn't get enough of.

But Damo had been royally messing up. None of this had been part of the plan, and it was starting to look like we had lost control for good.

When I found out that my boyfriend had a baby with some side chick, I fell into the arms of Damo. That was a year ago. I loved his swag, style and hustle. *He* didn't love his hustle, however. Even though he was getting money, he wanted to get it on another level. That's when he came up with the plan to break up Ross and Vegas' organization so that he could link up with one of them and then eventually get rid of the one that was left and wind up being the connect. But his attempts to get close to Ross failed miserably when he was fucking Divine. That young ass girl was so up Damo's ass that her only focus was on trying to be under him. She wasn't trying to hear anything else Damo was talking about.

Then he got her pregnant, and she found out about Treasure. So, that was a wrap.

"You were supposed to be getting close to Ross, not getting Divine pregnant!"

"Okay, and? Baby, damn! It was a mistake. I got this, though. Is their little boy band broken up or not?"

"Yeah, you did manage to do that, but you still haven't gotten to the connect. You still fucking with the middleman, when the plan was to get to their connect so that we can take this shit over."

"I'm getting there."

"How? Treasure is done with you. You don' scared her hoe ass into being faithful-"

"I was trying to get her to start back fucking with me so that we could make this shit happen."

My eyes rolled as I went on, "Well, that was a fucking fail. Then you pissed Vegas off. Now he not even fucking with you."

All of this had been going so well at first. It surprised the hell out of me that Divine and Treasure had no idea that they were fucking the same dude. It was amazing how some good dick could convince a woman to keep secrets from her loved ones. But I guess Damo and I had gotten too cocky because now it had all blown up in our face and he had no way in.

"And now you shooting at Vegas and shit. What the fuck was that supposed to do?"

"Show that motherfucker not to play me."

"Because he checked you for shooting at Ross? You sound stupid."

"Stupid?"

"Yea, stupid!" Just then my phone vibrated. I looked down and was surprised when I saw the text message from Vegas that read: *You at home?*

I smiled from ear-to-ear. Damo and I had originally planned for both of us to try to infiltrate Ross and Vegas' organization, but my attempts to get to Vegas had failed...well, maybe until now, I guess, because he had finally hit me up. I had always only been able to get to Vegas by sneaking in conversations when we were all partying. I had given him my number, but he'd never used it. And he had never given me his, no matter how much I tried to get close to him.

But now, he had finally reached out to me.

Game on!

My anger instantly subsided. I had been riding with Damo all this time because I wanted my baby to have everything he wanted. I also wanted to live the Queen Pen lifestyle while being at his side. But sometimes it took a woman to do a man's job.

"You know what?" I asked Damo with a smile. "I got this."

His eyebrow rose. "How?"

"Because..." I smiled. "Vegas just texted me and asked me if I was home."

An evil grin slid across Damo's face. "Word?" I could see his mouth salivating with the possibilities.

"Yeah. So, get out," I told him as I stood to go freshen up. "It's my turn to do this."

❦ 26 ❦

MELLO

“**D**addy, pleeeease? I want my tableeeet.”

“Oh my God, TJ!” I snapped. “We’re goin’! Chill, man.”

Paris looked at me strangely as I sped through the city back towards my pop’s crib. She had been looking at me like that since we left Sunshine’s birthday party a few hours ago. I had had a fucked up attitude ever since. Everything was fucking with me: how extra Paris had been, where my friendship with Heaven had ended up, how beautiful she was, and how much I loved her, despite everything telling me that I shouldn’t. I hated this shit. I couldn’t take seeing Heaven again. Not this soon. But TJ was steady whining about this fucking tablet. He wouldn’t even just let me get him a new one in the morning once we were back in Florida. He wanted it tonight and I knew if I wanted any peace, I had to go get it.

Once we pulled onto my father’s block, I saw his ride pulling out of the driveway. Heaven’s new Lexus was still in the driveway, though.

“Aye....um...” Paris was staring at me questionably, so I knew what I was about to say wasn’t going to go over well at all. “Why don’t you go to the airport without me?”

Her face scrunched up. “Huh?”

"I need to holla at Heaven. Just go to the airport. She'll drop me off."

"What?"

Yeah, I knew that wasn't going to go over well.

I grabbed the door handle. It was crazy how I was so eager to get the fuck out of that car and get to her. "Look, I need to talk to her about my father—"

"Mello, you sound—"

"*Just do it! Fuuuck!*" I snapped. Gawd damn, she was irritating!

She and TJ looked at me like I was a fucking monster. I took a deep breath, trying to calm down. But I knew she was going to keep arguing with me so I just got out.

Luckily, Paris was sliding into the driver's seat. She was still wearing a fucked up scowl. I bent down and told her through the driver's seat, "I'm right behind you. I promise."

"Okay," she said lowly.

I could tell by the look in Paris' eyes that she knew it was some bullshit in the game. But my need for Heaven was way stronger than I knew. I walked away from Paris and my son and jogged up the driveway. I heard the rental pull off fast as I heard music coming from the backyard faintly.

♫ *But I don't wanna give up*
Baby, I just want you to get up
Lately I've been a little fed up
Wish you would just focus on

Me
Can you focus on me?
Baby, can you focus on me?
Me
Me
Can you focus on me?
Baby, can you focus on me? ♫

I followed the angelic voice of H.E.R into the backyard where I found Heaven in a lawn chair. Music was flowing from her cell phone. She was staring off into space with tears streaming down her face. She couldn't hear me as I walked up on her. She didn't even know I was there until I was standing over her. She looked up slowly and nonchalantly as if she'd been expecting to see Ross. But when she saw me, she froze.

When I told her, "He's gone. I just saw him leave," she relaxed a little. But she still just stared at me as if she didn't know what to say.

But I did. "I love you."

We both were now frozen as my words lingered in the air.

When she just continued to stare up at me with those wide eyes, I sat down in front of her on the lawn chair and told her again, "I love you."

She broke down. Her tears were no longer silent. "Please don't do this to me."

"Why? Because you can't leave him?" I reached into my pocket. "Now, you can," I said as I forced a wad of money into her hand. "I got you. I can take care of you. *Now* tell me no."

I looked at her, daring her to say no. Fuck the rules. Ross didn't deserve our loyalty.

"I can't," she cried.

"Why not? You love him?"

"No," she confessed.

"Who do you love?" Her eyes fell to her hands, but I pulled them away. I wasn't about to let her talk herself out of leaving him this time. "Tell me who you love."

She watched me with tear-soaked eyes. I was waiting for my answer, but what she did was *show* me her love instead. She grabbed my face gently and kissed me. I slipped my hands on her waist and pulled her so close to me that I could feel as her nipples hardened to stone while I took her mouth.

Reluctantly, I pulled away. The guilt was eating at me. I loved her enough to tell her everything. I couldn't let her do something without her knowing the truth about Angel. "I gotta tell you something."

She saw the seriousness in my face and sighed. "Don't."

"It's import—"

"If it's gonna fuck up this moment, then tell me later."

I gave her what she wanted, which was *me*. Besides, as much as I wanted to tell her the truth, I didn't want anything to mess up this moment either.

She brought my mouth back to hers, and I let her. We kissed so passionately that I just knew I was going to take her body right there on that lawn chair. Fuck that flight back to Florida. If Heaven was rocking with me, then I was staying right here in the midst of the bull-shit with her.

This was perfect - this moment, her- it was all perfect and worth all of the drama... until Ross' voice suddenly shot through the air, "*What the fuck is going on?!*"

VEGAS

Princess' smile spread across her face as I stood in the doorway. It was as if she could see the hurt in my eyes and she was satisfied knowing that I had come to her.

She silently moved out of the way and let me in. I walked in feeling as heavy as I had when I walked out of me and Treasure's crib. I could feel Princess watching me as I entered her crib and flopped down on the couch. I was holding a bottle of Remy by the neck. I had been drinking straight from that motherfucker for the past two hours. I could hardly feel the liquor, though. I was drunk with anger, not alcohol.

Paris sat down next to me, wearing the same smirk on her face.

"You were right," I admitted to her.

She was only able to hold a haughty smile for so long while looking at the hurt in my eyes. It slowly slipped away and sympathy replaced it.

She shook her head, saying, "I told you she was fucking him."

She had. Princess had been telling me for the last couple months that she felt like Damo and Treasure were fucking. She claimed it was just her woman's intuition that had told her. She claimed she was just telling me to look out for me because she liked me so much that she didn't want to see me get played. Her liking me so much was why I figured it was a lie. I loved my woman that much not to listen to the next bitch. *I loved her that much.* I was ready to marry Treasure and give her the world, but she had made me look like a fucking fool. Not only that, but she had put a rift between me and my right hand that had damn near gotten us killed because she wanted to give that pussy up to the next motherfucka.

"You're better than that. You deserve so much more." Her hand was sliding up my thigh, so I knew she wanted to show me exactly what I deserved. She started loosening my belt. For the first time, I didn't stop her. Princess had only thrown that pussy at me subliminally, but I shut her done every time. In the two years since she had been mine, I had never touched another woman beside Treasure. *Never.*

But as I felt Princess' warm, wet mouth around my span of steel, that shit was about to change.

HEAVEN

Before I could say anything, Ross charged Mello. He had seemingly taken flight as he soared towards Mello. Mello had no time to react really. Before he could do anything, Ross' body collided with his. The force of their bodies' vigorous contact caused the lawn chair to topple over. I was tossed to the concrete patio underneath it.

I quickly jumped up and tried to pull them apart.

"Ross, no! Please?!" I begged. "Stop!"

Hearing my voice only made his anger intensify. He stood up over Mello and kicked him so violently in the stomach that I felt it.

"Arrrgh!" Mello held his stomach, rocking back and forth on the ground.

Then Ross bent down, grabbed Mello's head and smashed it into the ground.

"Ahhhh!" I screamed at a high pitch as Mello fell unconscious.

I ran towards Mello, but Ross was right there between us. His fist stopped me as it connected with my nose, causing a stinging pain to paralyze me. I was in a daze so I had no sense to fight back. I could feel him tossing me brutally around the patio. I also felt my body crashing into things. Ross' feet were connecting brutally with different parts of my body.

A gunshot brought me out of my daze. I hoped that it had killed Ross because I suddenly stopped feeling his blows. But as my eyes opened and focused, I saw Divine standing in the patio doorway lowering a gun down from the air and pointing it at Ross.

I jumped to my feet, feeling both the null and stinging pains of every blow Ross had landed on my body. Blood was running down my face from my nose and I could taste it as it seeped into my mouth.

"Divine, put it down!"

She wasn't looking at me. She was glaring at Ross. He wasn't afraid at all. He was looking at her as if she were a joke. But when he stepped towards her, she proved that she wasn't a fucking game.

Pow!

She fired another warning shot that barely missed his side.

"Divine!" I shouted.

"I'm sick of this motherfucker putting his hands on you," she said through gritted teeth as a tear streamed down the side of her face.

"I got it, Divine." We all suddenly looked at Mello, whom we hadn't noticed had come to. He was now standing behind Ross pointing his piece at his head. "Y'all go in the house," he told me and Divine.

Ross laughed. "Oh, y'all little motherfuckers think y'all run something?" His laugh was menacing as he reached into his back and pulled out his piece as well.

I was weak with panic. "Just stop! All of you, stop!"

"Son, what your weak ass gon' do with that gun?" he taunted Mello.

"Mello, I got you! I will shoot this motherfucker!" Divine spat.

Ross sneered. "And you better hope you get a good shot off before I manage to put one in this punk bitch."

"Pleeeeease!" I cried. "Put the gun down, Ross!"

"Fuck y'all!" he barked. "I took care of all you motherfuckers, and this is how you repay me?! My son, Heaven?! You've been fucking my son?!"

Divine lost her hold on the gun once she heard that. Her stance got weak and she looked at me in disbelief. I cringed in shame.

"Ross..."—" I started, but I was forced to stop, however, when I saw Mello making a sudden movement out of the corner of my eye. Ross and Divine had seen it too because they both raised their guns. It was as if time stood still. I saw everyone ready to kill one another. I saw my sister approaching them, putting herself in the line of it all, ready to fire one into Ross. I ran into the middle of them all, refusing to allow anyone to die because of me.

But before I could make them hear my plea, a shot rang out.

Pow!

Then.... everything went silent.

TREASURE

I couldn't sit in that house. I needed Vegas, but he wasn't answering the phone. I had driven by every spot where I thought he would be, but I didn't find him. So, I gave up. I called Heaven over and over again, but she wasn't answering. I couldn't go home, so I was on my way to her house since I knew she was home the last time I had talked to her.

I gasped when I pulled onto Heaven's block and saw police cars and ambulances surrounding her house.

"Oh my God!" I pressed the gas and sped towards the house. But I could only get so close because the police had a portion of the street barricaded. I threw my car in park and bolted towards the house. The commotion had drawn neighbors out of their houses. I had to push my way through the crowd to get as close to the house as I could.

The house was illuminated with red and blue lights. I watched in fear as police officers walked back and forth. My fear was magnified to horror when I saw the yellow tape enclosing the backyard.

A scream suddenly left my throat and pierced the air. I now had everybody's attention. I ran past the blue barricade towards the driveway, but was quickly stopped by a police officer.

"Let me go! Let me go! What happened?! Tell me what—"

I suddenly stopped when I saw Vegas watching me. He was talking to an officer a few feet away from me. I ran towards him. "What happened?!"

He barely looked at me.

"Vegas, please?" I begged. "What happened?"

He grimaced and told me reluctantly. "I'm trying to see myself. I came over here to holla at Ross and all this was happening."

"Fuck is you doin' here, motherfucker?!" Ross' voice suddenly shouted behind us.

I spun around, hoping that Heaven was with him, but she wasn't. Ross was being escorted out of the house alone by an officer. He charged through the lawn towards Vegas, spewing, "Get the fuck away from my house, bitch!"

"Ross, what happened? Where is Heaven?" I asked.

He didn't hear me. He just kept spazzing out. "Yo' bitch ass tried to kill me and you got the nerve to be at my house? Fuck all you snake motherfuckers!!" He was barking like a fucking maniac.

"Ross!" I tried to go to him, but the police officer near me stopped me. I looked at her, pleading, "Please? My best friend is in there. She's like my sister. Please?" I cried as I zeroed in on the yellow tape behind her. "What happened?" I asked the officer. "Did somebody get killed?"

I didn't need her answer. I knew that somebody was dead. I knew what yellow tape meant. The officer actually looked so sympathetic for my tears. Her mouth opened and closed repeatedly. My eyes begged her for an answer just as I could see paramedics coming out of the backyard. My knees buckled as I saw the black body bag. The officers caught me. I gripped her arms trying to gain my composure. I looked for Ross, hoping to get an answer from him, but both he and Vegas were frozen. Ross' anger subsided as they both stared unbelievably at the body being carried towards the morgue van.

Through my tears, I looked desperately at the officer holding me. "Please, tell me," I begged. "Who is it? Who got killed?'

to be continued....

When The Side Nigga Catch Feelings 2, the finale, is coming VERY soon! Get ready to 1-CLICK!

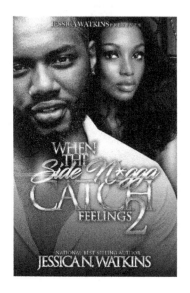

ABOUT THE AUTHOR:

Jessica N. Watkins was born April 1st in Chicago, Illinois. She obtained a Bachelors of Arts with Focus in Psychology from DePaul University and Masters of Applied Professional Studies with focus in Business Administration from the like institution. Working in Hospital Administration for the majority of her career, Watkins has also been an author of fiction literature since the young age of nine. Eventually she used writing as an outlet during her freshmen year of high school as a single parent: "In the third grade I entered a short story contest with a fiction tale of an apple tree that refused to grow despite the efforts of the darling main character. My writing evolved from apple trees to my seventh and eighth grade classmates paying me to read novels I wrote about kids our age living the lives our parents wouldn't dare let us". At the age of twenty-eight, Watkins' chronicles have matured into steamy, humorous, and realistic tales of African American Romance and Urban Fiction.

In September 2013, Jessica's most recent novel, Secrets of a Side Bitch, published by SBR Publications, reached #1 on multiple charts.

Jessica N. Watkins is available for talks, workshops or book signings. Email her at authorjwatkins@gmail.com.

Follow Jessica social media:

Amazon:
http://www.amazon.com/author/authorjwatkins
Facebook:
http:///www.facebook.com/iwritedopebooks
Facebook Group:
http://www.facebook.com/groups/femistryfans
Instagram: @authorjwatkins
Twitter: @authorjwatkins
Snapchat: @authorjwatkins

OTHER BOOKS BY JESSICA N. WATKINS:

SECRETS OF A SIDE BITCH (COMPLETE SERIES):
Secrets of a Side Bitch 1: https://goo.gl/zgLora
Secrets of a Side Bitch 2: https://goo.gl/5ptSSn
Secrets of a Side Bitch 3: https://goo.gl/BPgD4U
Secrets of a Side Bitch – The Simone Campbell Story:
https://goo.gl/rbnGPZ
Secrets of a Side Bitch 4: https://goo.gl/J1t1YW

CAPONE AND CAPRI (COMPLETE SERIES):
Capone and Capri: https://goo.gl/Qk14iy
Capone and Capri 2: https://goo.gl/hoY96X

A THUG'S LOVE (COMPLETE SERIES):
A Thug's Love: https://goo.gl/jcN3PP
A Thug's Love 2: https://goo.gl/6UHWqN
A Thug's Love 3: https://goo.gl/uqsvT6

NIGGAS AIN'T SHIT: (COMPLETE SERIES):
Niggas Ain't Shit: https://goo.gl/pcwQuP
Niggas AInt Shit 2: https://goo.gl/1eC7pr

EVERY LOVE STORY IS BEAUTIFUL, BUT OURS IS HOOD SERIES:
Every Love Story Is Beautiful, But Ours Is Hood:
https://goo.gl/KNyCg7

Every Love Story Is Beautiful, But Ours Is Hood 2:
https://goo.gl/wJ1yvN
Every Love Story Is Beautiful, But Ours Is Hood 3:
https://goo.gl/wJ1yvN

CAUSE AND CURE IS YOU SERIES:
Cause and Cure Is You: https://goo.gl/pt5jNd

LOVE, SEX, LIES (COMPLETE SEREIS):
Love, Sex, Lies: https://goo.gl/FdKXXL

Love Hangover (Love, Sex, Lies 2):

https://goo.gl/fwoB6A

Grand Hustle (Love, Sex, Lies 3): https://goo.gl/CQ58VL

Love Drug (Love, Sex, Lies 4): https://goo.gl/ZTmqy3

Bang (Love, Sex, Lies 5): https://goo.gl/WxNSCD

Love Me Some Him (Love, Sex, Lies 6):

https://goo.gl/J7GYDU

Good Girls Ain't No Fun (Love, Sex, Lies FINALE):

https://goo.gl/BCuhFu

In order to receive a text message when future books by
Jessica N. Watkins are released, send the keyword
"Jessica" to 25827! Please be sure to leave your review
of this novel!
Jessica would love to hear your thoughts!

Made in the USA
Monee, IL
24 May 2021